The Legendary Warriors

History's most powerful heroes!

Robert of Penrith and his illegitimate half brother, Piers, were raised as differently as possible, but they've become reluctant allies since a deadly raid on their father's land left them exiled. Now they are determined to rise up, to reclaim their birthright and become fierce warriors of legend that the world will remember forever!

But their journey won't just be shaped by revenge and redemption. Because these warriors haven't considered the power of romance...

Read Robert's story in:
The Iron Warrior Returns

And read Piers's story in:
The Untamed Warrior's Bride

Both available now!

Author Note

My new series The Legendary Warriors was, quite literally, inspired by superheroes. I wanted to create medieval warriors based on character archetypes we all know and love. In *The Untamed Warrior's Bride*, Piers of Grevershire is a bastard son who grew up fighting to survive. He's fiercely protective and won't hesitate to unleash his temper when it means keeping his loved ones safe. But when he competes to win the hand of the beautiful Lady Gwendoline, he falls hard for the woman who sees him as more than a lowborn serf.

Gwendoline recognizes the man Piers wants to become, and she finds joy in someone who views her as an equal and encourages her love of archery. But their daring escape from her father's iron command will put their very lives at stake...

If you'd like me to email you when my new books come out, you may subscribe to my author newsletter at www.michellewillingham.com/contact. I always love hearing from my readers.

MICHELLE WILLINGHAM

—

The Untamed Warrior's Bride

Recycling programs for this product may not exist in your area.

ISBN-13: 978-1-335-72372-7

The Untamed Warrior's Bride

Copyright © 2023 by Michelle Willingham

For questions and comments about the quality of this book, please contact us at CustomerService@Harlequin.com.

Harlequin Enterprises ULC
22 Adelaide St. West, 41st Floor
Toronto, Ontario M5H 4E3, Canada
www.Harlequin.com

Printed in U.S.A.

RITA® Award finalist and Kindle bestselling author **Michelle Willingham** has written over forty historical romances, novellas and short stories. Currently she lives in southeastern Virginia with her family and her beloved pets. When she's not writing, Michelle enjoys reading, baking and avoiding exercise at all costs. Visit her website at michellewillingham.com.

Books by Michelle Willingham

Harlequin Historical

The Legendary Warriors

The Iron Warrior Returns
The Untamed Warrior's Bride

Untamed Highlander

The Highlander and the Governess
The Highlander and the Wallflower

Sons of Sigurd

Stolen by the Viking

Warriors of the Night

Forbidden Night with the Warrior
Forbidden Night with the Highlander
Forbidden Night with the Prince

Warriors of Ireland

Warrior of Ice
Warrior of Fire

Forbidden Vikings

To Sin with a Viking
To Tempt a Viking

Visit the Author Profile page
at Harlequin.com for more titles.

To Kristin M. for being such a
wonderful mentor and support.

To everyone in the class of 272—especially
Keiran, Taylor, Grace, Matt, Henry, Jess, Chelsea,
Rylan, Brendan and Greg—thanks for your
friendship, your humor and all the memories.

Prologue

'Now, remember who you are. Say it again.'

Wenda of Grevershire stared down at him, her blue eyes revealing a stony indifference.

'I'm the true heir to Penrith,' Piers replied. He tried to sound brave, though a chill threaded through his guts. His stomach gnawed with hunger, but he knew better than to ask his mother for food. She'd cuffed his ear when he'd mentioned it last night. They had travelled for three days, and now they stood outside the castle keep and the surrounding walls of Penrith.

'This is where you belong,' Wenda told him. Though his mother's gown was made of silk, it had worn down over the years. The hem had frayed, and the blue colour had long since faded. Even so, she carried herself as a lady. 'You are going to live here in the castle and work at whatever tasks they give you. Learn this place,' she insisted. 'You'll have to if you intend to rule over it one day.' Her eyes gleamed with intensity, laced with anger.

Piers stared at her, not knowing what she meant by that. He could never rule over Penrith, despite her claims. He couldn't be anything more than what he was—a bastard son his father knew nothing about.

Wenda handed him the small bundle of his belongings, and he suddenly realised what was happening. 'You're leaving me?' His voice revealed his uncertainty, and he tried to stand up straighter. He was eleven years old, and somehow, he'd thought she was coming too.

'I must,' she said. 'But heed my words and remember them. I was betrothed to the Earl of Penrith before you were born. A betrothal is the same as a marriage, binding in the church.' Her eyes glittered with fury, and she stared at the fortress. 'He may have abandoned me, but you are his true heir. You were born first before he set me aside and took that harlot as his wife. And I will have my vengeance on Degal. I swear it on my life.'

Her words bordered on madness, and Piers looked down at the ground. Wenda gripped his hair and forced him to look at her. 'Learn about the family, all their secrets. Find the whore's son Robert and befriend him. Earn his trust.' She smiled slowly. 'And when the time comes, you will take your place at Penrith.'

When the time came for what? He didn't ask her but gripped the bundle in his hands.

Then Wenda rested her hand on his shoulder. 'Gleda will help you. She used to be my maid, years ago. She will give you a place to sleep.'

A hollow feeling of loss surrounded him. She truly planned to leave him here with these strangers. The iciness tightened, numbing him deep inside. 'Will I see you again, Mother?'

'You will,' she agreed. 'But not for some time. They need to accept you first. Let them believe you are alone.'

Piers wanted to hug her, but Wenda pulled away when he tried to step towards her.

'There's one more thing.' Her voice held a coolness, and something about her tone made him want to shrink away. 'The harlot's son has been ill. I've sent a vial of special medicine for Robert. Give it to Gleda along with the letter I wrote.'

'She can read?' he interrupted. He had never learned how.

'Yes, she can read. The letter tells her of the medicine and how to make more. Tell her to burn the letter after she's read it.'

Wenda rested her hands upon his shoulders and bent down. 'It is very important that the harlot's son takes his medicine every day. He may be ill, but this medicine will help him.'

The slight smile on her face made him uneasy. Something about her words did not sound truthful, but Piers dared not accuse her of lying.

'Now take this letter with you and go to the gates,' she said. 'Tell the guards you have a message for Lord Penrith. Deliver it to him and then find Gleda later that night.'

'What does the message say?' he asked.

'It tells him that you are his son. You will meet your father for the first time, and he will allow you to stay.'

His nerves turned his skin cold, and Wenda straightened. 'Go now, my son. And I promise that one day, you will be Lord of Penrith. It's time for your new life to begin.'

She gave him no embrace, only a slight push. Piers forced back his fears, knowing he had to be strong.

He didn't understand why his mother was sending him away, but he wanted to believe that one day she would return.

But despite her vow, he never saw her again.

Chapter One

England—1205

The sound of someone in her room sent her blood racing. Lady Gwendoline reached for the knife she kept hidden beneath her mattress and quietly sat up in the darkness.

Her heart pounded, but she didn't scream. At least, not yet. She had one opportunity to gain the upper hand, and she needed the element of surprise.

The footsteps came closer towards the bed, and she silently crept out the other side, the dagger hilt clutched in her palm. She held her breath, wondering if it was better to run or confront the intruder.

But then, the stranger took another step towards the bed. Was he trying to attack her or kill her? Fear roared through her, yet she saw no choice but to make her move. If she didn't, he would strike first.

Gwen held her breath and stepped behind him, pressing the blade to his throat. 'Looking for someone?' She didn't know who this man was or what he wanted, but she was not about to become his victim.

The man was tall and lean, but she could feel the hard muscles beneath her hand. His hair was roughly cut against his neck, and his scent reminded her of pine trees within the forest. In the darkness, she could not see his face.

'I was looking for you, Lady Gwendoline.' His voice was deep and resonant, but to his credit, he didn't move.

Gwen tightened her grip on the knife. 'How did you get in my room?' And more than that, *why* was he here? Was he trying to attack her?

'I know this castle well,' was all he said.

She didn't know what to make of that, but she needed to call out for the guards outside her door. Yet, something in the man's demeanour made her hesitate. His hand reached up to her wrist, but instead of trying to take her knife, he slid his fingers across her arm in the barest caress. The heat of his hand stunned her, and she hardly knew what to do. She'd had suitors before, but none had affected her like this. His touch seemed to reach deep inside, awakening sensations she'd never imagined.

'Don't touch me.' She pressed the blade deeper, and he released her immediately. 'Why are you here?'

'Because I wanted to see you before the competitions.' His voice was low and resonant, and something about him made her skin tighten. It was entirely wrong, but she felt a forbidden thrill at having her arm around this man.

'You're one of my suitors, then.'

'I am.'

Her father Alfred was hosting a tourney for her hand in marriage on Midsummer's Eve and had invited dozens of suitors. He'd told her that she could have her choice from among the competitors. And this man was clearly seeking an advantage.

Her emotions tightened, for she was uncertain about marriage. Her father had promised to let her choose… but he'd gone back on his word before. She was trapped within a prison of his rules, and she'd learned to feign ignorance, behaving like the perfect daughter. But inwardly, she wanted to escape these invisible chains. The last thing she wanted was to go from one cage into another.

This man clearly believed she would behave like any shy, terrified maiden. Perhaps he thought he could coax her into seduction or win her affections. His presence both unnerved and intrigued her. She'd never imagined anyone would go to these lengths to see her alone. But her brain warned that this was not a man who would grant her the independence to live her life as she wanted to. He would make demands, bending the rules to suit him.

She gripped her blade tighter, knowing she could never wed a man like him.

He reached for her hand gently and pulled the blade back just enough so he could face her. Then he released it, allowing her to keep the blade at his throat. 'I'm not going to hurt you.'

'Men who aren't planning to hurt me don't usually sneak into my room,' she pointed out. But even so, she couldn't quite understand what it was about this man that tempted her. His voice held the edge of longing and, in the darkness, she found herself breathless. He was more dangerous than anyone she'd ever met.

Call out for help and be rid of him, her brain warned. And yet…perhaps it was the safety of her guards that made her more daring.

'How else could I see you?' the man asked. 'Or talk to you before the competitions?'

'Why would I want to talk to you? You're a stranger to me.' Her arm was beginning to ache from holding the blade to his throat.

'My name is Piers of Grevershire,' he told her.

She didn't know anyone by that name, but she lied, 'I don't care who you are. I want you to leave my room before I draw this blade across your throat.'

'Not yet.' His voice was a rough whisper, and his hands moved to span her waist. She went motionless, and the sudden heat of his hand on her spine made her conscious of his touch and the masculine scent of his skin. He said nothing but moved his fingers against the base of her spine in a gentle caress. No man had ever touched her like this before. She didn't know what to do, but when his hands moved higher, her skin broke out into gooseflesh.

A wicked desire kindled within her, making her want to lower her blade. But it was only his means of lowering her defences while he laid siege to her common sense.

'What are you doing?' she whispered in return.

'I want to know more about you,' he answered. He continued his relentless assault on her senses, and she swallowed hard, knowing she had to send him away.

'I'm going to call for my guards,' she said, putting her hand between them.

'You're not,' he predicted.

His bold statement evoked her defiance. 'Why wouldn't I?'

'Because as you said before, you can take care of yourself. And I'd wager you're curious about me. You won't know more if they kill me.'

'I don't care anything about you,' she shot back. 'You're in my room, and you need to go.' In desperation, she tried to push him away, but in one swift motion he disarmed her and tossed the blade away.

Terror clawed at her and she took a deep breath, planning to call out for the guards. Without her blade, she was helpless against this man. But all he did was rest his hands upon her waist.

'I will leave in a moment,' Piers said softly. 'But before I do, I want to know something about you that no one else knows. And I'll tell you something about me. If you ask.'

'I don't want to know you.' Her words broke off when he caught her left hand in his. Gently, he explored her fingertips, his thumb grazing against her calluses.

Her heartbeat pounded at his touch, and she couldn't help but imagine his fingers moving over other parts of her bare skin. Why did he have this effect on her? She couldn't understand it, and she wondered how she could convince him to leave.

'But I do know something about you now,' he said quietly. His thumb stroked the crease of her second and third fingers. Then he took his thumb and circled her palm before he pressed his hand to hers. 'Something that I suspect few people know.'

'You know nothing.'

'You're an archer,' he predicted. 'And this is where

you release your bowstring.' He touched the callused part of her fingers. 'You don't practise as often as you'd like, and you probably haven't told your father.'

Her eyes widened at his statement and she pushed at him again, trying to seize what was left of her composure. How had he guessed? It was her secret, one that only a few of the soldiers knew. She loved archery, but she only practised when her father was away. He wanted her to be the obedient daughter, one who never touched a weapon. She'd learned to shoot in secret, but when she'd revealed her skills to her father, he'd been furious.

'I'm impressed,' Piers said, lifting her palm to his lips. Then without another word, he released her hand and disappeared into the darkness. She heard the slight movement of stone behind the tapestry. So that was how he'd entered her room.

Gwen exhaled a sharp breath, completely undone by what had just happened. But more overwhelming than his presence was the unexpected compliment. He didn't seem to disapprove of her ability to shoot a bow, the way her father did. Instead, his voice had held admiration.

That was unexpected.

She closed her eyes and sank down on the bed. It had been such a mistake allowing this man to talk to her... and yet, he'd stayed just long enough to talk to her. He could easily have made more demands, refusing to leave until she called for her guards. Yet, he'd provoked an unexpected interest.

Do not fall into his trap, she warned herself. *He's just like all the other suitors who want to seize command of Penrith by claiming your hand in marriage.* It had been foolish not to call out for help.

Yet somehow…she'd believed Piers when he'd said he wouldn't hurt her. She didn't know what to think of this man's boldness—whether to fear him or admire him.

But as she climbed beneath her coverlet, she couldn't help but wonder when she would see him again.

The next morning, Piers awakened in the stable, wondering if he'd made a mistake by going to see Lady Gwendoline in secret. He wasn't like her other suitors who had wagons of gold, acres of land, and a noble name. No, he had nothing to offer her, save himself. And if he was to have any chance at claiming her hand in marriage, he had to win her affections in secret. Only then did he have a chance.

His secret visit had been an impulse born of desperation, and it had fallen apart the moment she'd put a blade to his throat. But despite her insistence that he leave, she hadn't been entirely immune to him. And that made him question whether to try again.

She'll never agree to wed you, the voice of reason warned. *She won't want a bastard.*

There was no question of that. He'd even had wild thoughts of kidnapping her before he'd slipped into her room. But Lady Gwendoline was not meek or helpless—and he liked that about her.

He hadn't lied about being one of her suitors—but if she learned the truth about him, it was over. He'd only learned about this tourney from his half-brother Robert. The new earl had promised his daughter's hand in marriage to the winner…and command of the lands at Penrith. The thought was staggering.

Piers had laboured in the fields at Penrith since he

was a young boy, along with the other serfs. It had been backbreaking work, but he'd survived. And if he'd slept among the dogs, at least he'd had shelter.

But now, he had a chance to rise beyond his low birth. This tourney might change everything. He could win the hand of Lady Gwendoline, whose beauty and courage fascinated him. He'd never met anyone like her…and he wanted to know more.

He'd travelled here in secret, away from his brother. Although he knew Robert intended to compete, Piers had decided to challenge him. To Robert, this tourney was about regaining his birthright.

To Piers, it was far more. He'd lived in his brother's shadow all his life…but this time, he intended to live a different life than the one he'd endured.

After their father had died, he'd gone into exile with his brother at the ruins of Stansbury, along with two other prisoners who had escaped. Morwenna and Brian had lived with them, and they had quickly become friends.

One night, Robert had built a fire for them, and Piers had sat opposite him while Morwenna and Brian slept.

'How long are we staying here?' he'd asked Robert.

'I don't know. But better here than the abbey. I've no wish to become one of the monks.'

Piers tossed a limb on the fire, and sparks rose into the night sky. 'What do you want to do?'

'I want to train,' Robert said. 'We'll get weapons from my uncle. I need you to help me get stronger.' He stared into the flames, as if remembering the night they'd fled Penrith. 'I was a coward when we left, and my father died because of it. I can't be weak any longer.'

Piers said nothing, but guilt weighed upon him. 'You've never been weak.'

'I was ill for years,' Robert protested. 'The people believed I would die.'

Piers stared down at the ground. 'You're better now.'

'Aye, but what if the illness returns? I have to get stronger. I need to fight back to regain my lands.'

'You won't get sick again,' Piers had said, pushing back the knot of guilt.

But during those two years in exile, they had laid some of their enmity to rest. He'd trained alongside Robert, pouring his frustration into swordplay. They had learned to fight against each other, and although he still resented Robert's station, at least now Piers had an opportunity to change his life for the better.

He'd let Robert believe that he was staying behind at Stansbury, but instead Piers had followed them on their journey. As long as Robert didn't know he was here, it would be easier to carry out his plans.

The competitions would not begin for a few more days, so Piers could bide his time. This time, he would bring gifts and leave them for Lady Gwendoline. Perhaps during the daytime, she might tolerate his presence and give him a second chance.

He'd been careful to hide his belongings inside the hidden passageway. No one knew about it, save him. He'd explored all of Penrith's secrets as a boy, and he knew this keep better than anyone. Many times, he'd hidden within these tunnels when trying to escape a beating. Stealing food was necessary for survival, but he'd learned stealth quickly, after suffering bruises and bloody noses.

He had shelter below ground, and though it was cold, there was no risk of being seen. He would wait for the right opportunity to see Lady Gwendoline again, and this time he hoped to win her affections.

In truth, he'd never courted a woman in his life. He'd kissed a few girls at Penrith when he'd been an adolescent, but during the past two years, the only woman he'd seen at Stansbury was Morwenna, whose heart fully belonged to Robert. She was more like a sister, and her brother Brian treated him like an older sibling. They had been the only true family he'd known, and they had travelled here with Robert. But if either saw him at Penrith, they would suspect his intentions and tell his brother.

This morn, Piers had kept his face hidden, spreading fresh rushes in the Great Hall while the earl and Lady Gwendoline broke their fast. He'd stolen glimpses of the lady, noting her perfect manners and the way she smiled at her father. Something about her demeanour felt false, as if she were living an illusion and saying what the earl wanted to hear. This wasn't the same lady who had placed a blade against his throat.

In all honesty, he preferred her courage. And he knew exactly what gift to bring to her. He had no silver, but he didn't need it for this.

'Murdering bastard,' he heard a man mutter beside him as they cleared away the leftover food.

Piers glanced at the man, knowing he couldn't ask questions. But he wanted to know more about their hatred. 'May he rot in hell,' he answered in a soft voice.

At that, the man gave a grim nod. 'He'll get what's

coming to him.' When he studied Piers, he said, 'I've not seen you in some time. You shouldn't have come back.'

Piers met the man's gaze squarely. 'You didn't see me.' The man's gaze turned wary and Piers added, 'And if you want the new Lord gone, you'll keep your mouth shut.'

'I want nothing more than that.' With a nod, the man warned, 'But have a care. Penrith already executed one of our men who did nothing wrong. The earl is dangerous.'

'After I wed his daughter, he'll return to his lands at Tilmain. He won't be the earl here for long,' Piers said softly.

The man appeared pleased to hear it. 'God willing. There are others wanting to be rid of him.' Then he lowered his head and before he departed, he added, 'Not all the soldiers belong to the earl. Some are the king's men, and they keep themselves apart. You'd do well to disguise yourself among them. They don't know all of Penrith's men, so another soldier wouldn't be noticed.'

Piers inclined his head in agreement. After the man left, he ate some of the remaining food. Several of the dogs came up to him, their tails wagging. Damn it all, even the dogs remembered him. He tossed them a few scraps on the way back to the kitchens, and they continued to follow.

He commanded them to stay when he reached the armoury. Most of the soldiers were training outside, and Piers hid himself in the shadows until he was alone. Then, he chose a chainmail hauberk, a helm, and a better sword. He tested the weight of it, pleased with the new weapon. He'd hidden his training sword inside the secret passage near Lady Gwendoline's room. This steel was of better quality. He agreed with the man's suggestion of disguising himself among the other soldiers to learn what he could about the earl's defences.

Before he left the armoury, he searched for Gwendoline's gift. It took some time, but he found a bow and a quiver of arrows. No one would miss them, for there were nearly thirty bows lined against the wall. He deliberately chose a smaller weapon, not knowing if she had the strength for a longbow. Then he found a heavy cloth and wrapped the bow and quiver up together.

Piers crossed the room and went to the back corner where he pushed back the rushes and lifted up the wooden trapdoor leading to the storage chambers below ground. He followed the winding tunnels past the wine cellar to another storage chamber that led up the stairs to the kitchens.

He waited until no one was looking and then hurried outside. He walked behind a group of soldiers and then made his way towards the main keep.

Within a quarter of an hour, he was back inside Gwendoline's chamber. She was already there, talking to her maid. Piers waited until the maid left before he emerged from behind the tapestry.

'I brought you a gift,' he said.

Gwendoline let out a cry of shock and spun around. 'I vow, I'll have men seal up that wall by the end of the night.' She glared at him, already holding a blade in her hand. 'You should not be here, Piers.'

In the daylight, she was even more beautiful. This day, she wore a gown of light blue, and it accentuated her fair hair and blue eyes. Piers kept his distance and set the cloth bundle on her bed. With his hands up, he slowly backed away. 'I don't obey orders well.'

'Then you need to learn how,' she shot back.

'Do I?' He removed his helm, drawing back his hood. This time, he wanted her to see his face, to know him.

She faltered then, eyeing him as if she expected him to attack her. But he made no move forward, giving her time to grow accustomed to his presence.

'You can open your gift,' he said. 'I think you'll like it.'

She never took her eyes from him. 'If I do, will you leave?'

'You might not want me to leave,' he answered.

She gave a heavy sigh and strode towards the bed. 'Fine. I'll look at it. But then you must go.'

He watched as she pulled back the rough covering and revealed the bow and quiver. For a moment, she stared at the weapon as if she didn't know what to do with it.

'If there was time, I would have a master carver make a true longbow for you,' he said. 'One made of yew.' He moved closer to her and saw how she gently lifted the bow, running her fingers along it. 'But I didn't know if you've used a longbow before. Or if you're strong enough to pull the bowstring.'

'I shot one a few weeks ago,' she confessed. 'But my father didn't know. He won't allow me to keep this.'

'Why not?' He took another step closer while she selected an arrow, studying it.

'After he learned I'd been practising archery in secret, he burned the last bow I had. I've had to borrow weapons since then. I can only practise when men are careless and leave their bows out.' She turned to him and her face had gone pale. 'Much as I might want to keep this, I cannot accept your gift.'

'Don't let Alfred know you have it,' he said. 'Keep it hidden beneath your bed, if you must.'

She held his gaze for a long time. Her eyes held traces of fear, but he didn't close the distance, not wanting to upset her. It was dangerous enough to be inside her chamber. He sensed that she wanted to keep the weapon but was afraid of anyone finding it.

'I believe a woman should be able to defend herself,' he said quietly. 'You deserve that right.'

On the night he and Robert had fled Penrith, their friend Morwenna had been attacked by a soldier. Piers had never forgotten that feeling of helplessness while he and Robert were chained. They'd managed to kill the guard before the man could seriously harm her, but Piers had made a personal vow never to let a woman be hurt like that again. Not if he could do anything to stop it. And since that day, he and Robert had trained Morwenna to fight and defend herself.

'Don't let your father see the bow.' Piers regarded her and added, 'I don't see a reason why you shouldn't have any weapon you desire. Even a sword.'

Her expression shifted into a wry smile. 'I don't think I could lift a broadsword.'

'In time you could. If it's what you wanted,' he said. In her eyes, he could see that the fear and distrust were still there. He didn't want to frighten her any more than he already had, so he decided it was time to go.

'Enjoy your gift,' he said. 'I'll return to you tonight.'

Chapter Two

For a long time, Gwendoline simply stared at the bow. No one had ever given her a gift like this before. Men had given her flowers, ribbons, even gifts of food or drink. But never a weapon.

She ran her fingers down the wood, feeling the curves. With her fingers, she tested the taut bowstring, and a sudden rush of emotion flooded her. How had he known that she would want this? He'd done nothing except touch her fingers. But somehow, Piers had sensed a deeper part of her, a part that no one else knew about.

Who was he? She needed to learn why he'd gone to such lengths to see her. Today was the first time she'd seen his face, and she couldn't deny that he was handsome. His dark hair was slightly longer, his blue eyes vivid. He had a strong jawline and a firm mouth that fascinated her. His shoulders were broad, revealing strength, and despite the forbidden nature of their meetings, she found herself attracted to him.

She chose an arrow and nocked it to the bow, aiming away from the door as she pulled back the bowstring.

It had been weeks since she'd dared to shoot, and she wondered if her aim was still steady. If only she could go down into the bailey and spend an hour with a straw target, then she would know. But her father would never allow it. She suspected that he'd punished the guards who had set up a target for her while he was away.

She sighed and returned the arrow to the quiver. Carefully, she wrapped up the bow and arrows and slid them beneath her bed.

'I don't see a reason why you shouldn't have any weapon you desire.'

Somehow, she believed he meant that. Piers had such raw strength, he wouldn't be intimidated by a woman who could shoot. She sat down on her bed, wondering what it would be like to have that freedom.

He wasn't like any of the suitors she'd known in the past. Last night, he had touched her spine, his hands tracing her skin as if he were learning the shape of her. Though it had been wrong for him to slip into her room—she'd nearly stabbed him—never had she imagined that the same man would give her a bow and arrows.

What other suitor would have done such a thing? All the men she'd known before had treated her as if she were made of glass, too delicate to defend herself.

Piers was different. He didn't follow the rules, and somehow he intrigued her. She should have been terrified that he'd broken into her room. She should have screamed and demanded that her men take him away.

Instead, she'd been caught up by the forbidden moment. Gwendoline imagined his hands upon her bare skin, and the very thought fascinated her. Even now, she remembered the heat of his palms against her waist. She wondered what it would be like to have a man press her back on the mattress, his weight upon her body. Though she had never before known an intimate touch, she'd heard stories from the maids. And somehow, she suspected that a night with Piers would be passionate and wild, nothing at all like the predictable existence that trapped her now.

She closed her eyes and let out a sigh, pushing away the vision. What would it be like to wed a warrior instead of a nobleman? Unpredictable, most likely. She sensed that Piers was not a man of wealth, even if he had a title. Otherwise, there would be no need for him to seek her out in secret.

He had come to her alone in the darkness, but not once had he harmed her. Beneath his rough ways, she sensed a caged beast who wanted far more. And she understood that restless feeling of being trapped.

If she didn't choose wisely, her marriage could become the same prison she'd lived in for eighteen years. She wanted a husband who would value her thoughts and grant her the freedom she craved.

But she doubted Piers would be that man. He was here to win command of Penrith, and his only reason for slipping inside her room was to gain her favour before the other competitors. When it came time to choose someone, he would be no different from the others, no matter what he said. Men wanted obedient wives, not someone with opinions.

Her father rarely let her make any decisions at Penrith. He told her what to do and when to do it. And whenever she felt the urge to protest, he softened and told her he only wanted what was best for her.

Ever since her mother had died, after a terrible fall down the stairs five years ago, Alfred had tightened the invisible chains. His overprotective nature had grown so bad, Gwen was finding it more difficult to endure him.

She longed for so much more in her life. She wanted the freedom to know every person on these lands by name, who their children were. Especially whether they had enough food to eat and a roof over their heads. That was her responsibility, though her father had not permitted her to take on the full role of Lady of Penrith, despite her requests. One day, perhaps.

A knock sounded at the door, and after Gwen called them to enter, her father strode into the room. 'Were you lazing abed, my daughter?'

His words annoyed her, but she sat up and forced a smile she didn't feel. 'Only daydreaming.'

'Well, some of your suitors have begun to arrive. I want you to dress in a finer gown and greet them.' He crossed his arms and regarded her. 'I know we spoke of you choosing your husband. But it must be a man who can provide for you, one who will allow us to make a strong alliance.'

And there it was, her freedom slowly dissipating. 'So, you've decided to choose my husband now? I thought you gave me your word.'

Alfred laughed softly. 'Let us say that I will narrow the candidates. You may choose from the ones whom I have deemed appropriate.'

'What about the competitions?' she asked. 'You

said the men would compete in contests of strength and speed. Does that not matter any more?'

'If he is a man worthy of you, I am certain he will win several of them,' her father predicted. 'You have no cause to fear.'

She nodded, though she was starting to believe her father would go back on his word about allowing her to choose. There was no doubt that Piers would win several, if not all the competitions. His physical strength was undeniable. But would he meet her father's requirement of having a good family and lands? That much was uncertain. Or would he be different from the other men and allow her more freedom? He had brought her the bow, but beyond that, she knew nothing about him, save his name.

'Send Aelish to help me fix my hair, and I will join you in the Great Hall,' she promised. Though she didn't need her maid's help, it was a means of sending him away.

Her father appeared pleased and said, 'Gwen, I am glad you are not like other young ladies who try to defy their fathers. I know you understand that I am only trying to help you find the very best marriage. Your sons will one day inherit Penrith, and you must protect them, just as I've protected you.'

She wanted to tell him that she could guard herself well enough, but it was easier to simply nod. 'I will speak with the men who have arrived.'

'There is one man who might suit you well enough,' he said. 'Gareth of Watcomb is his name. His father is an earl, but Gareth is a younger son. He would be glad to learn from me until he can govern Penrith alone.'

Gwendoline didn't miss that there was no mention of her ruling over Penrith. 'So, while my husband commands Penrith, I am meant to simply stand aside and bear children?' Though she kept a false smile on her face, it was difficult not to let her irritation show.

'Is that not the role of a woman?' her father countered. 'Your husband must protect and provide for you. You will have silks to wear, a soft bed to sleep in, and all he would ask in return is for you to remain dutiful and give him heirs.'

If that was marriage, then it was the same prison she was trapped in now. Gwen didn't want to merely be a decoration—she wanted to play a bigger role in governing Penrith. Right now, her father prevented her from having any contact with the people here. And it was becoming harder to accept that, despite his claims that it was dangerous. There had already been one attempt on his life, and his overprotective nature bothered her. Hiding away from the people would do nothing to improve their relationship.

'I often feel as if I'm locked away,' she admitted. 'You won't even let me talk to the serfs. How can I ever become Lady of Penrith?'

'That's not something you should worry about now,' her father warned. 'I won't let my only daughter fall into their hands. They would kill you if they got the chance. Or have you forgotten the man who tried to stab me?'

'No, I haven't.' And yet, it seemed that there was more he hadn't told her about that incident. There was an aura of fear among the serfs, an iron control that her father held over them. 'But I don't understand why he did it. We helped the people rebuild their homes, provided them with food—'

'They were rebellious to our king, along with the former earl.' Her father's voice had turned sharp. 'Do not question my methods, Gwen. You don't have the stomach for what must be done to maintain peace.'

She fell silent then. She'd heard whispers about her father's ruthless nature, but there was no denying that Alfred had achieved the outcome he wanted. No one broke his laws, and every time she gazed at the fields beyond the castle, she could see the grain ripening in the sun. Still, she sensed that there was a cruel side to him, one she didn't want to see.

'Now then, we will not speak of the past. There are men awaiting your presence below stairs. Put on a smile and greet them as a true lady.' Her father walked to the door, adding, 'Give them a chance. I think Gareth would be a good choice for you.'

After he'd gone, Gwen clenched her fists. She was tired of being treated like an object with no value except to give a man heirs. The sense of restlessness ached inside her to be something more. After her mother had died, she knew what it was to feel lost and alone. Despite her father's efforts to rule, she saw the echo of her own fears in their faces. Perhaps by helping the people, she could give her own life purpose.

But as long as Alfred reigned here, he would never allow it. And she suspected that the husband he chose would be a weak man, one easily commanded.

Gwen pushed back the rising resentment. Though she wanted to believe that her father only desired what was best for her, it was becoming more difficult to justify his behaviour. After the death of her mother, she'd understood his overprotective nature. But now, it was wearing thin. As she clenched the coverlet, it took several moments before she found her calm once again.

If only she could escape the life that had been foreordained for her. She wanted to take control of herself and see the world as it truly was, no matter how dangerous. Only then could she become the person she wanted to be.

Watching Lady Gwendoline among the other suitors had soured Piers's mood. He'd remained in the guise of a soldier, for it gave him the opportunity to watch over her. She had greeted several of them in the Great Hall, men who had come to win her hand in marriage.

She wore the blue gown he'd seen earlier, and her blonde hair was bound up beneath a veil. As four men came forward to greet her, she smiled and made conversation with each one. He'd known her suitors would begin arriving, but it spurred an unexpected jealousy. He didn't know why he'd become so possessive—the competitions would begin soon, so of course the men would be here.

But seeing their wealth and nobility heightened his unease. These men had more than he could ever dream of. Why should Gwen be interested in him at all? She was unattainable, a woman so far out of his reach, she might as well be the stars above him. No matter how hard he tried, he would never be enough.

Even if he won her affections, they had nothing in common. He couldn't understand the world she lived in, any more than she could understand what it was like when no one cared if you lived or died. Robert might claim to care, but it was only out of duty. His noble brother had always been responsible, nearly a saint. Whereas Piers was, and always would be, a sinner.

Even if he did win Penrith, he had no idea how to behave like a nobleman. But he refused to let that discourage him from his goal. For now, he would concentrate on winning the lady's hand, and he would learn the rest later.

As the hours passed by, Gwen's expression grew strained. She kept her manners, but she seemed disinterested in the men. Then her father spoke to one of them, and the suitor approached the dais, offering his hand.

Gwen gave an answering smile, but it didn't seem genuine. Then the man escorted her outside the Great Hall. Piers waited for her father or other guards to follow and watch over her, but no one did.

He suspected this was the man the earl had chosen for his daughter. Piers could see the suitor's fine clothing and the way he admired Gwendoline as if she were a golden chalice. The man's attention irritated him, even though there was no reason for it.

Piers waited until no one was watching him before he went outside to watch over her. They were walking within the castle grounds in full view of everyone, and he maintained his position. At least, for now, she was safe. Then they moved towards the staircase that led to the parapets. Piers tensed, wondering what the man intended. There were several towers along the parapets, places where no one could see them. His instincts went on alert, and he decided to follow.

Piers walked down the main stairs, only to be stopped by the captain of the guards. 'I don't know you.'

He stared at the man for a long moment, and finally the captain asked, 'Are you one of King John's men?'

Piers gave a single nod. 'I'm under Lord Penrith's orders at the moment. And he has asked me to guard his daughter. If you'll excuse me.' He didn't wait for permission but pushed his way past the captain and went towards the stairs on the opposite side of the inner bailey. Lady Gwendoline was walking alongside the suitor who had fair hair and was shorter in stature. Though he might simply be courting the lady, Piers wasn't going to stand around and allow them to be alone.

He hurried up the stairs, keeping his distance from them. As they walked the perimeter, he saw the man's hand move to Gwen's spine.

Don't touch her, Piers wanted to snarl.

He couldn't understand the fierce annoyance that grew stronger with every moment that passed. But if that man laid another hand on her, Piers was tempted to tear it off.

The man escorted her towards one of the towers, and Piers never took his eyes from them. He continued walking in the same direction, but they didn't leave the tower right away. Soon, he heard a slight muffled cry, and at that, Piers broke into a run.

Just as he'd feared, he found the knave gripping Gwen's hair, his mouth upon hers. She had her blade unsheathed, but the man had pressed her against the wall.

Piers seized the man by his tunic and tore him away. A black rage erupted from within him that this man had dared to touch Gwendoline, seeking to harm her. He shoved the man back against the wall, and it took everything he had not to unleash his wrath against the suitor.

'Are you all right?' he asked Gwen.

'I—Yes. I'm—'

'Take your hands off me,' the suitor snapped.

'Don't speak,' Piers warned. A dangerous part of him wanted a fight, wishing he could release his fury and punish the man, who had dared to touch her.

'I'll say whatever I wish,' the man answered.

With that, Piers struck him hard across the face. His fists crunched against bone, and he took satisfaction from the blow when the man crumpled to the ground.

'Piers, don't,' Gwen urged. She kept the blade in her hands and reached for his arm. 'Just escort me back and leave him where he is.'

'Did he hurt you at all?' he asked. No man had the right to force a woman, and he would gladly hit the man again, truth be told.

But Gwen took a step towards the parapets. 'I wouldn't have let him hurt me. I could have stopped him.' Her defensive tone held an air of frustration, as if she'd wanted to guard herself. But he wasn't about to stand aside and let someone harm an unarmed woman.

'I won't let any man harm you,' he swore. 'Not while I am near.'

She was shaking her head, eyeing him as if he'd become a wild beast. 'You didn't have to hit him.'

'I won't apologise for that,' he said. 'He deserved it after what he did.'

'He only tried to kiss me,' she said. 'It was nothing.'

'Did you want him to kiss you?' he demanded. 'Or did he try to force you?' He'd seen the way the suitor had shoved her against the wall. If Gwen had been will-ing, she wouldn't have drawn her blade.

She stepped out on to the parapets, and he followed, stepping over the unconscious suitor. 'I wasn't willing. But he's not the first man who has tried to kiss me.' With a sigh, she leaned back against the parapets. Piers tried to come closer, but she put up her hand. 'Don't come near me right now.'

He stayed motionless, recognising her fear. 'I only meant to defend you.'

From the wariness in her eyes, she didn't trust him yet. He'd likely overstepped the boundaries, and now, he didn't know what to say or do.

'I don't need you to defend me. Or have you forgot-ten last night?' Her eyes flashed with annoyance, and he let out an unsteady breath.

'I couldn't let him hurt you,' he muttered with a sigh. 'Nor any man.'

'I wouldn't have allowed it,' she countered, holding up her knife. 'He was an inconvenience, not a threat.'

'You shouldn't have to endure the attentions of a man you don't want.'

At that, she sent him a sidelong glance. 'Like you?'

Her words were a blow and caught him off guard. Did she truly believe his behaviour was the same as her attacker? He'd meant only to defend her. Confusion struck him, for he'd expected gratitude, not annoyance. Piers crossed his arms, leaning back against the tower to grant her physical distance. Though he didn't want to retreat, he recognised that his presence was only mak-ing matters worse.

Perhaps it had been his temper. He'd wanted to tear the man apart, and it was possible that he'd frightened her, which was never his intent. Better to give her space to let her feel safe again.

'Go back to the keep, Gwen,' he said. 'I'll stand guard a few paces back, so no one bothers you.' He paused and added, 'I hope you liked the bow.'

He didn't give her a chance to answer him but walked a short distance away towards the opposite tower. She returned towards the main keep, and he kept his word by guarding her several paces back. At least then she wouldn't feel threatened by his presence. From across the parapets, he saw her uncertain stare.

He wouldn't apologise for beating the man who had dared to touch her. But neither did he want her to fear him. He sensed that she didn't see his actions as protection—she saw them as threatening.

A darkness enfolded him as he kept his gaze fixed upon her. When he looked at Lady Gwendoline, it was a vivid reminder of all the things he would never have. He was lowborn, so how could he even think she would ever want a man like him?

Piers closed off the uncertain emotions, walling them off inside him. Aye, he'd frightened her, but there was nothing to be done about it now. He could not stray from the path he'd chosen. His mother had died trying to make him the heir to Penrith. He'd sworn that he would build a different life for himself, and he would do everything in his power to convince Gwen to marry him. Afterwards, he would keep her safe, allowing her the freedom to do as she pleased. And perhaps one day, she might not see him as a monster.

'What happened?' her father demanded. 'Gareth of Watcomb came to me and said one of my guards attacked him.' The earl's face was crimson with fury as he strode into her bedchamber. 'Tell me who it was, and I'll have him flogged.'

Gwendoline raised her chin to face him. 'Gareth was the one who attacked me,' she said coolly. 'I did not want his attentions, and I asked the guard to defend me.'

From the look on her father's face, he didn't believe her. 'You were in full view of everyone.'

'Not when we reached the tower,' she said. 'I tried to push Gareth away, but he would not listen. I called out to the guard for assistance.'

'Which guard?' her father asked softly.

But Gwen knew from the look on his face that he intended to punish Piers. She stared back at the earl and answered, 'I don't know his name. They all look alike to me.'

'Then I will ask Gareth to point him out to me,' her father said. 'This will not go unpunished.'

She could not believe he was defending her attacker. 'And what if Gareth had raped me? Would you defend him then?'

Her father sent her an exasperated look. 'You're overreacting, Gwen. Gareth is from one of the noblest families in England. He knows the meaning of honour. He, along with any of the other suitors I chose, would make an excellent husband for you.'

Her anger rose hotter. Overreacting? Because a man had tried to force a kiss? 'I will not choose him,' she insisted. 'Any man who thinks I would yield so easily is not a good man.'

'You hardly know him,' her father said. 'Give him a second chance.'

She refused to even consider it. But the more she argued with her father, the more stubborn he would become. He would never yield in a disagreement.

'We still have a few more days before the competitions begin,' she said. 'There are other suitors arriving from farther away. There may be another man even better whom we both prefer. Let us not quarrel about it now.'

He held her gaze for a moment before at last he relented. 'All right.'

Though she didn't want to, she embraced her father. Then she spoke the words that would soothe his ire. 'I know you only want what's best for me.'

Her words had the intended effect, and he softened. 'I do, indeed. Now remain in your room and embroider something or weave, or whatever it is you want to do now.'

He patted her head, making her feel as if she were six years old. But she masked her emotions and braved a smile.

Only after he'd gone did she tear off her veil and throw it hard at the bed, releasing her own anger. It was then that she noticed the cluster of wildflowers on her pillow. The yellow and white blooms dissipated her frustration, and she recognised them for what they were—an apology.

She hardly knew Piers at all. He was like a ghost, stealing into her room, leaving her gifts. There was no doubting he was a strong warrior, a man who could easily slay an enemy. But she sensed he was holding back secrets. Why else would he disguise himself or use hidden passageways to find her?

* * *

After a time, there was a knock at her door. She called out for the person to enter, but instead of a servant, she saw Piers standing at the entrance. He didn't come inside her room but instead stared at her.

'I came to ensure that you are unharmed.'

'I don't need your protection, Piers. Or your flowers.' Though she knew why he'd given them, it was only a reminder that he could invade her room at any moment.

'I know you don't,' he said quietly. 'I am sorry for frightening you. But I won't apologise for defending you.'

'You need to go,' she warned him. 'Gareth complained, and he may try to make trouble for you. My father wants you punished. If he does, I—'

'I don't care about your father,' Piers said. 'I came to see you.'

He didn't move, didn't press her for more. Instead, his gaze held hers in silence. And she realised that he had come to her door deliberately, so as not to frighten her again.

'What do you want from me, Piers?' she asked.

'Everything,' he answered honestly. She almost smiled, for it was not at all what she'd expected him to say. Then he continued, 'But I thought you might want to practise with your bow.'

'I can't,' she said. 'My father would see, and he'd never allow it.'

'There's a way outside the castle where he wouldn't see you,' Piers said. 'If you want to go, I'll take you there.'

Although the thought of escape was appealing, she

knew better than to go alone with a man who wanted her. Piers was dangerous and not at all someone she could trust.

'You seem to know a lot about this castle,' she accused. 'How?'

He paused a moment before admitting, 'This isn't the first time I've been to Penrith.'

She waited for him to say more, but he held his tongue and would not say more. Then he asked, 'Do you want to leave or not?'

Although she welcomed the idea of practising with her bow and escaping the castle for a few hours, it wasn't wise to go off alone with him. But her longing for a chance to breathe fresh air and escape her father's rules was tempting.

'I don't trust you,' she admitted. 'Why would I go with a stranger?'

'Because your father won't allow you to practise,' he said. 'You want to leave these walls and do something forbidden. And you know I'll keep you safe.'

'And who will keep me safe from you?' she demanded.

'I swear on my life that I will never hurt you.' He held both hands up in silent surrender. 'And I want a chance to redeem myself.'

Was it worth the risk? Her brain warned her that it was a terrible idea. She didn't know this man at all, except that she was attracted to him, and he'd defended her. He had already admitted he was one of her suitors, and this was his way of being alone with her for a longer period of time.

He could have overpowered her at any moment—

especially on the first night. Yet, whenever she'd demanded that he not touch her or ordered him to leave, he'd obeyed without question.

She longed to shoot her bow. It had been weeks since she'd had that feeling of power, the knowledge that she could pull back the bowstring and embed her arrow in the target. Somehow, she doubted that any man here would allow it.

You cannot trust him, her brain warned.

But then she heard herself ask, 'If I agree, where would you take me?'

'Just into the forest,' he offered. 'There's an underground passage that leads outside the castle grounds.'

While her brain warned her that this was unwise, a reckless side of her was tired of living beneath her father's orders. She did want to leave the castle and experience a moment of freedom. Perhaps it was worth it, if for no other reason than to find another way out.

She went over to her bed and reached beneath it to pull out the bow and quiver of arrows. 'All right. Show me the way.'

Within the hour, Piers led her through the wall behind her bed and along the narrow passageway that continued underground. He ducked low as he brought her past barrels of wine to the last tunnel.

It was nothing short of a miracle that she'd agreed to come with him. She had offered him a second chance, and he wasn't foolish enough to spurn it.

'I never knew all this was here,' Gwen breathed. 'I cannot believe it.'

Piers brought her to the end of the passage and then

stopped near the exit. 'This one leads to the barbican gate. But if we go out this way, we'll be seen.'

'I thought you said there was another passage that goes beyond the walls.'

'There is,' he agreed. 'But I wanted to warn you that it's narrow and difficult to go through. Your gown may be ruined.'

She shrugged as if she didn't care about the gown. 'My father wouldn't even notice if I never wore it again. We'll go outside the castle grounds.'

He was glad of her cooperation. 'Then follow me. I'll carry your bow for you once we're inside.' He started pulling out loose stones to reveal the hidden passageway. Even his brother Robert didn't know of its existence. Piers had only learned of it when he'd gone exploring one day. It appeared that someone had tried to seal up the passage long ago, but the mortar had come loose. He'd spent enough time hiding in these tunnels that he knew every inch of them.

As they moved through the tunnel on their hands and knees, he carried Gwen's bow for her. He pushed past the spider webs with his hands, squeezing through the passageway.

'I can hardly believe I'm doing this,' Gwendoline remarked. 'I shouldn't trust you—I know this. But I haven't had an adventure like this in I don't know how long.'

'When do you have to return?' he asked.

'By the afternoon, before the evening meal,' she said. 'We have a little time.'

They continued crawling on their hands and knees to

get to the end of the tunnel. By the time they reached the exit, they were inside the forest.

He helped Gwendoline stand, and she stared out at the woods in awe. Sunlight gleamed through the branches, illuminating the greenery. 'This is wonderful, Piers.' Her smile held such brightness and joy, he was struck by her beauty. 'Where will we go to practise?'

He led her through the trees until they reached the stream. 'I'll show you.' They followed a path along the water's edge, and he helped her cross the stream at one interval, lifting her over the water so her gown and shoes would not get wet. When they reached a small clearing, he bade her, 'Wait here.'

He took out a piece of leather and some rope from a bundle he'd brought with him. Then he set up the leather target between two trees, pulling it tight and tying it down.

'Should we not just shoot at a tree?' she suggested.

'It will be easier to retrieve the arrows from leather,' he answered. 'And the wood isn't good for the arrow-heads.' When the target was set up, he returned to her side. 'Go on, then. Give it a try.'

Gwen had already withdrawn an arrow and nocked it to the bow. Her face held such joy, he'd never expected this. Did archery really mean that much to her?

He could tell from her stance that she had shot a bow before, but her arm strained slightly, as if she'd lost some of her strength.

'What is your true name, Piers?' she asked as she took aim at the target.

He didn't know what to tell her at first. He could hardly say he was from Penrith. But he also didn't want to lie outright. Instead, he gave her the name of his mother's lands. 'I already told you. I am Piers of Greversshire.'

She released the arrow, and it struck the bottom of the target. 'I've not heard of Greversshire before.'

'It's small,' he lied. 'I would be surprised if you did know it.' Especially since the house and lands were in ruins. His mother had been an only child, and after she'd died, the lands had been claimed by a cousin whose lands adjoined theirs.

Gwen released two more arrows, each one striking the bottom of the leather. With a sigh, she admitted, 'I'm out of practice. It's been a few weeks since I've been able to shoot.'

'At least you struck the target,' he said. 'It's more than others could do.'

She finished shooting her arrows, and after Piers retrieved them, she regarded him. 'Your turn.'

He hesitated, for he'd planned on spending this time with her, letting her have that freedom. 'It's all right. You can continue practising.'

'No, I want to see what you can do.' She smiled and held out the bow, her eyes gleaming with interest. 'Do you even know how to shoot?'

'I do.' He'd used a bow and arrow to hunt their meals. He, Robert, and Brian had hunted together during the past two years. They'd remained in hiding after the king's men had burned Penrith and killed his father Degal. Shooting a bow had often been the difference between eating or starving.

'Show me.' She handed him the bow and an arrow. Piers drew back the bowstring, taking aim at the target. He was fully conscious of Gwendoline's nearness as she stood behind him. The faint aroma of her skin allured him, and he couldn't deny that he wanted to impress her. Just before he released the arrow, he kept his arm steady and turned his head to catch her gaze. He released the arrow and heard her audible intake of breath.

He knew, without looking, that he'd struck the centre of the target. The look of admiration in her eyes told him everything he wanted to know.

'Do that again,' she urged.

He nocked an arrow, took aim, and embedded a second arrow beside the first. Then a third. Gwendoline appeared delighted and said, 'Show me how to shoot like that.'

Piers held out the bow, and when she took it, she stood beside him. He made no move to touch her, but the scent of her drove him to madness. He grew distracted by her slender form, for he wanted to take her in his arms and kiss her. He could easily spend an hour exploring that beautiful skin with his mouth.

Though he'd come with the intent of winning Penrith, this woman held him spellbound. He couldn't deny that he wanted her badly, even if he would never be the sort of man she wanted.

She pulled back the bow and took aim. He adjusted her elbow and touched her forearm. 'Lift it slightly higher. Now release it.'

This time, her arrow was closer to the centre. She turned to smile at him, and her mouth was so near, the temptation was overwhelming.

'Again,' he commanded. He moved his hand to her waist and adjusted her hips as she took her aim towards the target. Her smile faded, and when she looked back at him, he got lost in her eyes. She was staring at him as if she didn't understand the heat rising between them.

Although he was taking advantage of the situation, he drew her close and helped her aim once more. She made no protest but let him adjust her bow. For a moment, he savoured the feeling of having this woman in his arms. Never in his life had he imagined he would spend time with a woman like Gwen, much less hold her. Her innocence was his undoing.

But it didn't matter whether he desired her. Once she learned the truth, she would never want him in return. He could only keep the deception going for so long until her interest turned to hatred for his lies.

He steeled himself against the inevitability. Aye, she would despise him, but that was to be expected. No matter what he had to do, no matter who stood in his way, she was going to be his one day…and Penrith along with her.

Chapter Three

She should have asked him more questions. Gwendoline sat on her bed for a long moment, wondering what she'd done. It had begun as an archery lesson—but it had ended with her feeling unsettled and restless.

Piers had kept his word and had only helped improve her shooting. But during the time she was in his arms, she'd felt a stirring inside her. His strong arms had enveloped her when she'd pulled back the bow and, behind her, she'd felt the body of a warrior. In his arms, she'd been conscious of his strength and the scent of his skin. She could easily have turned around and been in his embrace. Once, his mouth had been so close to hers, she'd wanted him to kiss her. In his eyes, she'd seen the darkness of desire, and she'd wanted to taste it.

But he'd left her alone, just as he'd said he would. Gwen let out a breath, wishing she'd taken advantage of their time together. She'd had hours to find out more about him, but she hadn't asked him nearly enough. She'd been so caught up by the thrilling freedom of being able to shoot her bow again that she'd forgotten all else.

She couldn't deny that she'd loved every moment of the archery lesson. Even when his arms were around her, he had been careful not to cross that boundary. Under his guidance, she had adjusted her shooting and it had made a strong difference.

It had been such an unexpected gift to hold a bow again, she found herself drawn to this man. For a moment, she allowed herself to dream of what it would be like to be wedded to a man like Piers. He was fierce, strong, and he'd sworn never to let anyone harm her. But now, instead of being frightened by him, she found him intriguing. And unlike the other men she'd known, he did listen to her, even if it was hard to concentrate in his presence.

Would he allow her to voice an opinion or rule alongside him? Was it possible that Piers might be different from her other suitors? She was almost afraid to hope. With a sigh, she hid her bow and quiver of arrows once again.

Within a few moments, she heard a knock at her door. She called out for the person to enter, and her maid Aelish came inside. 'We have a visitor, Lady Gwendoline. It's a lady that our soldiers found at the gates with only a single guard. She was robbed and has asked for shelter.'

Sympathy welled up within her at the woman's fate. 'Was she hurt? Should we send for the healer?'

Aelish shook her head. 'Only upset and lost, I think.'

Gwen rose from the bed and strode towards the door. 'Let us go and greet her, then.' She could only imagine how the woman was feeling, and she would do everything in her power to make her feel safe.

She hurried down the stairs, and when she reached the Great Hall, she saw that the doors were already open. Gwen strode towards the entrance and outside, she saw a young maiden standing at the bottom of the stairs. The woman wore a green gown and a darker cloak, and her appearance was rumpled, as if she'd lost her veil. Her brown hair seemed to be falling loose from its arrangement.

The woman raised her chin and squared her shoulders, but despite her outward air of confidence, there was fear in the young woman's eyes. She glanced at her guard and then the others, as if she were overwhelmed.

Gwen hurried to the woman's side and came to greet her. 'I am Lady Gwendoline. Come inside, and you can join us. We were just about to eat.'

'My name is Morwenna.' The woman glanced around her, and her guard remained farther back.

'I'm so sorry for what happened to you,' Gwen said. 'Aelish told me you were robbed on your journey. Are you certain you're not hurt? Can I get you anything?'

'I'll be all right.' Morwenna's voice was barely audible, and Gwen linked her arm with the young woman's. It was meant to be reassuring, but she could feel the slight tremor, as if Morwenna had not yet recovered from the attack.

'Come and sit beside me,' Gwen offered. 'You'll feel better once you've had food and drink.' She led the young woman to the dais, and one of the maids took Morwenna's cloak.

Although she was sympathetic to the woman's plight, part of her was grateful for another woman to talk to.

They seemed to be of a similar age, and it seemed like forever since she'd had a friend to confide in.

The scent of roasted capon made her mouth water. A servant offered a portion of the meat to her father. Alfred then sliced off a wing and gave Gwen some. It surprised her that he hadn't served their guest first, but before she could offer any to Morwenna, the servant was already in front of her.

The moment Morwenna saw the man holding the food, her eating knife clattered upon the table. Then she tried to hide her reaction by saying, 'Forgive me. I fear that my weariness has caught up with me.'

Gwendoline didn't entirely believe that. She suspected it was still fear lingering after the attack. Though she couldn't imagine what Morwenna had suffered, undoubtedly it would take time for her to feel safe around men again. But she offered her sympathy. 'I understand. I will find a place for you to sleep, and you may stay with us until your father arrives.'

The lady nodded, but Gwen didn't miss how the woman's eyes followed the servant. It made her wonder whether there was a problem of some kind. 'How many men attacked your travelling party?' she asked gently.

'I…don't really remember.'

'And what of your guards?' Gwen enquired. 'How many are missing?'

The woman lowered her gaze. 'I don't know. It all happened so fast, and one of my guards, Brian, brought me here. I'm not sure what happened to the others. I suspect they went to find my father.'

But there was a tell-tale flush of guilt on her face. Gwen couldn't tell whether Morwenna was nervous or lying for some reason. For now, she decided to play along and pretend she believed the young woman.

As they ate and conversed, Gwen glanced around for some sign of Piers among the soldiers, but he was nowhere to be found. It was clear he was keeping his presence hidden, almost as if he didn't want anyone else to know he was here. Her mind centred on that certainty, and she thought about his claim that he'd been to Penrith before. He seemed to know this castle better than anyone. And she could think of only one reason why he knew the estate as well as he did.

She'd heard rumours that the former earl had a son who had disappeared. Was it possible that Piers was that son? It would make sense why he wanted to wed her. And certainly, the earl's son would know Penrith and all its hidden secrets. It also explained why he might give a false name. If he'd kept himself hidden to survive, then it made sense. The idea took root within her, but she needed to know more about him.

After the meal, Gwendoline led Morwenna to her chamber. The woman appeared awestruck at the room. 'Are you certain this is all right? I could find another place to sleep.'

'No, you'll stay with me,' Gwen promised. 'I imagine you must be exhausted after the day's events.'

'I am,' Morwenna agreed. She walked over to the bed and touched the coverlet as if she'd never seen anything so fine. More and more, Gwen was convinced that Morwenna was holding back secrets. But was she here to cause harm? It didn't seem so. She decided to bide her time and find the answers she wanted.

'Should I ask Aelish to come and bring you a shift?'

'I'll just wear the one I have on,' Morwenna answered. She remained standing beside the bed and lowered her gaze.

'I will lend you clothing, if you have need of it,' Gwen promised. 'In the meantime, I'll have a servant light a fire for us.'

She opened the door and, within a few moments, a young lad came to build a peat fire in a brazier. Soon, the space filled with warmth, and she sat down across from Morwenna. Though Gwen was itching to ask the woman more, she sensed that it would take time to gain her trust.

'Is there anything else you need?' she asked.

'No, you've been very kind. I'm grateful for your help.' Morwenna pulled a stool over beside the brazier and came to warm herself.

'Have you been to Penrith before?' Gwen pulled another chair up nearby her.

'Years ago,' Morwenna admitted.

Good. Then she might have seen the former earl's son. Gwen continued, 'I heard…rumours that the former earl had a son. Do you know what happened to him?'

There was a sudden flash of emotion that crossed the woman's face, but she quickly masked it. 'I know he was taken captive the night the king's men came. After that… I cannot say.' She shook her head, offering nothing else.

The more she thought of it, the more Gwen believed that Piers had to be the missing heir. Although she didn't know if he would try to see her again tonight, she intended to ask him. And one way or another, she would have her answers.

* * *

Piers awakened when he heard footsteps approaching and saw the flare of an oil lamp. In the darkness, he saw Gwendoline illuminated by the light.

'What are you doing here, Gwen?'

Never had he imagined he would see her within the hidden tunnels. How had she ever managed to find him? His first instinct was that she was in trouble somehow. But from her calm expression, that didn't seem possible. Why had she come in search of him?

'I thought that I might find you here,' she remarked. 'You seem to be remaining in hiding.'

He sat up, and Gwen set the oil lamp down, joining him on the ground. 'You're going to get your gown dirty,' he warned.

'I got it dirty hours ago. And it doesn't matter,' she said, leaning back. For a moment, she seemed to be thinking about something. Then she turned to him. In the dim lamplight, she studied his face. 'I came because I want answers from you. Who are you, Piers? And don't say Piers of Grevershire. I don't believe that. You know Penrith far too well to have only been here once or twice.'

Clearly, Gwen was not a woman to abandon her curiosity. And he wasn't about to fall into a trap that could cost him her hand in marriage. Instead, he tried to divert her attention. 'Did you enjoy the archery today?'

She smiled at that. 'I did, though I know you're trying to change the subject. I asked you a question.'

'And I'm choosing not to answer.' He reached out to cup her cheek. 'I am here to compete for your hand in marriage, Gwen.'

'You shouldn't keep calling me that,' she warned, pulling back from him. 'It will anger my father.'

'Does it anger you?' He didn't care at all about her father's wishes, but he didn't want to offend her. He preferred calling her by her name, for then he could think of her as a woman instead of lady of the castle.

'No, but…you should only call me that when we're alone,' she acceded.

'Like now?'

She nodded in the lamplight as if she'd suddenly grown aware of what she'd done. 'I suppose.' For a moment, she seemed to grow shy. 'You're not a man of wealth, are you?' she whispered. 'And I think I know why you're hiding your past from me.'

She likely believed he was Robert, but Piers wasn't about to tell her the truth about who he was. Better to let her believe he was the heir instead of a bastard, at least until he gained her consent to wed.

Instead, he knelt before her and drank in her features in the golden light of the lamp. 'I'm not the sort of man you're used to. My past was…difficult.' He drew his hand to her nape, and she froze at his touch. He waited to see if she would pull away, and when she made no protest, he threaded his fingers into her silken hair. 'I came here to compete for the right to marry you. And I'm not going to give that up without a fight.'

She rose to her knees and took his hands in hers. A flare of rigid need struck him, and he wanted to kiss her, to tempt her beyond her wildest dreams. But she'd already been attacked once. He didn't want to risk her ire, and it took every last thread of control not to frighten her.

'I know what you really want. And it's not me.' She lifted her chin to regard them. 'You want Penrith, just as the rest of them do. Perhaps more because it was once yours.'

He didn't deny it. But he couldn't bring himself to speak.

'Degal of Penrith, the former earl, was your father,' she predicted.

Piers said nothing, allowing her to draw her own conclusions. Instead, he reached out and touched a finger to her lips. 'Is this why you came in secret to see me? To press me for answers?'

She took his finger away. 'Yes. I want to know the truth about you, Piers.'

'And what if I don't want to tell you?' he ventured. 'At least, not yet.'

'Then that means you have something to hide.' She stared at him in the darkness. 'You don't have to deny it. I know you lost everything when he was executed.'

'I don't want to talk about the past,' he hedged. 'I'd rather talk about the future.' Her expression held him spellbound, and he needed to know more. 'What is it you truly want, Gwen?' he gritted out, fighting back against the brutal urge to capture her mouth. 'Tell me what it is, and I will give it to you.'

'I want to be in command of my own life,' she answered. 'I want to escape my father's prison and truly be Lady of Penrith.' She kept her hands on his shoulders, and her touch only deepened his longing. 'From what I see of the people, there is misery. Mayhap from the rebellion years ago. I know they don't like my father. I want to help them, but I am powerless to do anything.'

'And will that change when you marry?'

She lifted her shoulders in a shrug. 'Not unless Alfred returns to Tilmain. And I fear that he won't want to.'

'If you wed a man without a spine, I vow that Alfred most definitely won't go.' Piers moved his hands to rest at her waist. He didn't press her for more, but he waited to see if she would pull away.

'What is it that you want, Piers?'

You, he almost said. But then he thought about Penrith and the birthright that should have been his. He understood why Wenda had been furious after Degal had abandoned her, leaving her pregnant and alone. But his desire to govern Penrith had nothing to do with Wenda's vengeance and everything to do with his own desire to change his life.

'I want a second chance,' he said at last. 'I want to rebuild what was lost here. And to do that, I need your help.'

Her expression transformed into a slight smile. 'I suppose you're telling me what I want to hear.'

'No, if I were doing that, I would be telling you that you're beautiful.'

She did laugh at that. 'But you're not saying that at all, Piers.'

He took a risk and rested his palm against her cheek. 'I already know there's more to you than what the others see.'

Her smile faded, and she pulled back from him. 'But I don't know you at all.' He sensed her nerves but didn't move.

'Do you want to?' he asked quietly.

'Yes.' In the faint lamplight, her expression had turned pensive. She leaned back against the wall and drew her knees up. 'I do want you to fight in the tourney,' she said. 'I admire your strength.' Her gaze fixed upon his shoulders, and he tensed as he wondered what she thought of him. 'And you're right. You're not like any other man I've known.'

Her touch seared him to the bone, making him crave her even more. 'I'll fight if that's what you want from me,' he vowed. 'And I intend to win.'

She was staring at him with such intensity, he said in a husky voice, 'But what I want most of all is to kiss you right now, Gwen.'

She paled, and he didn't move at all, waiting to see what she would do. In the tunnels below ground, the air was cool, and she shivered.

He wanted to draw his cloak around her, to capture her mouth and tempt her. But he didn't want her to compare him to the suitor he'd struck down.

'But you're not going to?' she whispered.

'It's your choice. If you want me to kiss you, I will. Or if you want me to stay back, I won't move. You're in command.' He saw the indecision in her eyes and remained seated across from her, unmoving.

'I don't know what I want,' she admitted. But she drew closer and rested her hands on his shoulders. 'Except my freedom.'

Piers leaned in, knowing she was a lady of innocence. He'd never kissed anyone like her before, and he didn't really know why she was considering it. He suspected it had to do with the rebellious side to her.

He waited a moment longer and then lightly claimed

her lips in a silent question. She yielded to him, her mouth softening beneath his. Her hands framed his face, and he deepened the kiss. Though he hungered for more, he wouldn't risk frightening her. But even so, he couldn't stop himself from sliding his hands through her hair.

'I know you're the earl's son,' she murmured against his mouth as she kissed him again. 'I would stake my life on it. But don't worry—I won't tell anyone.'

He stiffened at her words but didn't acknowledge them. Instead, he slid his tongue against her mouth, asking her to open for him. When she did, he entered her mouth and felt her gasp. But even then, she touched her tongue to his and her hesitant response only made him want her more. She was gripping his shoulders, leaning in as he took her offering.

The kiss was a gift he'd never expected. For her to willingly kiss him awakened him to a hunger for more, a desire that pushed past the boundaries between them into a fierce temptation. She kissed him with the softness of an innocent, but her lips only reminded him of what he couldn't have.

Piers didn't want to pull back, but he did at last. Her breathing was unsteady, her hair falling against her face. 'You cannot come to see me in my room again. I have a guest staying with me. Morwenna is her name.'

Morwenna was in the castle? He swiftly hid his response, for that meant the risk of seeing Robert was higher. He knew they'd made camp in the forest somewhere…but why would Morwenna come here? Piers had successfully avoided everyone thus far—but now, he'd have to be even more careful.

'Is she a friend of yours?' he asked Gwen, even though he knew everything about Morwenna. She was the miller's daughter who'd been hopelessly in love with Robert for years. She was spirited and fierce, but what he didn't know was why she'd come to the castle. It was far safer for her to remain in the forest.

'No, I've just met her. She claims that she was robbed during her journey and only has one guard. We've sent word to her father, but I suspect there is more she hasn't told me.' Gwen lowered her gaze. 'I will find out, but in the meantime, you cannot visit my room. My father is going hunting the day after tomorrow, and I plan to accompany him. You can meet me in the forest on that day.'

Piers hesitated, for the risk of being caught was even greater out in the open. He knew Robert was visiting with the people of Penrith, learning what he could about the new Lord. Though his brother was unlikely to come on a hunting trip, Piers couldn't dismiss the possibility.

And yet, Gwen had asked him to come. It gave him hope that she was truly considering him as a suitor, despite the way he'd avoided her questions. For now, he would let her believe whatever she wanted—it would make no difference in the end.

'I will come,' he agreed. 'There is a path leading through the forest with a drop-off and large rocks below. It's not far from the stream.'

'I know the place,' she said.

'Then I will meet you at the bottom of that hill near the rocks.' He leaned in and stole another kiss. 'You'd better go before Morwenna discovers you're gone.'

'She left before I did,' Gwen said against his mouth. 'I don't know where she went, but I'll find out.'

Piers suspected Morwenna had gone to meet with Robert in secret, but he said nothing. 'I will meet you in the forest the day after tomorrow,' he promised. 'And when the competitions begin, I intend to win.'

She reached out to touch his face and smiled. 'Good.'

The morning of the hunt, Morwenna seemed nervous about something. She'd worn the same rumpled green gown from the day she'd arrived, but in the daylight, Gwen noticed that it was an older dress that fit poorly. More and more, she was convinced that Morwenna was not a noblewoman. But why was she here? She intended to get the answers, but slowly.

'You can stop pacing now,' Gwen said. 'We'll be leaving soon.'

'Am I pacing?' Morwenna sighed and sat on the bed. 'I'm sorry. I don't mean to be a bother.'

'You're not.' Gwen drew closer. Yesterday, the young woman had confided that she hadn't told the entire truth—that her father was dead and she had nowhere to go. Morwenna had also admitted that there was a man whom she cared for, who was coming to Penrith to compete for Gwen's hand. She believed the young woman, especially in regard to the suitor. Morwenna's face had filled with sadness and longing, almost as if she were resigned to losing him.

'I'm just…thinking about the competitions.' Morwenna let out a heavy sigh and reached up to the golden pendant she wore. 'I can't stay here for too much longer, I know. You've been very kind.'

'You don't have to be afraid,' Gwen insisted. 'I haven't told my father anything. Or I can try to help you contact your mother's family.'

'Perhaps,' she whispered. But there was a sadness on her face as if she didn't believe it was possible.

'You have choices,' Gwen argued. 'Whether *he* arrives or not. There will be plenty of men at the competitions, if you want to choose a husband from among them.' As far as she was concerned, Morwenna was welcome to any of the men, as long as it wasn't Piers. She only wished she could be sure he was the earl's son. He was hiding so many secrets.

'But this is your tourney,' Morwenna reminded her. 'And I do hope you'll find your own perfect husband.' She smiled at Gwen and reached out to squeeze her hand in silent support.

'I hope so.'

It had been so long since she'd had a female friend. Though she knew Morwenna was hiding secrets, her friendship had seemed genuine. They had talked for long hours into the night, and Gwen learned that they had a great deal in common. It felt as if she had an ally of sorts.

Just as the sun began to rise, they went to join her father and the others. It seemed that Alfred was distracted for some reason. He continued to search while they rode through the forest, as if he were looking for something. When they reached the stream, they dismounted and waited.

Gwen didn't know whether they had caught sight of deer, but the waiting continued for a while. She was wondering how she would ever manage to slip away from the others to meet Piers.

A sudden rise of anticipation brought a chill of nerves. She hadn't seen him at all yesterday, and she wondered where he'd been or what he'd done. It was strange to realise that she'd missed him, despite his overbearing, secretive ways. The only problem was that she couldn't slip away until her father was preoccupied during the hunt.

But then Morwenna came to her aid. The young woman caught the attention of Alfred and motioned to both of them. She nodded towards the far end of the stream, as if asking for permission to relieve herself.

Though her father wasn't pleased by it, he gave a shrug. Gwendoline dismounted and accompanied Morwenna as they left the others. 'Where are we going?'

'Somewhere we can talk,' Morwenna answered. 'Don't you find the waiting dull?'

At that, Gwendoline beamed. 'I knew I liked you.' But this was about more than the waiting—it was her opportunity to leave. They continued walking through the forest, following the stream. Dry leaves crunched beneath their feet while above them, the trees were filled with greenery and morning sunlight.

When they were within a short walking distance of the oak, Morwenna excused herself. 'I need a moment. You can keep walking, and I'll catch up. Meet me by that large tree ahead.'

'I can wait for you,' Gwendoline offered, though she didn't truly want to. She wanted the chance to be alone, but it wasn't right to abandon the woman.

'No, I'd rather have…privacy,' Morwenna countered. 'I'll be there soon.'

Gwen was careful to hide her elation. Now was her chance to leave. As soon as Morwenna turned her back, she hurried towards the stone outcropping Piers had described. She could no longer see Morwenna through the thick trees, and she found the path leading down to the rocks. She held on to her skirts as she descended to the bottom of the hill. Just as she'd hoped, Piers was waiting for her, leaning back against one of the stones.

Her nerves returned at the sight of him, for the last time when he'd kissed her, they had been almost in darkness. Here, in the light of day, she suddenly felt shy. He was just as handsome and rugged as she remembered, his blue eyes staring at her as if he couldn't believe she was here. He wore leather and chainmail, his dark hair cropped against his neck.

Then he held out his hand to her. 'You came.'

She put her hand in his and admitted, 'I cannot stay long. But I—'

He cut off her words, claiming her mouth in a kiss. She didn't know what she'd expected, but it certainly wasn't this storm of breathless need. He pressed her back against the stones and pulled back for just a moment. 'I've been craving a taste of you, Gwen. If this isn't what you want, go back now.'

She didn't move, but her heartbeat thundered in her chest. 'Wh-what are you going to do?'

'I'm going to tempt you,' he answered. 'If that's what you desire.'

His words sent a secret thrill through her as she moved towards him. 'I cannot stay long. But I don't know if—'

He cut off her words and kissed her hard, as if he

couldn't get enough. But instead of frightening her, she found it exciting. He was a handsome warrior and, despite his ruthless ways, it seemed that he saw her in a way no one else did.

He didn't chastise her for wanting to shoot a bow; instead, he'd taken her to practise. He'd helped her improve and had spent time with her during these past few days. And when an overeager suitor had dared to touch her, Piers had taken him apart. She couldn't deny that with this man, she felt protected.

She'd been the obedient daughter for so long, following her father's rules. And just now, for a moment, she wanted to break every last one of them. She wanted to savour this man's brutal wildness, the savagery of being claimed, while rebelling against the rules she had to follow.

Gwen wound her arms around his neck and kissed him back. His hands moved to her backside, and Piers pulled her hips to his, making no secret of his arousal. The hard ridge of him evoked an aching desire between her legs and she had no interest in gentleness.

Piers kissed her with a fierce intensity, his tongue plundering her mouth. Her body ignited with fiery need, and when he wedged his knee between her legs, he lifted her up to sit on his thigh. The sensation of having that pressure between her legs evoked an unfamiliar longing.

Knowing that it would end soon—that she had to go back before anyone discovered she was missing—only made the kiss hotter. This man was forbidden, and she loved the way he made her feel. His mouth moved lower against her throat, and shivers broke over her skin. She was drowning in unfamiliar sensations, and the pressure of his knee suddenly drove her desire to a fever pitch.

'If we had time, I would pull your gown to your waist and taste every inch of your skin,' he murmured as he took her mouth hard. She was crumbling apart, and he seemed to know how to move his knee against her intimately, making her imagine he was filling her body with his. 'I would kiss your breasts and learn what pleased you.' As if to underscore his words, his hand moved over her bodice, near her breast but without touching it. She let out a gasp, for her imagination made her envision his caress. An aching sensation spiralled within her womanhood, and she grew wet, yearning for this man.

'I would spend hours,' he swore. 'And I wouldn't stop pleasuring you until you couldn't bear it any longer.'

'I already can't bear it,' she moaned. 'Piers.' He continued to kiss her as he moved her against his knee, and she felt the relentless pressure building higher.

'If I were your husband, I would tempt you every night,' he said. 'Even now, all I want to do is lift your skirts and sink deep inside you.'

He gentled his kiss, nipping it lightly. 'Do you want me, Gwen?'

She could barely breathe, but she murmured, 'Yes.' She drew back from the kiss, knowing she had to go now before they discovered she was missing. 'But y-you have to win the tourney on the morrow.'

'I will,' he swore. 'And you will choose no other man but me.'

She could hardly breathe after he lowered her from his knee. Her body was aching with an arousal she didn't understand, but she wanted this man. More than ever, she was convinced that he was the true Earl of Penrith. He belonged in this place and knew every inch of it.

If she chose him as her husband, it offered a fitting end to his plight. Their marriage would return the title he'd lost, and one day their sons would claim the land. Somehow, it was a way of healing the past.

But she could never let her father learn the truth. Her only hope of gaining Piers as a husband was to continue the deception and let Alfred believe that he was the son of a powerful lord instead of a traitor.

'I will see you on the morrow,' she promised. And though it bothered her to turn back to the others, there was no choice. Morwenna would be looking for her, as would her father. These stolen moments were all she had. And somehow, they would have to be enough.

She raced back up the path and picked up her skirts. There was no time to wait for Morwenna, but she rejoined her father. Alfred had a cool expression on his face, and he stared at her with disapproval.

'Where were you?' he demanded.

'I was…taking care of my needs,' she lied, keeping her voice quiet. 'I'm sorry if it took some time. Were you successful in your hunt?'

'Where is Morwenna?' he demanded.

'I assume she's near the stream,' Gwen said. 'We both had to…'

Before she finished, her father seized her wrist and forced her to walk with him away from the others. 'Are you trying to make a fool of me, Gwendoline? Do you think I'm so ignorant that I don't know when a young woman is sneaking away to be kissed?'

The colour drained from her face, and she hardly knew what to say. There was no excuse she could give, so she remained silent.

'Aelish confessed to me that you left your chamber two nights ago.' Her father kept his voice in an iron whisper. 'I don't know what you think you're doing, but no daughter of mine will play the whore. I have men in your chamber right now, sealing off the passage you used to escape.'

She hardly knew what to say to him, though she was certain her expression had given her away. But finally, she said, 'I have done nothing wrong, Father.'

'Don't lie.' His words were frigid, warning her of dire consequences. 'I know every suitor who has arrived at Penrith. And the only man I'll allow you to wed is Gareth, who is not here.'

Her face turned scarlet, and she tried again to answer. 'You're wrong. I—'

'Silence,' he snapped. 'When I learn who it was, I'll have him flogged.'

She said nothing, for at that moment one of the men shot a deer. There were cheers among the others, and her father left her side as they went to retrieve the carcass. Gwen glanced behind her, but there was no sign of Morwenna. Only after the men began cleaning the deer did she see the woman approaching. Gratefully, she went to join her, for it was exactly the distraction she needed.

But her heart hadn't stopped pounding. Alfred had guessed what she'd been doing, and if she showed any attention to Piers at the tourney, her father would know the truth.

What should she do? She had to marry—there was no choice in that. Her father wanted her to wed a man of his choosing. But after meeting Piers, she found it difficult to imagine marrying anyone else. She liked his bold recklessness and the way he cared nothing for the rules. Around him, she could be herself. And that freedom was intoxicating.

It made sense why he'd been careful to tell no one who he was and why he'd remained in hiding—else someone would recognise him in the castle. But during the tourney, he would have to reveal himself.

Gwen risked a glance back at the trees, wondering whether she could trust Piers. Or was he only using her in an effort to win back his lands?

Chapter Four

It was nightfall when Piers joined the other suitors at the competition. Penrith blazed with the glow of nearly one hundred torches. The inner bailey had been divided into four areas, each set up for a different competition. Colourful banners hung from all over the castle, and he heard the sound of bards singing and playing the lute. The air held the heady scent of roasting meat, and dozens of men gathered in the bailey.

He stood behind most of them, staring at Gwen. She was exquisite in her gown of white with a silver torque around her throat. In the light of the torches, she appeared almost otherworldly, like an angel. For a moment, it reminded him of how unworthy he was of her. Morwenna stood beside Gwen, wearing a borrowed crimson bliaud.

The men in front of him wore finely made armour, and some of their sword hilts were gold with embedded sapphires or rubies. Piers had left his training sword behind for it was so brittle, it might shatter with any force at all. The other sword was the one he'd stolen from the armoury, and he feared someone might recognise the weapon. The last thing he needed was more attention.

Piers wore simple clothes with no colour or embellishments. But despite his poverty, he was here to win the contests. He would marry Gwendoline and reclaim Penrith, regardless of her father's wishes. After their stolen moment in the forest, he suspected he could convince her to come with him willingly.

His half-brother Robert stood near the front of the competitors, and Piers was careful to stay away from him, keeping his face hooded to obscure his face. Though it had been less than a sennight since he'd seen Robert, he was torn between wanting to soundly defeat his brother and being glad to see him once more.

Everything would change between them if he succeeded in winning Gwen's hand. Robert would be furious, accusing him of stealing his birthright. But Piers wanted a different life…and he wanted Gwen. He yearned to have her, for she challenged him even as she allured him.

Soon, Lord Penrith moved to the front of the stairs to address all of them. 'Tonight, we begin a series of contests. Those of you who choose to join will compete for my daughter's hand in marriage. There will be games of skill and prizes for the winners, but it is your chance to show her your strength and abilities. By tomorrow, she has promised that she will choose a husband from among you. And if you are not chosen, there is another lady who wishes to marry. You might consider the Lady Morwenna after Gwendoline has made her choice.'

Piers planned to watch Robert to see which contest his brother would enter first. Then he intended to compete in a different competition, one where Robert wouldn't see him.

After a time, the suitors divided among the different events. Piers chose archery as his first contest while Robert joined the wrestling matches. Gwen was with Morwenna, and they went to watch the fighters while Piers competed against the other archers.

Although he wanted Gwen to watch him, it was unwise to reveal his presence just yet. Not only to her, but also to Robert. His brother would fight for Penrith with everything he had, and Robert was the one competitor strong enough to defeat him.

Piers chose an arrow and aimed at the straw target. As he did, he thought of the day he'd taken Gwen shooting. He would never forget the softness of her body in his arms as he'd helped her adjust her aim. She had loved the freedom of practising with her bow, and he wanted her to have that opportunity.

He never should have kissed her in the forest. In her eyes, he'd seen the interest. But it was only because he'd allowed her to believe that he was the true heir. She thought he was Degal's legitimate son, and Piers had said nothing to deny it. But only a bastard would lie to gain her consent to the marriage. He wasn't a man of honour or nobility—he was ruthless, using every means to get what he wanted.

All he could do was enjoy whatever time was left before she learned the truth and looked upon him with regret.

Piers pulled back his bowstring and struck the centre of the target each time. It took no effort at all to defeat his opponents in this first round. For the second competition, he decided to join the sword fighting. He handed his bow to another competitor and kept to the shadows, trying not to be noticed. Then he saw Gwen approaching the archers who were starting the next round.

For a long moment, he studied her features. Her beauty went beyond a lovely face—she had courage. Even if she were not the heiress to Penrith, he wanted this woman. And that meant fighting for her and facing his brother.

It might as well be now, for there was no sense in delaying the inevitable. He saw Robert awaiting his turn, and Piers quietly gave his name to the man directing the fighters.

'Do you have armour?' the man asked.

Piers shook his head, once again to avoid the others recognising his stolen chainmail. The man pointed towards a wooden table. 'Choose armour and a sword.'

He selected a chainmail hauberk and cowl, then a sword. He tested the weight and feel of the weapon, and it was similar to the other one he'd taken. Piers kept his back to the fighting ring while he donned the chainmail. Then he picked up the sword and chose a wooden shield.

'You'll fight your opponent over there,' the first man said.

Piers crossed the space to the ring where Robert was waiting. It was time to face his brother and fight for what he wanted. He lowered his hood and gave a slight smile to Robert.

His brother stared at him in shock. 'What are you doing here?'

Piers didn't answer but made the first move, swinging his sword towards his brother's neck. Robert blocked him, and Piers leaned in closer. 'I thought I'd court the Lady Gwendoline. She is a beauty, is she not?'

The taunt had exactly the effect he'd intended. His brother could keep a cool head when fighting other opponents, but not with him. Even now, he could see Robert struggling to keep his temper. 'Stay away from her,' his brother growled. 'She's a high-born lady.'

And you're a bastard.

Piers could almost hear the unspoken words, along with the silent assertion that he wasn't worthy. Robert knew exactly how to make him angry, and his own fury began to rise.

'So she is,' Piers answered. 'And I've a right to be here, the same as you.' He continued his attack, his sword striking hard until the sound of metal rang out in the bailey. His sword slipped past Robert's defences and nicked him on his chin. Blood welled up, and his brother lunged forward while the crowd shouted around them.

Piers caught a glimpse of Morwenna and Gwendoline watching. Seeing Gwen renewed his energy, and he fought back, defending every blow as Robert circled.

But this fight was about more than Gwen or even Penrith. It was about his frustration over the life he'd been given and his desire to change it. He hungered for the life of an earl, not because he wanted wealth or to live in a castle. He wanted the power that went with it, the means of changing lives.

He had endured the life of a serf, going hungry in the wintertime. He knew what it was to be invisible to his overlord—to live a life where he didn't matter. If he were Earl of Penrith, he would change everything. Piers understood the serfs' frustration at injustice. And with Gwen at his side, they could make a difference.

Robert's emotions were visible, and he grew reckless, hacking with his sword until Piers could only defend himself. He pushed back, causing his brother to stumble, but before he could gain the advantage, his brother swung at his head.

The weight of the chainmail made the fight even worse. Sweat ran down his face, and he wondered how long it would continue. Robert wasn't going to surrender. He would fight until he could no longer lift a sword. Piers's arms ached as he parried blows and continued his own attack.

But then Gwen shouted, 'Stop! This match is over.'

Piers was already swinging his sword when his brother turned towards her voice. He tried to stop his motion, but Robert barely avoided the blow.

The women hurried towards them, and Gwen said, 'I declare this match a draw.' Worry lined her face, as if she'd known this was more than a competition. 'You will both dine with me and the Lady Morwenna.'

Robert sheathed his sword, and Piers handed his sword to one of the other fighters before stripping off his armour. He caught a glimpse of a blush on Gwen's face when she saw him without a shirt. Then he donned his leather tunic and turned to join her.

She reached out to take his arm, and Piers couldn't stop his smile. It didn't matter who had won the match. As far as he was concerned, he held the greater victory.

* * *

Gwendoline didn't have a good feeling about the banquet. Although her father's expression held a smile, she recognised that look. It was a warning to her.

They took their places on the dais—she on her father's right side with Piers beside her. She introduced him to her father as Piers of Grevershire, and Alfred's expression never wavered. *Careful,* her instincts warned. She could not allow him to think that Piers was the man she'd kissed. She had to remain as indifferent as possible.

Morwenna sat beside Alfred with the other man on her left. Gwen hadn't met him yet, but he introduced himself as Robert of Inglewood. From the look of concern on Morwenna's face, Gwen suspected that Robert might be the man Morwenna had spoken of earlier— the one she'd wanted to marry. The young woman had grown alarmed at the sight of them fighting and, for a moment, Gwen had felt the same.

She was trying to discern if there was something between Piers and this man, Robert. The fight between them had gone beyond any ordinary match. It almost seemed personal in some way. If she hadn't stopped the fight, she was convinced that one of them would have been seriously hurt.

When she glanced over at Piers, he appeared uncomfortable on the dais. His face held an empty stare, as if carved from stone. When a serving girl offered food to him, he hesitated. It was as if he didn't know quite how to respond.

And then, suddenly, she went cold at the realisation. If Piers were the son of a lord, then he would know to offer her a portion of the food. He would be at ease seated beside her on the dais, for this was where a no-bleman sat during every meal.

Instead, he remained motionless, like one who had never sat at the high table before. And God help her, she suspected something else. What if Piers wasn't a lord, or the son of a lord? What if he'd lied to her? If that were true, then he could not be the heir to Penrith. With that uncertainty, all her dreams came crashing down. Who was this man? And what did he truly want?

For now, she avoided the problem by lowering her voice. 'Take some of the food and put it on my plate. Then choose for yourself.'

He obeyed, giving her entirely too much food. But she could discern his discomfort. Her own suspicions magnified until she didn't quite know what to do. If he'd lied to her, how could she ever trust him as a possible husband? Secrets she could tolerate, but never lies.

Then again, he'd never answered her question about who he was. Perhaps that was why. Her emotions rose higher, and she intended to confront him as soon as they were alone. It was time for the truth.

Her father was speaking with Morwenna, asking her about a pendant she was wearing. Gwen picked at her food, noticing that the young woman was getting increasingly upset.

But then Alfred turned to them. 'So, your name is Piers, is it? I've never heard of a place called Grever-shire.'

Gwen was starting to believe the place didn't exist. But Piers faced her father and answered, 'It's north-west of here, near the coast.'

'And who is your father?' Alfred asked.

Gwen's discomfort heightened, but Piers replied, 'My father is dead. My mother was Lady Wenda. I was born at Grevershire.'

She studied Piers closely, but when she looked for signs of deception, there were none. He answered her father's questions without hesitation.

'And you think that by winning some of the matches today I'd consider you as a potential husband for my daughter?' Her father's expression held amusement, and she sensed that Alfred intended to humiliate Piers.

'No.' Piers faced the man, and in his blue eyes she saw a silent challenge. 'I don't think you'd consider any man good enough for her.' He glanced over and met her gaze. 'None of us is good enough.'

And something in his words unsettled her doubts. He was right that no man would likely ever be good enough for her father. For so long, she'd obeyed Alfred blindly, believing that he was trying to help her find a good husband. But the first man he'd suggested had been terrible. Alfred had chosen a suitor who had thought it was all right to force himself upon her. She couldn't imagine marriage to a man like Gareth.

But when Piers took a drink from his goblet, his eyes never left hers. No man had ever looked at her in this way, as if she meant everything to him. Time and again, he'd given her the choice on whether to kiss him. And he'd tempted her, making her feel utterly desirable.

She was starting to question everything. So what if he *was* a man without wealth or lands? Did that truly matter? He was a man of strength and power, and if he needed her help to govern Penrith, she would gladly give it.

At least Piers had discovered her love of archery and had given her the gift she truly wanted. He'd respected her wishes, and she didn't believe he would treat her as if she were only good for bearing children. But would he ever tell her the truth about who he was?

Morwenna and Robert excused themselves from the table, and Piers leaned in. 'Are you considering Robert as one of your potential husbands?'

She kept her voice low and answered, 'I think he is more interested in Morwenna.'

'I agree. Does that bother you?'

She shook her head. 'Morwenna has become a friend during the past few days. She mentioned a man she cared for, and I suspect it's Robert, though she denies it.'

Piers gave a nod. 'I agree with you. But I believe he's here because he wants Penrith. Like most of the others.'

'The way you do?' she suggested.

He didn't take the bait but simply said beneath his breath, 'You already know that's not all I want.'

Her body warmed to the words, even while her brain reminded her that Piers was holding back information. She simply didn't know what to do about it.

After a short time, Morwenna and Robert returned to the table. Her father stood at that moment and announced, 'My daughter has chosen five men who will remain at Penrith. She will choose an appropriate husband from among them, with my permission.'

Gwen blinked at that, for she hadn't chosen anyone. Alfred's decision had been entirely his own. But she hadn't missed his last words—*'with my permission.'* That last part was a clear warning to her.

But he did name the men who had won the competi-

tions thus far. Robert and Piers were chosen, along with
Gareth, who had wisely kept his distance. She knew
he'd only been invited because of her father's woeful
attempts at matchmaking. Then there were two other
men—one who had won the footrace and another who
had won the spear-casting competition.

'Let us have music and dancing,' her father ordered,
and the musicians began to play.

Gwen saw an opportunity to escape and stood. To
Piers, she said, 'Come, let us dance.' Then she looked
over at Morwenna and Robert. 'Join us, won't you?'

The men pushed back the trestle tables and opened
up the space for dancing. Gwen almost expected Piers
to protest, but he surprised her by taking her waist and
spinning her around. She let herself enjoy the night as
she danced with the men and women. Once, when Piers
had his arm around her waist again, she caught an intense stare from him, as if he was thinking about their
shared kiss in the forest.

She flushed but held his gaze in hers. There was so
much she didn't know about this man, and he held so
many secrets. Was he low-born? Or had he simply been
fostered in a place where they had not taught him how
to behave like a lord? She needed answers, and though
she wanted to trust him, something held her back.

After the dance ended, she returned to the table, and
he poured her a cup of ale. She took it gratefully, but
she didn't miss her father's annoyed stare. Piers didn't
seem to care what Alfred thought of him, and she supposed that was a small mercy.

Several moments later, she noticed that Morwenna
had returned. The woman appeared uncomfortable, and

Gwen slid over to sit beside her. 'You don't look as if you're enjoying yourself, Morwenna.'

Her friend forced a smile. 'It's just a little overwhelming. I've never seen so many suitors.'

Gwen thought a moment, and then an idea occurred to her. If Piers wouldn't give her the answers she wanted, perhaps Morwenna could gain information. She asked, 'Have you met Piers of Grevershire before? He's quite handsome, but… I know little about him.' She hoped Morwenna would take the hint.

'Do you want me to find out?' Morwenna offered.

Gwen smiled, for she did indeed. 'Please. Come, and I'll arrange it.' She led Morwenna over to Piers, who was drinking a cup of wine. When he glanced up at her, his eyes turned wary.

'This is Lady Morwenna,' Gwendoline introduced her. 'And this is Piers of Grevershire.'

She thought she detected something between them, just a fleeting glance of uncertainty. But then Morwenna said, 'I am glad to meet you…my lord.'

Then Piers glanced back, as if to ask Gwen what she was doing. The truth was, she didn't know. This was about gathering information more than anything else.

'Morwenna would like to dance,' Gwendoline told him.

Piers inclined his head and held out his hand. He led Morwenna out among the dancers. They seemed to be talking together, and Gwen watched, wondering if the young woman could learn more on her behalf. But before she could determine anything else, her father sat beside her once again.

'He's the one, isn't he? The one you've been meeting in secret.'

At first, she felt herself fumbling for excuses. She didn't want to lie, but she also felt her arguments losing ground. Instead, she lifted her chin and faced him squarely. 'As I told you before, I've done nothing wrong.'

'Forgive me if I don't believe you. But more to the point, you'll never marry a man like this… Piers of Grevershire. Or whatever lies he's telling you. I don't care how many competitions he wins. He's not for you.'

Gwen wasn't at all surprised, though it pained her to hear his confirmation. 'Father, I—'

But he only cut her off. 'I had hoped to attract more powerful men to wed you, men who could make true alliances with me. I may send word to a few others. There are some who are still capable of giving you a child.'

Still capable? Then that meant these men were as old as her father, if not older. She suppressed a shudder. *Say something*, her brain warned. 'Father, I thought you would let me choose.'

Alfred laughed at that. 'I said you could choose from among the men *I* select for you. These men aren't powerful enough as allies. They're worthless to me.'

'But…what about…?' *What I want?* she almost said. She stopped herself because it was clear that he didn't care. This wasn't about marriage. It was about increasing his own stature and making new allies. He still had the lands at Tilmain, which his steward was governing on his behalf. And Penrith had become his upon the king's command.

Her father stood from the table and went over to

speak with Morwenna. For a moment, Gwen sat in silence, feeling as if she had no voice at all.

When Piers returned from the dancing, she could hardly look at him. Everything she'd hoped for had come crashing down. She was truly trapped in this place, and an escape was impossible.

'You're upset,' he said quietly. 'What's happened?'

She shook her head, unable to find the words. But Alfred would return in a moment, so this was her last chance to speak with Piers. After tonight, she might not see him again.

'He's not going to let me wed a man of my choosing. I am only allowed to choose from among the men he picked. And he hasn't chosen any of you. He was trying to attract the attention of powerful lords, but none of them came.'

Piers leaned in, and she felt the warmth of his breath against her cheek. 'What do you want, Gwen?'

'I don't know,' she whispered. 'I tried to argue with him, but he won't listen to anything I say.'

'With a man like the earl, it has to be his idea,' Piers said. 'And I've always known he wouldn't allow you to wed me.'

'Then why did you come?' Her bleak future seemed to spread out into nothingness. She'd been naive to imagine that her father would allow her to choose.

'Because I don't need his permission to take what I want,' he said. 'When you're ready to leave Penrith, you're going to come with me. We'll wed in secret.'

While part of her was thrilled at his offer, her brain was wary. 'I don't even know you, Piers. I know nothing about your family or where you're from. You haven't told me the answers I need.'

He took her hand in his and stared at her. 'I've told you no lies, Gwen. My mother was from Grevershire. And she did have noble blood.'

Though his admission made her feel slightly better, she still wondered what else he hadn't told her. 'What of your father?'

'I will tell you all of it after we are wed,' he promised.

She faltered, knowing that there was a reason why he'd kept secrets. He was indeed hiding something, but what? And why was he so insistent on marrying her so quickly? It was entirely too fast, and she wasn't ready to think of it.

'I don't think a marriage should begin with secrets,' she said. 'I prefer honesty.'

Piers faced her and said, 'Then don't marry me yet. I can still take you away from Penrith. You can go wherever you want to go, or we can come back here. If you want an escape from your father, I can give that to you.'

That much she believed, though she wasn't sure of him. 'I need to think about it.'

He raised her fingers to his mouth and kissed them. 'Whatever happens, whenever you're ready to leave, Gwen, just say the word.' Then he reached up to her hair and pulled a ribbon free, keeping it as a token. She stared back at him, feeling as if her heart had unravelled just as easily. She didn't know this man or even what she wanted.

But he kept her hand in his, stroking her palm with his thumb. His touch deepened below her skin, making her crave so much more. Her breasts grew tight within her bodice, and between her legs she ached, remembering their stolen moment in the forest.

In a low voice he murmured, 'I'll return this ribbon to you later. One day, I hope you'll wear it for me. And nothing else.'

She let out a shuddering breath, and he gave a wicked smile before he turned to leave the banquet.

Piers intended to slip into Gwen's room tonight. He hadn't pressed her for an answer, but he would ask her again. He'd taken extra bread, nuts, and a few pieces of cooked venison, hiding the food discreetly inside his tunic for their travels. The earl hardly noticed when he departed, so it was easy enough to slip inside the stables.

Piers chose two horses, and he intended to take Gwen riding during the night until they reached the ruins at Stansbury before dawn. After that, he would get a priest from the abbey to wed them, and he would take her away—possibly to his mother's ruined estate at Grevershire—until they could make their final plans.

This wasn't at all what he'd wanted, but his plans kept shifting. On one hand, it was better because Gwen might come willingly. But on the other, her father would hunt them. It was a grave risk.

Yet, when he'd kissed her hand upon leaving the banquet, he hadn't missed the fleeting glimpse of hope in her eyes. This woman was worth fighting for. She wasn't a soft, innocent maiden afraid of the world. No, her courage attracted him, and he admired the way she spoke her mind. She would need that strength to face what lay ahead.

Her father's competition and his quest for more allies be damned. Piers would claim Gwendoline as his bride and, somehow, he would find a way to take back Penrith and give her the life she deserved. Even if she hated him.

He packed the food and travelling supplies into a small cloth bundle that he tied to one of the horses. Then he returned through the narrow passageway that led to her room.

But when he reached the entrance, the air smelled wrong. He pushed at the hidden doorway, but it wouldn't move. Damn Lord Penrith for this. Somehow, the earl had learned of this entrance and had sealed it off.

Piers bit back a curse, for now he would have to go back through the tunnels and through the main keep to reach her chamber, which heightened the risk. He backtracked and returned to the Great Hall. One of the spiral staircases led up towards her chamber, and he approached it—only to be stopped by two guards.

'You're not going anywhere,' came a voice from behind him.

Piers turned and saw the earl. Alfred's expression held a rigid fury. For a moment, Piers simply stared back. He supposed he was meant to back down, to apologise and walk away. Instead, he used his full height to meet the earl's gaze, and he crossed his arms.

'You will not see my daughter again, Grevershire,' the earl snapped. 'Or whoever you truly are. You'd do well to leave in the morning.'

'Oh, I will be leaving,' he agreed. But with Gwendoline at his side.

The earl seemed to sense what he hadn't said. Piers turned to look at the guards at the staircase, and Lord Penrith ordered, 'Take this man out of the keep. See to it that he doesn't return.'

For a moment, Alfred reminded him of the former earl, his father. Degal had refused to acknowledge him, though he'd allowed Piers to live at Penrith. This man behaved in the same manner, treating Piers as if he wasn't worth the dirt under his feet. It didn't matter whether he had wealth or not. All that mattered to Lord Penrith was the blood that ran through his veins. And he would never be good enough for Gwendoline.

The two guards came up on either side of him, and Piers didn't move. Instead, his gaze locked with the earl's in a silent challenge. Then Piers turned to walk outside, followed by the guards. The moment they reached the stairs, they seized him by the arms. Piers struggled and demanded, 'What are you doing?'

'We have orders to hold you prisoner until the earl learns who you are.'

'Do you?' He'd been itching for a fight and now he had the opportunity. He had no intention of becoming their prisoner.

The men tried to tighten their grip, but Piers was stronger. In one swift motion, he twisted hard and brought his dagger up to the man's throat. The soldier staggered backwards with a deep cut, and Piers lunged at the other soldier. He unleashed his temper, letting the anger take him.

The soldier struck him with a mailed fist, but Piers remained standing. Pain radiated through his face, but he returned the blow with his own fists, striking hard. The soldier tried to move backwards, but Piers kicked him in the stomach, causing his opponent to fall down the stone stairs.

The first soldier attacked again, while blood ran down his throat. Piers dodged the blow and then punched his fist hard into the man's shoulder.

For a time, everything blurred. He was dimly aware of more men coming to restrain him, and only raw fury kept him standing. He dodged a blade, only to be struck a ringing blow against one ear.

But he ignored the pain. He'd always known taking Gwen would be nearly impossible, and now the moment had come for him to steal her away. It didn't matter whether she was ready or not—their time had run out. And no man would stop him.

He could only claim Penrith if she was his wife. Although she wasn't ready to wed him yet, he believed that if they journeyed together alone, he could convince her. She was the key to his future—and he could never leave her behind.

A battle lay ahead of them, a fight that would take time to win. But with Gwen at his side, he believed they could overcome the obstacles. The people of Penrith needed a new leader, and Piers had to convince the serfs to rise up against the earl and overthrow him. Only then could he and Gwen claim their places and ensure a better future.

Though he hadn't finished making plans—and truthfully, he didn't know how to achieve all his goals—he would take it one step at a time. But first, he had to fight the earl's men.

Piers seized one soldier's helm and used it as a weapon against the other man, smashing his nose. The first man hesitated, and Piers used the chance to escape. He hurried down the stairs, knowing they would call for more soldiers. Just as he reached the bottom, the other soldier shouted in warning.

Several men tried to close in, but Piers ducked into a crowd of onlookers with his dagger in hand. Swiftly, he made his way towards the hidden entrance to the tunnels and flung open another door outside so the men would believe he'd gone that direction. Then, he had only seconds to disappear.

He slipped into the tunnel and closed the hidden entrance behind him. The narrow space was cramped, but at least no one could follow.

He waited, listening as the men entered the outbuilding in search of him.

Within another hour, he heard a separate commotion outside. He thought he heard Morwenna's voice, and when he slipped from his hiding place, he spied her beside another man. They were arguing, and Piers gripped his dagger, wondering if Morwenna needed help. Then the man cursed, and Piers suspected she had escaped his attentions. He let out a breath, thankful that she'd been able to defend herself.

Time dragged onwards, and he forced himself to wait. Patience was more important than all else right now. If he tried to go up the stairs to Gwen's room too soon, he would be caught again.

No, better to watch and wait. He had a little time now, and he would make his plans carefully. And when the time came, he would take her.

Chapter Five

Morwenna never came to her room that night. Gwen had seen her talking with Robert earlier and hadn't wanted to disturb them. But as the night continued onwards, she started to worry. Gwen opened the door to the hall outside her bedchamber, only to find it heavily guarded. It infuriated her to see it, but she would speak to her father later about it.

'Send Aelish to me,' she ordered the man. Her maid might have the answers she sought, even though she no longer trusted the woman. Aelish's loyalty belonged only to the earl, as she'd proven when she'd betrayed Gwen's disappearance to her father. Even so, her maid would probably know what had happened to Morwenna.

Within a quarter of an hour, Aelish arrived, her expression appearing uneasy. 'What do you need from me, my lady?'

'I want to know what has happened to the Lady Morwenna. Is she safe? Has anyone seen her?'

'It's very late, my lady. I'm sure she's found another place to sleep.'

Aelish wasn't meeting her gaze, and Gwendoline suspected she was lying. 'What aren't you telling me, Aelish? What has happened?'

Her maid hesitated but eventually answered, 'Lady Morwenna…isn't a lady. Lord Penrith discovered that she's a serf pretending to be of noble blood.'

Aelish's declaration wasn't surprising. Gwen should have expected something like this. Morwenna had always seemed nervous and uncertain. But then again, the woman had admitted her father was dead, and she had nowhere to go. Gwen had been kind to her, becoming a friend during these past few days. Now, she was certain that Morwenna had come to Penrith because of Robert. She'd dressed herself as a lady in an attempt to get closer to him. Had she been in Morwenna's position, she might have done the same.

'What did my father do?' Gwen asked.

'He sent her away, my lady.'

Though she should have expected it, Alfred's command annoyed her. He'd never even bothered to let her know—he'd simply made up his mind and sent Morwenna off. At the very least, Gwen wished she could have said farewell.

Aelish began to help her with the laces of her gown, and Gwen undressed until she wore only her shift. Afterwards, she dismissed her maid. It felt as if her life had been upended and broken into pieces. She wanted to see Piers again, to talk with him about possible plans. But the only way she could see him was if she tried to find him. And given the way her father had sealed up the passageway and kept her room heavily guarded, none of the soldiers would allow her to wander around the castle.

Gwen lay back on her bed, wondering what to do now. Should she take Piers's forbidden invitation to leave the castle? He had spoken of taking her away to wed in secret. And although she wasn't ready to agree to marriage, she *was* thinking of escaping Penrith.

What would it be like to flee this place on horseback with a man like Piers? A flush suffused her skin at the thought of spending her nights sleeping beside him. His kiss had set her on fire, making her crave his touch. She'd never felt anything like it before, and it awakened her to desires she'd never known.

If he were here now, he would press her back against the coverlet, covering her body with his own. She closed her eyes, imagining it. His kiss would be wild, untamed.

It was reckless to even imagine escaping. But even so, she walked over to her trunk and began searching through her belongings for a simple travelling gown. She didn't know if she had anything at all. She dug through the gowns until she came across something she hadn't seen before—a wrapped bundle. When she loosened it, she saw clothing that belonged to a boy. Had this belonged to Morwenna? Gwen began to see the possibilities. If she disguised herself as a serf, it was far more practical for travelling. She held on to it for a moment, envisioning running away with Piers.

But then, she set the thought aside. Although it sounded thrilling, she knew it couldn't be real. More likely, her father would send twenty men to track them down and bring her back. Alfred might even have Piers killed.

She sobered at the thought. Piers didn't deserve that—and her father had already proven himself unreasonable when it came to her choice of a husband.

With a sigh, she closed the trunk, abandoning the idea. Why was she even considering running away with a man she barely knew? No, she couldn't do this. At least not until she had the answers she sought.

Two days later

The waiting was killing him. Piers had kept himself hidden, and he'd only managed to reach Gwen's door once. Her father had imprisoned her in her room, and worse, Morwenna was now the earl's prisoner. Somehow, Alfred had learned she was only the miller's daughter, and he meant to have her flogged tonight for impersonating a noblewoman.

Robert and Brian were working together to get her out, and Piers had no doubt they would succeed. But his greater challenge was helping Gwen escape—that is, if she would agree to it. He'd disguised himself as a soldier once again, and this time, he planned to bring her food.

Piers walked up the stone stairs and saw the two guards outside her door. One was the captain who hadn't recognised him earlier. Now, however, he stared hard at Piers.

'We'll take the food for Lady Gwendoline,' the captain said.

Piers handed him the tray. Then in one motion, he took off his helm and swung it hard at the second guard. The captain had no time to react before Piers punched his fists and connected with the older man's jaw.

The wooden tray clattered to the ground, but he hit the older man again until the captain dropped unconscious. The other man was bruised and bleeding, already on the floor. Then Piers picked up the fallen food and the flask and pushed the door open.

'Piers.' Gwen stared at him in shock as he closed the door behind him. She started to run to him before she faltered. It was almost as if she were afraid to come close.

He ignored her hesitation and set down the food. In two strides, he pulled her into his arms, keeping her in an embrace. She clung to him, and he breathed in the scent of her hair, savouring the forbidden moment. Though he knew it was a mistake to get too close to this woman, he had already made the decision to take her from Penrith. She might despise him, but he didn't care.

When he drew back, her cheeks were blushing. 'What's happening? Why am I being held prisoner by my father?'

The mention of Alfred sobered him. 'Your father doesn't want you to know that he took Morwenna prisoner.' He didn't know whether to tell her more, but Gwen would ask questions if he didn't offer an explanation. 'She was not…who you thought she was.' It was weak but the best he could do.

'She's the miller's daughter,' Gwen said. 'I've known that for a few days now.'

It startled him that she already knew. His suspicions sharpened, and he had to ask, 'Were you the one who told the earl?'

She shook her head. 'No, in truth, I like Morwenna. And even if she is a serf, what of it? Does she not deserve the chance to wed a good man? Why should the circumstances of her birth affect her future?'

It was the last thing he'd imagined she would say. Though it was unlikely, a shard of hope cut into his defences, making him wonder if she could ever care for a man like him—a bastard.

Piers forced back his emotions, knowing it could never happen. Though she wanted her freedom, she didn't want to marry him and likely never would.

He took her hands in his and asked, 'Do you want to help her?'

She smiled at that. 'Of course, I do.'

Now, her eyes sparkled as if she were imagining an adventure. He couldn't deny that there was a terrible risk…but he was willing to chance it for her sake.

'We'll need a horse,' he said. 'Can you make the arrangements?'

'I don't…think I can. I'm supposed to be a prisoner, remember?'

He uttered a low curse, for it had been a stupid thing to say. Any man here would recognise her. But then he thought a moment and asked, 'Did Morwenna leave any of her belongings here? She had some of her brother's older clothes.' Wearing them would be critical to helping Gwen leave this place.

She walked over to her trunk and dug inside until she withdrew a bundle. When she unwrapped it, she pulled out a tunic, hose, and a cap. 'Should I disguise myself?'

Piers nodded. 'Tell the stable master that you are bringing a horse to his lordship. He won't question you.' Though he didn't know if that was true, he wanted

Gwen to feel more confident about leaving. He reached for the battered cap and set it upon her head.

Gwen twisted her braids into the cap, hiding her hair. He stared at her for a long moment, not truly knowing what they were doing. They might be caught, and it was likely they would have difficulty saving Morwenna and Robert. But he could see the eagerness in her eyes, and her beauty left him speechless. He cupped her cheek, needing to touch her. He stroked her face with his thumb, and her smile faded as she covered his hand with her own. For a moment, she closed her eyes, and he wanted nothing more than to claim her mouth in a kiss. This woman captivated him and, no matter what happened, he would willingly shield her body with his own. For a long moment, he simply studied her, memorising her features.

'Bring the horse to the barbican gate,' he said at last. 'Try not to let them see you.'

She held his hand and asked, 'Are you going to get her out?'

He hoped it was possible, but he couldn't answer that. 'I'll do what I can,' was all he could say. 'Something happened earlier. Soldiers were searching everywhere. I think Robert might have freed her, but from what I've heard, it went wrong.'

Her expression turned worried, and she asked, 'You'll be careful?'

He nodded, though a rescue would be both reckless and dangerous. Involving Gwen was a risk he shouldn't take—but he didn't want to leave her behind.

She seemed to sense his concern and asked, 'Will you return to me?'

In her voice, he heard a softness, an emotion he hadn't expected. She was afraid, but her fear was for him. No one had ever really cared what happened to him. And for this woman to voice such a question utterly disarmed him.

In answer, he crushed her mouth to his, kissing her hard. Gwen returned the kiss, and the taste of her quenched a thirst he hadn't known was there. He didn't have the words to tell her what she meant to him—all he could do was show her.

Her tongue met his, and he ravaged her mouth, his mind imagining what it would be like to lay her down on the bed. He could spend hours exploring her body, finding what brought her pleasure.

But there was no time now. They had to leave before Robert and Brian were discovered. With reluctance, he broke the kiss and said, 'I'm going to wait for you in the hallway while you change your clothes. Then I'll lock the door, so no one knows you're gone.' He would have to get rid of the soldiers who had guarded her earlier.

He closed the door behind him, wondering if bringing Gwen with him would endanger her. But no matter what happened, he could not leave her behind.

She would be his, no matter how many battles he had to fight.

Gwen kept her head lowered, hoping no one would notice her. Piers had bound the two soldiers who had been guarding her door with ropes, gagging them before he locked them away in a chamber nearby. She knew it was only a matter of time before the men were discovered.

Exhilaration rushed through her at the thought of escaping Penrith with him. Aye, it was still an impossible idea. But after she'd been treated as a prisoner for two days, all loyalty to her father had begun to fade. She'd done nothing wrong, and he was punishing her with only food and her embroidery to keep her company. Never had she imagined he would take Morwenna prisoner with the intent to flog her.

True, the young woman had lied about her past. But Gwen couldn't bring herself to be angry. Morwenna had had nowhere else to go, and she'd followed the man she loved. It wasn't wrong to seek her heart's desire, and her actions had harmed no one.

Gwen slipped into the stables, walking towards her mare. But then she stopped herself, realising that it would draw too much attention. She needed a lesser horse, one of the geldings that wouldn't be missed. For a moment, she stared at the horse stalls, realising that she would have to saddle the horse herself. The other stable boys were sleeping with the dogs, and she didn't know if she had the strength to manage it.

You must, she told herself. There was no other choice but to haul the heavy saddle to the horse and do her best to fasten it to the animal.

Outside, she heard the sound of shouting and soldiers gathering. Fear rushed through her, for she didn't know if they were searching for her. Or were they were trying to find Piers? She didn't know.

Though the saddle was unbearably heavy, Gwen struggled to move it atop the horse. The bridle and reins were easier, but it still took far too long to prepare the horse. And then there was the problem of reaching the barbican gate without being discovered.

Her heart hammered in her chest as she guided the animal out. Dozens of soldiers were gathering, and she overheard them talking about the woman escaping.

So Morwenna had made it out, but the soldiers were in pursuit. Gwen frowned, not knowing what to do. But the moment she started towards the gate, one of the men stopped her.

'You there. What are you doing with that horse?'

'Captain's orders,' she answered, trying to lower the tone of her voice to sound like a boy. 'Lady Gwendoline escaped her room.'

The soldier let out a curse and shook his head. 'Where is the captain?'

'Near the barbican gate,' she lied. 'I'm taking the horse to him now.' Her brain spun off, wondering what else she could say, but then the soldier was called to join another group. He ignored Gwen and strode over with the others.

She wanted to breathe a sigh of relief, but there was no time. Instead, she tried to take the horse towards the gate. Instinct warned her to look near the last outbuilding by the gate. Though she saw only shadows, she sensed that Piers was there.

Her skin went cold, for she saw the soldiers moving directly towards him. Piers picked up the fallen body of a man, and she couldn't tell who it was in the darkness. They were going to take him if she didn't do something.

The soldiers were shouting at one another and amid the commotion, she called out, 'Piers! Take the horse!'

He was carrying someone unconscious on his back,

and he stopped when he heard her voice. Though she wanted to run to him, it would only draw more soldiers. Terror rose within her, knowing that his life lay in her hands. If she made the wrong choice, Piers might die.

More than anything, she wanted to run to his side and help him. But if she dared take the risk, it would draw more attention. She froze in place for a moment, waiting to see what he would do. And then she saw him carrying Robert, one of her suitors. The man was gravely injured, and it made her stop and wonder why Piers would save him. What had become of Morwenna? Had she escaped?

Gwen patted the horse's flank and sent the animal towards him, feeling as if her plans were tearing in half. There was a connection between Piers and Robert. They'd nearly killed each other in one of the matches earlier—but why would Piers save him now? She couldn't understand it. But he managed to get the horse and pulled the wounded man over the animal. Then he stopped a moment and looked at her.

She shouldn't leave. And yet…how could she stay after what her father had done? In spite of her fears, she ran hard towards them. They reached the gate, and Piers struck down the guards with a mailed fist and his shield, ordering her, 'Run to the drop-off where I met you in the forest. And don't stop!'

She obeyed blindly, racing through the gate and outside. It was so dark, she could barely see where she was going. Brambles caught at her clothing as she tore her way through the woods. For now, she worried more about escaping than finding the path. She didn't know whether Piers had made it out with Robert or whether they had both been caught.

But although fear made her heart pound, she also felt a sense of excitement. She had left her old life behind and now she would make a new one for herself. The only question was whether she would wed Piers or not.

She found her way towards the stream and followed it until she discovered the drop-off with the large limestone boulders. Carefully, she gripped slim tree trunks to aid her balance as she made her way down to the bottom of the hill. Then she waited in the darkness.

It seemed as if time had slowed down, dragging on until she wondered what had happened to them. Then, at last, she heard the sound of footsteps crunching against dried leaves. She pressed herself back against the limestone until she heard Piers whisper, 'Gwen.'

'I'm here.' She didn't wait for him to say another word but ran to him and held him close. He gripped her body against his, and she felt safe at last in his arms.

'I need your help,' he told her. 'Robert is wounded.' He took her hand in his. 'I hid him in a cave for now, but he's badly hurt. Will you come with me?'

'I will,' she agreed. 'But who is Robert to you, Piers? Why would you save him?'

He paused a moment and sighed. 'I've known him for years. He's…like a brother to me.'

She sensed there was still more he was holding back, but if they had been friends for years, it made sense that he would save him. He led her through the darkness, up the hill and down a different path until they reached another outcropping of stone. It was only a small shelter, but she saw the body of a man inside.

Her healing skills were only adequate, but she'd learned a few things about treating wounds. 'How badly is he hurt?'

'His head and his left arm are wounded. He hasn't woken up.'

Gwen loosened Robert's tunic, trying to see his arm. It appeared that Piers had tried to stop the bleeding, but the bandage was soaked through. 'Can we build a fire?' She needed to see his wounds better, and she didn't know if they would have to cauterise the wound to stop the bleeding. It also bothered her that Robert had not awakened once. She worried that it might mean that he was bleeding inside.

'A fire would only draw them to us,' Piers argued.

'I need light to see his wounds,' she insisted. 'Can you make a torch at least? We can put it out after I've tended him.'

He didn't seem happy about it, but he understood her reasoning. 'What else will you need?'

'Water, bandages, and I'll need garlic, if you can find it for me…mayhap in the morning after the sun rises.'

'I'll get the water, and you can cut bandages from this.' He took off his tunic and handed it to her. Then Piers went to the back of the cave and fumbled through another bundle that she hadn't seen. He took a bowl from the bundle and then returned outside.

Gwen could feel the warmth of his body heat on the tunic. Though she didn't like destroying his clothing, there was no other choice. She tried to take strips from the hem and used her knife to cut what she needed. Then she cut some of her own tunic to make a rag.

Within moments, Piers had brought her a wooden bowl of water. He used flint and a knife to strike a spark and made a torch out of a dry limb and some of the cloth. Then he held it for her while she worked. Gwen dipped the rag into the water and loosened the bandage on Robert's arm. Although it was still bleeding, she washed the wound and wrapped it tightly, binding it up. Then she did the same for his head, wrapping that wound as well.

'I will need the garlic as soon as you can find some,' she said. 'It will help stop a fever if I pack it into his wounds.' A healer had told her that once, and it seemed to be true.

Gwen washed the blood from her hands, and then Piers extinguished the torch. Robert had moved slightly while she'd treated him, but he had never regained consciousness. It bothered her, though she said nothing to Piers.

At last, she had finished, and she gave Piers what was left of his tunic. He balled it up and put it beneath Robert's head as a makeshift pillow. Then he came and sat beside her with his head lowered.

'We've done everything we can,' she told him.

And then he pulled her into his lap, kissing her deeply. She could feel his rigid arousal pressing against her, and she inhaled sharply. 'Thank you for tending him,' he said roughly.

She pressed her palms to his bare chest, startled at the strength there. He went motionless at her touch, and she explored him with her fingertips, noting the ridges of his stomach and the hard pectoral muscles of his chest. He was stronger than she'd imagined, and this was the first time in her life she'd ever had the opportunity to touch him like this.

He caught her wrists with his hands. 'Careful, Gwen.'

She understood his warning. But part of her didn't want to be careful. She had risked everything by coming with Piers, and she had chosen him. She wanted to be reckless and wild, ignoring caution and seizing what she wanted.

She pulled her hands free and stared at him. In the darkness, she couldn't read his expression, but she took his palms and brought them beneath the tunic upon her bare skin until they rested below her breasts.

'You don't know what you're asking of me,' he growled. 'Don't let yourself believe I'm one of your gentle suitors, Gwen. If you offer this to me, I'm going to take it.'

In silent answer, she drew his hands higher until they cupped her bare breasts. And then his thumbs grazed her nipples. She jolted at his touch, feeling an aching response between her legs. He caressed the erect tips, and she pressed herself against his hard length to ease the sensations she was feeling. Though she didn't know what he would do next, she wanted him so badly. She pulled his head down and kissed him, threading her tongue with his. He gave an answering groan and gently stroked her nipples, as she moved against him.

'God above, Gwen,' he hissed. 'You don't know what you're doing to me.'

No, she didn't know, but she gave in to her own impulse, touching his bare chest and then pressing her

mouth to his shoulder. At that, he took the tunic and
pulled it over her head before he grasped her hips and
moved her until she straddled him. Before she knew
what was happening, his hot mouth covered her nipple.

She barely muffled her shocked cry and was suddenly grateful for the darkness. It embarrassed her
to think that Robert might regain consciousness, that
they weren't alone. But as Piers swirled his tongue over
her nipple, she could barely control the sensations that
flooded through her. Between her legs she grew wet,
and she pressed against him out of instinct. The thick
ridge of his erection only deepened her need, and he
continued to torment her breasts, making it hard for
her to breathe. She'd never known this existed and for
a moment, she wondered if he intended to claim her
innocence. She was burning up inside, her body aching for release.

'Piers,' she murmured.

Her breathing was shaky, and he spoke against her
lips. 'Do you want me to give you pleasure, Gwen? Do
you want to know what it will be like when I fill you
with my body?'

'I want you,' she said, fighting to gain command of
herself. 'But this isn't the place for…more.' Her face
burned red, but she forced herself to finish. 'I don't
think we should—'

He cut off her words with another kiss. 'I won't claim
you here. Not yet. But I want to show you more. If you're
willing.'

'Willing to do what?'

He reached for the ties of her hose and loosened
them. Then he slid his hand inside, and she felt his fin-

gers slide against her wetness. She tensed, so afraid of what would happen next. And yet, he didn't do anything except cup her, making her imagination conjure up even more.

He kissed her again, and this time when his tongue slid against hers, he echoed the movement by sliding one finger inside her.

She gasped, her nails digging into his back. She'd never felt such pleasure before in her life, and it threatened to overwhelm her. But Piers didn't stop. Instead, he caressed her deeply, and she squeezed against the single finger. The sensations mounted deep inside her, and he began to circle his thumb above her entrance. She shuddered, her body straining to reach for something she didn't understand.

And when he took her breast into his mouth again, she utterly lost control. She cried out as waves of pleasure crested over her, and she bit her lip to stop from screaming. He continued to stroke her, and his thumb brushed against a sensitive place. The pleasure only doubled, and she couldn't stop herself from reaching for his shaft. He loosened his hose and drew her hand against him, and she felt the rock-hard heat of his flesh.

He guided her on how to stroke him, and when she found a rhythm that pleased him, his own breathing shifted.

'I want to be inside you right now,' he gritted out. He slid a second finger inside her, and as she squeezed him, she closed her eyes, imagining it. 'You're mine, Gwen. No other man will have you. I swear to God.'

Piers showed her how to move her hand, and she quickened her pace, enjoying the heady feeling of power over him. She loved touching him, and over and over she slid her hand up and down.

'You're going to kill me,' he gritted out. 'But it's worth dying for.'

'Do you want me to stop?'

'God, no.'

She continued to squeeze him, sliding her hand up and down. His breathing was as unsteady as her own, and she heard him fighting for control. Then he let out a shuddering groan, tensing until she felt the warmth of his release against her palm.

He wiped her hand against his hose, and then he kissed her tenderly. Slowly, he stroked her intimately, his fingers moving inside her until the same intense pleasure began to kindle once more. She arched against him, seeking his touch until he circled his thumb against her. The sensation deepened, and she felt herself rising to the desire. She trembled against him, and when she squeezed his fingers, she felt herself straining hard. It was almost violent with the raw intensity of his touch until he commanded, 'Let go, Gwen. Come for me again.'

Within seconds, she broke apart, her body shattering as he pleasured her once more. She felt tears burning at her eyes, and she could hardly bear it. Her body continued to quake, but then he pulled her atop him, skin to skin.

She slept at last, utterly drained.

Chapter Six

Just before dawn, Piers awakened with Gwen in his arms. He couldn't remember the last time he'd felt such contentment. Watching her come apart at his touch had given him the same unforgettable pleasure. Even now, he wanted to awaken her with a kiss and run his hands over her beautiful body. In the morning light, he'd been unable to do anything except watch her sleep. He'd memorised her features, the curves of her body, and the softness of her expression.

It felt as if he'd stolen a priceless jewel, and he could hardly believe she'd come with him. And though he intended to bring Robert to safety, his greatest priority was keeping Gwen safe.

He gave in to his impulse and stole the kiss he wanted. She smiled against his mouth and kissed him back. Then she pulled back and reached for the fallen clothing. 'I'd better get dressed in case Robert awakens.'

He donned his own tunic, admiring her as she clothed herself. 'I'll try to find the garlic you need for his wounds.'

'And I'll see if I can coax him to drink water,' she said. 'Did he ever awaken?'

Piers shook his head, afraid of what that meant. Despite their differences, he didn't want his brother to die. He took a glance back at Gwen. 'I'll return soon.'

He wasn't certain whether he would find the garlic, but the greater purpose of venturing outside the cave was to discover where Penrith's men were and the nature of the threat. Piers knew better than to believe they were safe. They might be able to seek sanctuary at Colford Abbey, for Robert's uncle was the abbot there. But it was at least a day's journey from here, and he didn't know how Robert would fare.

He walked along the edge of the stream, searching for the garlic Gwen wanted. He couldn't find any, but as he continued searching, he saw another plant that stopped him cold. He stared at the black berries, a chill settling in his bones as the memories came flooding back.

He'd gone to visit Robert, slipping through the tunnel and emerging from behind the tapestry. No one had allowed him near the heir for nearly a year, but he'd wanted to see his brother for himself. He'd seen Robert lying upon his fine bed, his face pale as milk. For a moment, Piers struggled with what to say.

'You're very sick, aren't you?' he'd said. 'I thought they were lying to me.'

'Who are you?' Robert had asked in a rough voice. He tried to sit up, but then he hesitated before sinking back on the bed. On the floor beside it was a chamber pot that smelled of sickness.

'Piers,' he'd answered. He'd been in awe of Robert's

chamber, particularly the soft bed. Never had he seen anything so fine in all his life. Piers moved closer and touched the coverlet. 'This is yours?'

Robert nodded. 'Please go.' Exhaustion lined his voice, and Piers realised that his mother hadn't been lying. Robert was indeed very sick, more than he'd realised.

When he'd first come to Penrith, he'd believed Robert was the Lady of Penrith's son from a former marriage. He hadn't known that he and Robert were born of the same father—not until recently. But now, he wanted to know his brother and befriend him. He wanted to have family…a friend of his own. And perhaps Robert might want a brother too.

'You don't understand,' Piers said, trying to find the right words to speak the truth.

But Robert clenched his sheets and gritted out, 'What?'

Piers flinched at his tone and finally said, 'I'm your brother. I found out from the cook. I thought we could—'

'Get out!' Robert ordered. He reached beneath the bed for the chamber pot, and barely made it before he vomited.

Piers retreated, wondering if he should send for help. 'But…'

Robert pushed aside the pot, barely managing to lift his head back to the pillow. 'Just leave me,' he whispered. 'I don't want to be your brother.' Then he hardened his tone and stared back at Piers. 'Or your friend.'

The words had cut him so deeply Piers hadn't known what to do or say. Robert had slashed his hopes apart with only a few words. A hot anger rushed through him, resentment that his brother lived in a chamber of his own with a fine bed while Piers was forced to sleep in the freezing stable, hugging the dogs for warmth. And his brother didn't even want to know him.

In a fit of anger, he'd seized the vial of his brother's medicine and taken it into the hidden passageway, dumping it out on to the floor. If Robert wanted nothing to do with him, so be it. Piers would get his own revenge by getting rid of the young lord's medicine.

Rage flared through him with the desire to lash out at Robert. He didn't want his brother to be well, not if he was going to treat him the way Degal did. He wouldn't care if Robert died. Robert certainly didn't care about him.

To cover up what he'd done, Piers refilled the medicine vial with water from an animal skin he carried at his waist. The healer would give Robert the medicine, thinking it would help the young lord. And instead, the water would do nothing at all.

Silently, Piers replaced the vial in the chamber. A hint of guilt pricked his conscience, but he shut it down, telling himself that the young lord deserved it. It wasn't as if he'd put anything bad in the vial—only water. It was in God's hands what happened to his brother.

During the next few weeks, he'd continued to fill his brother's medicine with water, and in time, Robert grew stronger and recovered from his illness. It was then that Piers realised what his mother had done. She'd been secretly poisoning Robert with the help of her maid Gleda, likely with the intent of making Piers the heir instead.

By stealing the 'medicine' and throwing it away, he'd accidentally saved his brother's life.

He'd never told Robert about it. Nor had he spoken of the day when he'd poured several vials of medicine into Gleda's wine while her back was turned. The old woman had drunk the wine and fallen into a sleep from which she'd never awakened. But at least she could no longer poison his brother.

And for that, Piers held no regrets.

He now understood that Robert had sent him away out of shame. His brother had hated his weakness and wanted to be alone. But as he grew stronger, Robert started to venture forth from his room, though his new stepmother Clarine would not let him leave the keep.

Piers had begun working in the fields, and no longer did he visit the keep. But on the night two years ago when the king's soldiers had attacked and taken them captive, he'd realised that he didn't want his brother to die. He'd fought the men, only to be imprisoned himself.

Only after they'd escaped and gone into exile together, had they finally become friends. But he'd never told Robert the secrets of the past.

The knot gathered in his stomach as he pushed back the memory. Gwen didn't need to know about any of that. He was already aware of how miraculous it was that she'd come with him. She'd wanted her freedom and she felt the same attraction he did, but he was uneasy about their future. He had nothing at all to offer her except danger and poverty.

But with every moment he spent with her, something shifted. She looked upon him as if he were a hero. And part of him wanted to be that for her. He wanted to transform himself into someone else. He wanted to conquer Penrith for her sake and return to rule with her at his side…but he didn't know how.

Piers continued walking through the woods, and eventually found a place on the hillside where he dug up wild garlic. He didn't know if it would help stop Robert from getting a fever, but he gathered what he could.

Despite everything, Piers blamed himself for his brother's poisoning. If he'd never come to Penrith, Robert might not have become ill. But one thing was certain—he wouldn't let Robert die now—no matter what happened.

He climbed up the hillside towards the cave where they were waiting. With every step, he realised that the fight would continue—not only for his brother's life, but for his own.

No longer would he remain among the dogs, forgotten and alone. He'd lived in the shadows for so many years, he hardly knew what it was to be a leader of men. He didn't know how to become an earl—but he would find a way to take command of Penrith by convincing Gwen to wed him.

Only then could he become the man he wanted to be.

They spent the next day travelling together. Gwen sensed Piers growing distant, as if he were distracted by something. She tried to get answers from him about where they were taking Robert, but either he didn't know or he wouldn't tell her. Sometimes he would reach for her hand and hold it while they walked alongside the horse carrying Robert. It was a silent comfort to her, despite her uneasiness.

Her stomach was gnawing with hunger, but she said nothing to Piers. He'd barely eaten anything, either, and his entire concentration was on keeping Robert alive. Had they been best friends and rivals? Gwen wasn't entirely certain. But as they continued walking through the forest, it wasn't long before they heard dogs barking in the distance.

A ripple of fear flooded within her. She should have expected her father's hunting dogs to begin tracking her scent. Because of it, Piers changed their path to walk through the stream. Her shoes and skirts grew soaked in the cold water, but there was no choice. It was the only way to disguise their path.

'Piers, where are we going?' she demanded. She was starting to fear that he had no plan. He'd told her only pieces of the truth, and she didn't know what was happening.

'Colford Abbey,' he said at last. 'Robert's uncle is there.'

So, he intended to seek sanctuary with the monks. It made sense, though she didn't know how long they could remain there. What were his intentions? He'd mentioned marriage, though she'd told him it was too soon. But what about after that? She had avoided thinking about their future at first, but now her fears were growing stronger.

They travelled through the water until her feet grew numb and the sound of the dogs faded. Hours passed and the sunlight faded from afternoon into evening. Her feet ached from all the walking, but she was grateful that her father's men hadn't found them.

Piers stopped by the stream and helped Robert down. For a moment, the man's eyes flickered open. Gwen took a cup from their pack of belongings and filled it with water. She tried to get Robert to drink a little before he passed out again. When she met Piers's gaze, his expression was grim. 'We'll be there soon. He needs the help of a healer.'

Gwen agreed with him about that. For a moment, she sat upon one of the large rocks lining the stream and removed her shoes to ease the pain of her blisters.

The moment Piers saw them, he frowned. 'You're hurt. I didn't know.' Immediately, he knelt before her and reached for her foot. He touched her bare calf, and the heat of his hands sent a flush of sensation through her skin. As he examined her sole, she winced at the pain.

'I'm sorry,' he said. 'I should have let you ride with Robert. Do you want me to wrap it for you?'

'No, it's all right,' she said, pulling her foot back. But when he examined her other foot, his hands slid over her skin in a slight caress. She closed her eyes, savouring the moment. And when he met her gaze, she saw the flare of desire in his eyes.

She rested her hands on his shoulders while he knelt before her. And when she slid her palms to the back of his neck, he responded instantly, pulling her into a kiss. His mouth was unyielding, and she lost herself within the kiss, sliding her tongue against his. She burned for this man, wanting his hands upon her, and she answered his kiss with silent demands of her own.

She didn't understand these dizzying needs that took command of her, but she wanted his forbidden touch.

Part of her feared that her father's men would catch up to them soon. Their time together might run out.

'Nightfall,' he swore, after he pulled back from her mouth. 'We'll finish this then.' He helped put Robert back on the horse, and after she put her shoes on, he lifted her into his arms.

Gwen was startled by it and protested, 'I can walk, Piers.'

'No. It's my fault this happened.'

She could tell from the rigid expression on his face that he wasn't going to relent. Though she loved being in his arms, she didn't want him to be in discomfort with her weight.

'I don't want the rest of our travels tonight to burden you,' she protested.

'You'll never be a burden to me.' His voice warmed her, and she rested her cheek against his chest as he carried her.

Though she wanted to believe that she would make her escape and find her freedom, a voice inside warned that it could not happen. She should have taken all her jewels with her, for they needed a way of paying for their safety. Though they might flee the soldiers now, she worried about what would happen later.

Piers wanted her to wed him so he could return to Penrith and claim it. But she hardly knew him at all for he'd kept so many secrets. She was torn between the feelings in her heart and her head's steadfast warnings. Her father did not approve of Piers as her husband. It would be different if he had wealth and power, or even an army of soldiers—but he'd lost everything.

Even if she returned as Piers's bride, Alfred would try to kill him.

Don't think of it now, she told herself. Instead, she took comfort from being in his arms. For she didn't know how much time they had left.

Thankfully, the distance to Colford wasn't as great as she thought it would be. Within the hour, they reached the outskirts of the abbey. One of the monks was tending a garden, and Piers lowered her to stand. They walked together as he led the horse forward. When the monk raised his head and stood, Piers told him, 'My... friend Robert is wounded. His uncle is the abbot here.'

'I know who you are,' the monk answered. 'But you cannot stay here. Some of Lord Penrith's men are already inside. We were able to hide Morwenna and her brother, but if you seek sanctuary, they may capture you instead.' He glanced at Gwen. 'They're looking for her.'

A thread of fear wove through her, but she felt the need to defend Piers. 'I left home of my own free will.'

Piers's expression remained stony. 'That won't matter to your father.'

'Is there somewhere else we can go?' she asked. To the monk she said, 'Robert needs new bandages and a poultice to prevent fever. I've packed it with garlic, but if you have a healer...he really should stay here.'

Piers shook his head. 'If your father's men are here, Robert's not safe. Penrith's men wounded him when he tried to save Morwenna.'

She let out a heavy breath, knowing he was right. 'What should we do?'

'Father Oswald will want to help his nephew,' the

monk said. 'I could gather what you need from the healer and leave the supplies in a basket in the forest. You'll want broth to feed him as well.'

Piers nodded, and she could see him considering where to go. There was so little time, she felt the urge to leave as soon as possible.

'We'll continue travelling to Stansbury,' he told the monk at last. 'Leave the supplies near the rowan tree by the stream. I'll return for them later after I've brought Gwen and Robert to safety.'

Gwen's uneasiness grew heavier with every moment, especially since she knew at any moment one of her father's men might find them. Her worries intensified, forming a dull ache in her gut. She simply didn't know what to do. If they were caught, she would have no choice but to go back. Although she wanted to ask Piers about it, his entire concentration was on saving his brother's life. That was the higher priority at the moment.

Piers led the horse away from the abbey, careful to ensure that Robert didn't fall from the saddle. Gwen followed him down a narrow path that led up a hillside. It was late, and the sun was already rimming the horizon. Just as they were about to turn, something made her glance behind her. In the distance, she spied the glint of chainmail. The sight of the soldiers only heightened her terror. Within moments, she heard a man shouting, followed by the ringing of a bell.

Dear God. They were here already. Her fear sharpened, and she turned to Piers. He froze and instinctively began to hurry. But they were nearing a thinner part of the woods that opened into a clearing. It wouldn't take long for the men to find them. He cursed and un-sheathed a sword. 'I'll lift you on to the horse. Take Robert and ride deep into the woods. I'll cover for you.'

She faltered, realising the implications of his decision. 'No. My father will kill you if you stay.' She had no doubt that Alfred would be ruthless, and with the number of soldiers, they would cut him down before he could escape. 'You should take Robert and ride away. I'll stand and face them. They won't harm me.'

It terrified her to face Alfred's wrath, but she saw no alternative. Either she gathered her courage, or Piers would die. There was no other choice.

'Gwen—' Piers started to argue, but she touched her hand to his mouth.

'We don't have time. They're hunting for me. My father won't hesitate to punish you.' Though it tore her apart, she knew the truth. She had to make a choice between giving up her freedom or risking Piers's life.

And in that, there was no choice at all.

She couldn't allow her father to hurt Piers, no matter what it meant for her. If she surrendered, no one would hunt him or Robert. Her sacrifice meant their safety, though the thought of returning to Penrith made her heart ache.

'You have to go.' She embraced him hard, feeling as if her heart were cracking in two. 'There's no other way.' Somehow, she sensed that she would never see him again. The tears welled in her eyes, filling her with regret that this was the end. Her father would force her to marry someone else, and she simply didn't know if there was another way out.

Piers kissed her hair, holding her tightly. 'After I've

brought Robert to safety, I will come back for you,' he vowed. 'I swear it on my life.'

Gwen didn't know whether to believe him, though she wanted to. She kissed him one last time and then watched as he mounted behind Robert and spurred the horse into the woods. If he hadn't been trying to save his friend, they might have escaped. But it was impossible now.

She walked slowly towards the soldiers, removing her cap to let her hair fall to her shoulders. Just as the soldiers arrived, she stood before them, feeling as if her freedom had crumbled into dust.

As the men surrounded her, the frustration stretched tightly inside her. Once again, she was trapped in a life she didn't want, helpless to do anything. She wanted to lash out at the unfairness, to release her fury. Resentment added fuel to her frustration. She'd been given the barest taste of freedom, enough to now recognise the prison she'd been living in.

It broke her heart knowing that she had to willingly surrender to the life she no longer wanted.

The men gave her a horse and escorted her back to the abbey where a wagon was waiting. The captain said, 'My lady, we have orders to bring you back to Penrith immediately.'

'I know,' she whispered. He offered her food and drink, and she took both from him.

The wagon was covered with leather and heavy cloth to keep out the wind. They helped her inside, and she sat alone in the darkness as the wheels rolled along the road. Only then, did she let her tears fall while she drank the wine and ate the bread.

Though she wanted to blame her father, she had to face her own truth. For years, she'd been relying on others to grant her freedom. She'd been the obedient daughter, following orders blindly. She had never once made plans of her own, and it was time for that to change.

She removed her shoes and touched her sore feet, remembering how Piers had caressed them. He had cared for her, putting her needs before his own.

I want to be with him, she realised.

Even if that meant turning her back on the privileged life she'd known, embracing poverty. She might never be lady of a castle again. And yet, did that matter any more? It struck her that this was partly her fault for not making plans of her own. Piers had been trying to save the life of his friend and help them all escape. She should have shouldered some of the burden he'd carried.

A sense of firm resolution filled up inside her. This time, she would make better plans. Although she had to return to Penrith, it would only be for a short time. She would gather all the wealth she could, everything she needed to build a different life.

And when Piers returned for her, she would be ready.

Today, for the first time, Robert opened his eyes. The sense of relief that flooded through Piers was overwhelming, mingled with the crushing loss of Gwen. It was his fault that she'd been captured, but as soon as he healed Robert, he would find a way to bring her back.

He knew why she'd given herself up, but he blamed himself for it. He should have kept her hidden, and he should have covered their tracks better. Seeing the anguish in her eyes had sliced through him when they'd taken her, but there was nothing he could do except let her go—for they both knew her father would not harm her.

Though it had been a grave risk, he'd watched over Gwen for a short time to ensure she was safe before he'd left with Robert. He'd brought his brother back to a small cave he'd found only an hour's journey from the abbey.

'You're awake, I see.' Piers reached for a crust of bread and tossed it to his brother. He had tended Robert's wounds during the past few days, feeding him broth. His brother blinked a moment, glancing around with confusion. Likely he didn't remember what had happened.

'I thought you might be in trouble when I saw the soldiers searching.' Piers crouched down to look at him. Though Robert appeared startled, at least he was now conscious.

'Why did you save me?' His brother's voice was hoarse.

Piers didn't know how to answer that at first. Their relationship had always been strained over the years. And yet, when he'd seen his brother lying motionless, he'd known he couldn't let Robert die. He wasn't the sort of man who could walk away from someone, even if it might benefit him later.

'I probably should have let you bleed to death,' Piers admitted with a wry smile. 'But then I thought it might bring me an advantage later. You owe me a favour, Robert. And one day I'll collect on it.' The words were ruthless, but he wouldn't back down on this. His greatest priority now was going back for Gwen. During the past few days, she'd suffered in her father's custody, all because of him. He would do everything he could to remove her father from power at Penrith and restore her rightful place as lady of the castle.

Robert struggled to sit up, and he reached up to his forehead to the bandage there. He looked around at the small cave, as if trying to determine their whereabouts. Then he picked up the bread Piers had tossed at him and took a bite. The moment he did, his hunger got the best of him. Robert tore at the bread, eating it quickly. Piers handed him a flask of ale, and his brother asked, 'Where are we?'

'Not far from Colford. I didn't take you there at first because they were searching near the abbey. I think you've healed enough to go now.' And then he could finally go back for Gwen. Though it had only been a few days, it was killing him that she was at her father's mercy. He would have to find another way to get her out.

'How long have we been here?' Robert asked.

'We've been in this cave for two days,' Piers answered. 'But it's been five days since I found you.'

'What do you mean? How could it be a sennight?'

'We had to keep moving to different places. Lady Gwendoline helped us escape her father.' Piers paused a moment and then admitted, 'Lord Penrith kept her a prisoner when he took Morwenna, but she knew nothing about it. But on the night when I found you wounded, Gwen helped save your life.'

During those few days with her, it had only heightened his desire. She had captivated him, making him yearn to wed her. He'd never imagined she would choose to come with him, fighting to save his brother's life while fleeing her father. Because of her sacrifice, they'd escaped the danger. He intended to keep the vow he'd made, as soon as he brought Robert to safety.

'What about Morwenna and Brian?' Robert asked. 'What happened to them?'

'Morwenna is already at Colford Abbey,' Piers said. 'I'll take you to her. I saw Brian travelling south with some of the monks. I don't know where they're going, but I'm certain they all believe you're dead.'

'I'll send word to Brian,' Robert answered. 'Will you take me to the abbey?'

'We'll have to wait a little while until it's dark,' Piers warned. 'The earl is still searching for us.' That wasn't true at all, but his brother needed more time to regain his strength. Robert didn't seem to realise how weak he was.

His brother tried to stand up, but the moment he was on his feet, his knees buckled. He rested his hand against the stone wall to regain his balance.

'You took a hard blow to your head,' Piers said. 'I thought they cracked your skull. And you lost a lot of blood.' He held out a piece of dried meat and another flask, this one filled with water. 'I imagine you're starving. It was hard to force you to eat when you were mostly unconscious.'

Robert ate the meat and Piers gave him more bread, which he devoured. It was a good thing the monk had kept his word and had left them supplies. Without them, it would have been far more difficult to remain in hiding.

'You saved my life,' Robert acknowledged. 'I'm grateful for it.'

Piers shrugged. 'I suppose you'd have done the same for me.' But truthfully, he wasn't entirely certain. His relationship with his brother was on unsteady footing.

But Robert surprised him by nodding. 'I would have, aye. We may have been born from different mothers, but we share blood. That means something.'

He'd never imagined his brother would acknowledge their blood bond. For so long, they had competed against one another, fighting to come out on top. But the thankfulness in his brother's voice gave him the opening he'd needed. 'I saved your life, but there's something I want in return.'

At that, Robert tensed. 'What is it you want?'

He knew what his brother expected him to say, but he began with what was most important. 'Lady Gwendoline's hand in marriage,' Piers answered. 'She's mine. You will never lay claim to her as a bride.'

His brother met his gaze with speculation. 'And what about Penrith?'

He met Robert's gaze with his own. 'I'm not giving her up. Whether the lands are involved or not.' On this, he would never yield.

His brother paused before answering. 'I won't pursue Lady Gwendoline. But you'll have to fight that battle with her father.'

'Our fight has already begun,' Piers admitted, though he had not yet decided how he would save Gwendoline. He began to saddle the horses, preparing for their journey. He hoped Robert was strong enough to manage it, though he had his doubts. He was eager to leave, for that meant he could come back for Gwen. 'I don't know what will happen with Penrith,' he continued, 'but we both know you'd be dead if it weren't for me.'

'Neither of us can have the estate unless the king

intervenes,' Robert said. 'I think we should appeal to him and let him make the choice.'

Because then, the king would choose Robert. He would always choose a high-born man over a baseborn one. Piers gave a hard stare at his brother. 'You owe me, Robert.' If he'd left the man to die, the path to Penrith would be clear enough.

Instead, his brother answered, 'It's getting dark now. Let's go to Colford and speak of it later.'

The words were a means of delaying the argument. For now, Piers would keep the peace. But in the end, if fighting for Penrith meant fighting for Gwen, he would never surrender that battle.

Chapter Seven

Ever since her return, Gwendoline had been a model of obedience to her father. But whenever Alfred had ventured outside the keep to hunt or ride, she'd begun softening her approach to the guards. Gaining their trust was the key to making her escape.

'Good morn to you,' she greeted one of the younger guards within the keep who appeared more inexperienced. She gave him a flask of ale and bread. 'Could I ask you something?'

'Yes, my lady.' He devoured the bread eagerly, as if he'd not had enough to eat.

'I would like to visit outside the walls of the keep to see the serfs. Will you accompany me?'

His expression transformed, and he shook his head. 'It's no place for you, my lady.'

She ignored his warning and said, 'I've heard rumours that the people of Penrith are not treated well by my father or the king's men. Is that true?' She offered him another piece of bread that he accepted eagerly.

'The serfs work in the fields from dawn until dusk,'

he answered. 'They barely have water or food, and Lord Penrith has soldiers on all sides of the fields. If any man shirks his duty, they beat him. Sometimes they kill someone as an example to the others.'

Shock suffused her at his confession, along with fury that her father had done this. He'd treated them no better than slaves. Why had she ever believed Alfred's claim that he was bringing order to Penrith? If anything, he'd made their lives a misery. And she was just as responsible for their neglect. Ignorance was no excuse at all. She should have intervened sooner or recognised Alfred's cruelty.

'I want to see them,' she insisted. 'Today.'

For a moment, the guard seemed uneasy about the idea. 'The king's men won't like it.'

'And are they always guarding the serfs? Or is there a time when you and some of the other guards of Penrith are there?'

'A few hours before sundown,' he admitted. 'We change positions, and the king's men come to the keep. But, my lady, why do you wish to know?'

'Because the people are hungry, just as you are,' she answered. 'I want to bring them food and more supplies. And if you help me leave the keep to visit them, you will be rewarded.'

Beyond helping the people, it was also a way of getting the soldiers to relax their guard. If they saw her leaving regularly, it was easier to plan another escape.

'Lord Penrith will never let you leave these walls,' the soldier admitted. 'Not after you ran away.'

She kept her frustration veiled, though she should have expected this. 'Is there a leader among the serfs?

Someone who could come to me, and I could provide him with food and water for those in need?'

The guard thought a moment and then said, 'Henry the Fletcher. When I go out to the fields later, I can send him to you.'

'Thank you,' she said to the soldier. If nothing else, it was a start. 'You have been most helpful.'

After that, Henry the Fletcher came to see her each day after sundown. Gwen gathered food and supplies in secret, and he distributed them among the serfs. Although he didn't trust her, they had bridged a grudging sort of gap between them, so at least the people could get the food they needed. And in return, she hoped Henry might help her escape Penrith when the time came.

Though she wanted to believe that Piers would come for her, she knew it was naive to place all her hopes on him. It was far better to make her own arrangements than to expect him to save her. During the past few days, she had learned the rotation of the guards and had befriended the Penrith soldiers who guarded the barbican gate at night. Although she gave most of the men extra portions of food, she was particularly kind to those who might be on duty at night or in the morning.

'Ah, there you are, Gwen.' Her father approached her inside the Great Hall and motioned for her to walk with him.

'Good afternoon, Father,' she said demurely. She kept her gaze downcast, behaving as the perfect obedient daughter. It was also the best way to avoid showing any reaction to his words.

'The witnesses to sign your betrothal agreement to Gareth will arrive in the morning,' he said. 'After your…poor decision to run away, few men would have you to wife. I chose him from among your suitors as the winner.'

Though she had expected this, it tightened her nerves to realise how quickly her time was slipping away. She had already packed her belongings last night, and she'd also included the green gown that had once belonged to Morwenna. On a whim, she'd also gathered a few things that had belonged to the former earl and his wife, in case they belonged to Piers. He would want to have the memories of his family, and Gwen didn't want to leave the possessions behind. Now the only question was where to go. Should she go to the abbey in search of Piers? Or was it safer to travel to Tilmain? And then she questioned whether to leave today or in the morning.

'Did you hear what I said?' her father prompted.

'I did. Though I've already told you my thoughts on the matter.' Namely that Gareth was the last man she would ever consider marrying. The only reason her father had chosen him was because Gareth allowed Alfred to make all the decisions, and his family had influence and wealth.

Her father laughed softly. 'Gwen, I know what's best for you. And believe me when I say this will be a good marriage.'

For someone else, she added silently.

'May I go?' she asked him. 'I have preparations I'll need to make before the betrothal.' *Preparations to escape the castle and avoid the betrothal, that is.*

Her father smiled and nodded. 'I will see you to-night then.'

She gave no answer, for she had not yet decided when to leave. It might be best to go after the evening meal, for her father would not suspect her absence then. As she walked towards the keep, she stopped one of the stable boys. 'I want you to take more supplies to Henry the Fletcher.'

'Yes, my lady.'

'Come with me.' Then she walked with the boy towards the kitchens. To Wilfrid, the cook, she said, 'Give this boy a loaf of bread. And then prepare two bundles of food and ale. Send one to me and the other half with him.'

Gwen nodded to the boy and told him, 'The bread is for you and your family. Give the rest to Henry so he can divide them among those in need.' She wanted to ensure that the serfs had enough, especially since she would not be able to meet with Henry again.

The boy nodded and offered a smile. 'Thank you, my lady.'

She sent him on his way and noticed Wilfrid's approval. 'Your generosity has not gone unnoticed, my lady.'

'I regret that I did not help them sooner.' She met his gaze and added, 'Bring the food to me yourself. Tell no one of this.'

It was a risk to trust the cook, but she needed the supplies for travelling. She'd sewn her jewels into the hems of her gowns, and she would ask the stable boy to saddle a horse for her just after sundown.

Gwen walked up the stairs towards her chamber,

feeling an ache in her chest. More than anything, she wished Piers was here to accompany her. It was dangerous for a woman to travel alone, and she would have to ride all night.

She decided to start by travelling to Colford Abbey. At least there, the monks might know where to find Piers. And if no one knew where he was, she could leave word with Father Oswald that she was travelling to Tilmain. Piers could join her there later.

Although the estate was several days journey from here, no one there would suspect that she'd fled Penrith—the land belonged to her father, after all. And it would give her the time she needed to go even farther.

Gwen opened the door to her chamber and closed it behind her. Though she supposed she should feel a sense of adventure or excitement, only dread and fear filled her now. If she did not succeed in her escape, her father would likely imprison her until she was wedded and bedded by a man of his choosing.

This was her last chance for freedom.

At dawn, Piers left on horseback with supplies the monks had given him. He intended to ride to Penrith to keep the promise he'd made to Gwen. As he continued the journey, he went over the plans in his mind. It would be the safest to use the tunnels within Penrith to avoid detection, but he had to send word to her somehow.

He rode hard, only stopping once or twice to let his horse rest and get water. It would still take the remainder of the day to reach the estate.

But after a few hours, Piers heard what sounded like soldiers approaching.

He moved off the main road, trying to determine the source of the sound without being seen. But when he spied Gwen riding hard with the men in pursuit, he seized his bow.

He took aim at the first rider and struck him down. Then he took out the second man with another arrow. When the soldiers realised they were in range, they pulled back, which gave Gwen the time she needed to get away. Piers spurred his horse forward until she saw him.

Though he wanted to embrace her, there was no time. 'Stay with me,' he warned. 'Get your bow.' She obeyed and nocked an arrow to the bowstring.

'I'm so glad I found you,' she breathed. 'I've been riding all night.'

'I was on my way to bring you back,' he said. But it bothered him that she'd had to make her own escape. He should have been the one to rescue her. 'Can you shoot from horseback?'

'I've never tried it before,' she admitted.

'Don't try for a small target—just hit them however you can. Take the men on the right. I'll take the left,' he said. 'Once they've retreated, we'll change our direction and go west.'

He pulled back and took aim, striking another soldier. Gwen aimed for a soldier's chest, but instead, her shot struck his arm. Even so, it was enough to prompt the soldiers to pull back, giving them more distance.

'Come on.' He took her horse's reins and guided her through the woods. She needed time to rest before they continued.

They weren't far from the cave where he had tended

Robert. But if they tried to hide there, the men could surround and trap them in the space. It was better to keep moving.

'We're going to reach an open clearing soon,' he told her. 'When we do, ride as hard as you can. Don't look back, and don't stop.'

She appeared exhausted, but she nodded. He reached out to her while still on horseback and pulled her into a light embrace, kissing her temple. 'It's going to be all right, Gwen. I promise you.' He would die before allowing anything to happen to her.

'I can't go back to my father,' she said softly. 'Not again.'

He recognised the tremor of fear in her voice, and it only strengthened his resolve. 'I won't let them take you,' he said. 'This time, we'll stay together, no matter what.'

'I'm afraid he'll never stop hunting us,' she admitted.

'I'll take you home with me,' he swore. Which wasn't a lie. Stansbury had been his home for nearly two years. And if they could not remain in hiding there, they could continue to the ruins of his mother's home at Grevershire. Somehow, he would find a way to keep her safe. No longer did they have the choice of returning to Penrith to overthrow her father—not for a while. Instead, they would have to change their plans. It meant returning to exile for a time, but he wasn't about let her surrender to Alfred a second time.

Though he didn't understand the emotions Gwen had awakened inside him, one fact was clear—she belonged to him. He would fight for her, aye, even surrender his own life if that meant keeping her safe. But more than that, he wanted to raise himself up to be good enough for her. And one day, they would return to Penrith and reclaim it.

'We have to go now,' he told her when they reached the clearing. 'Are you ready?' She nodded, and he slapped her horse's flank. 'Go. Ride towards the hills. I'll be right behind you.'

Gwen broke through the trees and into the clearing. Once she was in the open meadow, she increased the pace until she reached a full gallop. Piers followed, watching for signs of the soldiers. They were farther back, and though he had bought them some time with his arrows, the men would not give up.

He kept his bow in hand while he rode, leaning forward against the horse. He increased his pace until he caught up to Gwen and then signalled for her to follow him. They needed a place to hide until nightfall. Her eyes held weariness, her shoulders slumped forward with exhaustion. Though it was dangerous, she needed to rest. He scoured the landscape, searching for any place they could take shelter.

Piers led them into another forest near the large hill and dismounted by the stream to let the horses get water. He lifted Gwen down and, the moment her feet touched the ground, her knees buckled.

He caught her and held her steady. 'Are you all right?'

She nodded. 'It's just that I've been riding since yestereve.'

'Have you eaten anything?'

'There was no time,' she admitted. 'I have a few things packed with the horse, but I just…couldn't.'

He tethered the horses and took out a blanket from his saddle bag and some bread. Then he led Gwen up the hillside, along a narrow path that made it impossible for anyone to follow in a large group. When at last they reached the summit, he led her over the top of the hill and to a smaller plateau where they would remain out of view. Then he spread out the blanket and gave her the bread. 'Eat something and then rest. I'll keep watch.'

'What about the horses?' she ventured.

It was indeed a grave risk to leave them by the stream, but the animals needed water. 'If the soldiers approach, we'll hear them. We have the high ground, and we can use our bows to take them out.' He'd counted nine soldiers remaining and sensed that another attack was coming.

Gwendoline appeared pale, and she only nibbled at the bread he'd given her. 'So many men.'

And then he realised where her fear was coming from. She'd likely never had to kill a man before. He could see the shock on her face and the uncertainty. He moved to sit beside her. 'I'll keep you safe, Gwen, I promise.'

Although she nodded, he could see in her shadowed eyes that she didn't quite believe him. 'I don't know if he'll ever stop hunting us, Piers. I only know that I can't go back. Not again.'

He didn't ask her what had happened at Penrith, but he could guess. 'You're safe now.'

'I know. And I trust you.'

Her words slid beneath his defences, pushing past the invisible walls he'd built around his emotions. He didn't deserve her trust, especially after all the secrets he'd kept from her. When she learned the truth, that he was a low-born bastard, she would hate him. He could only hope that she would give him the chance to fight for the future she deserved.

Gwen closed her eyes and drew up her knees. 'My father is trying to force me to marry Gareth of Watcombe.'

'No.' He would take her far away from here before he'd let that happen. He'd already beaten the man for daring to steal a kiss.

'It's not what I want either,' she admitted. She moved closer to him and leaned her head against his shoulder. 'But I don't know what to do. I thought I could run away, but my father will never stop. He will bring me back no matter how far I go. And he won't give me a choice in who I marry.'

'You could marry me instead.' Although he'd mentioned it to her before, he knew it was still too soon. He waited, fully expecting her to refuse.

Instead, her face shifted as she turned to look at him. Her eyes held a blend of startled amusement. 'Because my father can't force me to wed if I'm already married?'

A sudden hardness caught in his throat, but Piers nodded. She started to laugh, and her smile was blinding. 'Do you know, I think I will do it.'

Piers didn't know what had prompted her to agree to this. But she embraced him hard, and he held her close, breathing in the scent of her hair. She had no idea of how low she'd sunk. He was bringing her out of her sheltered, noble life and into one of nothingness. He could only hope that, one day, he could change it.

She drew back to look at him and then turned serious. 'But if I agree to this, I want no more secrets between us. I need to know everything about you.'

He stared back at her, still in disbelief that she'd

agreed to this. Part of him wanted to warn her against marrying a man like him.

Yet he heard himself saying, 'No more secrets, after we are wedded.' Even with that vow, he intended to delay telling her everything.

She deserves to know the truth, his conscience insisted. It had hung between them long enough.

But he didn't want to see the disappointment in her eyes when she learned he was a bastard. And what if she happened to conceive a child? Although he desired her with every breath in his body, the thought of her becoming pregnant utterly terrified him. Their child would be lowborn, like him.

The same thing had happened to his mother. She had believed she was marrying a nobleman, only to fall into shame after his father Degal had abandoned her. Would Gwen feel the same after she learned his secrets?

A heaviness rested within him that he was bringing her down. But she leaned in to kiss him, and he forgot the words he ought to say. Instead, he tasted the softness of her lips and, for now, he lost himself in her.

'Will you lie down beside me?' she asked. 'I'll only rest for a little while.'

It wasn't wise, but Piers couldn't refuse her plea. He lay on his side with her back pressed to his stomach. He wrapped his arms around her, keeping her head tucked beneath his chin. Gwen gave a slight shiver, but he suspected it was out of fear. Although it was utter torture holding her so close, he offered her what comfort he could. After a little while, he felt her breathing grow even as she fell asleep.

All around him, he listened for signs of the soldiers,

but he could hear nothing at all. They wouldn't stop their search; that was certain. But he didn't know how long they could rest until they had to continue their escape.

It was humbling to realise that Gwen had travelled so far alone, and she'd had to rescue herself. He should have saved her, and he couldn't forgive himself for that. Gwen didn't deserve to live her life fleeing from her father's men.

But in her sleep, she reached for his hand and drew it to her heart. He could feel the steady rise of her breathing beneath his palm. Somehow, she had faith in him, although he was unworthy. He didn't know how to become the sort of man she needed.

But one thing was certain. If she went through with the wedding, one day she would regret marrying him.

It was nightfall when Gwen awoke in Piers's arms. To her surprise, he was riding with her, holding her on horseback while she slept. Her horse was tied to his, and she didn't remember him waking her or putting her on horseback at all.

'I'm sorry,' she said to him. 'I didn't realise I was that tired.' She did feel better, though her body still ached from riding.

'I didn't want to wake you,' he answered, 'but we needed to leave. I couldn't let the soldiers find us.'

The reminder only tightened her fear, and she rested her hands upon his, seeking comfort. 'Where are they now?'

'Not far behind,' he answered.

From the tense expression on his face, the danger had

not lessened. If anything, the time they'd spent resting might have made matters worse. She inwardly cursed her weakness, though she'd been grateful for the sleep.

'I should get back on my own horse so we can ride faster,' she said. Being in his arms had made her feel safe, but it hindered them from travelling faster.

Piers slowed his mount and unfastened the reins. Then he lifted her on to her mare. She had no idea where they were travelling now, but she trusted him to bring them to safety.

'Where are we going?' she asked.

'West,' was all he could say. 'At least for now.'

It was in the opposite direction of Tilmain, but Gwen didn't argue. She increased the punishing pace of her mount and followed him, despite her discomfort. Already it was growing dark, and she could see the moon rising. It made her wonder how long they'd been riding while she was asleep.

Was there any hope of escape? She studied the horizon before them, wondering where they would take shelter again. Did Piers truly have lands that belonged to his mother's family? She knew so little about him, and he'd only shared pieces of the truth. She only wished he would share the rest of his secrets with her. He'd promised to do so after they were wedded, and she had to trust that he would.

After another hour of riding, she glanced behind them. It was then that she saw the flare of torches. Her heartbeat quickened at the sight. 'Piers,' she warned. 'Look there.'

He turned around and let out a curse beneath his

breath. 'They've found us. We need to ride fast and hope we can outrun them.'

'I'll follow,' she agreed.

He spurred his horse hard and took the lead. She urged her mount and soon enough, she was a slight distance behind him. The brightness of the moon reflected off a silvery ribbon of a stream that cut through the clearing.

But when she glanced behind, she saw only four riders. Where were the others? She'd been certain there were more than that. Her worst fears were realised when more torches appeared in front of them. Piers switched directions, but the men were already closing in fast, cutting off their escape.

'Come on,' he urged her, turning the opposite way. 'Ride towards the woods ahead of us.'

She obeyed, but her horse stumbled and reared up. She managed to keep her seat, but it was too late. Within moments, the soldiers surrounded them, and terror lanced her heart. Oh, God. What if they killed Piers?

He dismounted his horse and unsheathed his sword, preparing to fight. But she saw one of the soldiers draw back his bow. In one motion, she dismounted with her own bow and quiver and moved in front of him.

'Gwen, don't,' he warned, but she wasn't about to listen. Not with an arrow aimed at his heart.

'They won't hurt me,' she said. They were here to bring them back, but she knew the moment they took her into custody, Piers would be killed. Her only hope was to shield him as best she could.

Her heart was beating so fast, a rushing sound filled

her ears. The torches circled around them, and she fought back against the blinding fear.

'You're going to die,' one of the soldiers said to Piers. He was leering at them, and Gwen took aim at the man.

'Not if I kill you first.' Her words came out shaky, but she meant what she said.

The man started to laugh, and she thought she heard a faint sound from behind the men, though she couldn't tell what it was. Her hands were shaking at the prospect of having to kill one of these men, though she had no doubt in her ability.

'You've caused us a great deal of trouble today, Lady Gwendoline,' one of the men remarked.

She took a breath, trying to calm herself. Panicking would only cause matters to worsen. But her skin had grown ice cold, and it was becoming difficult to hold the bow steady.

Then there came a shout, and the men drew back at the sight of another soldier lying on the ground, his throat sliced open.

'Run!' Piers ordered her. It was then that she saw Robert, alive and well. She didn't know how he'd found them, but he held his own sword in readiness. This might be their only chance to survive. If she fled, some of the men would pursue her, giving Piers and Robert a better chance of winning the fight.

Gwendoline lowered her bow and picked up her skirts, running towards the woods. Though a horse would have been faster, there wasn't time for that now. She kept her weapon in hand, along with the quiver of arrows.

When she reached the woods, she was startled to

see her friend Morwenna waiting there. Oddly enough, Morwenna was dressed in the manner of a monk, wearing a shapeless, undyed garment. She and Robert must have been travelling in disguise.

'Are you all right?' her friend asked. She held a sword in her hand, her attention fixed upon the fighting ahead.

'Yes,' Gwen breathed. She didn't ask questions about how Morwenna or Robert had managed to find them, but she was deeply grateful for their intervention. At least now they had a chance of survival.

'Do you want to go deeper into the woods?' Morwenna asked. 'I could take you into hiding.'

The thought was tempting, but she knew the men were already in pursuit. 'No. I have my bow, and it will be easier to shoot the soldiers if any of the men try to follow.'

She worried that it would be difficult to see the men in the darkness. The moonlight reflected somewhat off their chainmail armour, but the darkness would alter her aim at such a distance.

Gwen nocked an arrow to her bow, watching the men fight. Piers and Robert fought back-to-back, their swords moving as they cut down their enemies. They moved together as if they'd practised for years, and she marvelled at their fighting skills.

'Two men, over there,' Morwenna warned, holding tightly to her sword. Gwen took aim at the first enemy, praying her arrow would strike true. A second later, he crumpled to the ground, and she swiftly drew another arrow. The other man kept running, but he moved sideways, making it difficult to take aim. She kept the bow steady, trying to predict where he would go. Then finally, she shot the arrow…only to miss.

The man continued to run, constantly changing his direction to thwart her aim. In the distance, she saw a rider thundering towards her, his sword raised. It was Piers and, behind him, Robert mounted another horse.

She pulled hard on her bowstring and released another arrow at the soldier, but her second one missed as well. Horror washed over her when she realised the man was going to reach them. She nocked a third arrow, but he was too close now. He raised his sword, prepared to cut them down. Before he could swing his weapon, Morwenna darted forward and stabbed him in the heart. Her reckless courage saved them both.

Gwen let out a shuddering breath, dropping the bow and arrows. A surge of relief flooded through her as the soldier slid to the ground. Morwenna's hands were covered in blood, just as the two men arrived. Robert reached her side and crushed her into an embrace.

Gwen was trembling as Piers took her in his arms. They were alive, and all their attackers were dead. It was terrible to think of so many men losing their lives, though she knew there had been no other choice.

Piers tucked her head beneath his chin, stroking back her hair as he held her tight. She could hear his own heartbeat echoing the pace of her own. But they were alive. And for now, it was enough.

'Are they all dead?' Morwenna asked.

'They are,' Robert answered. 'But we can't stay here. There could be more.'

Though Gwen knew it was possible, she couldn't let

herself think of that now. Her entire body seized up with fear, and she couldn't stop the tremors. Piers pulled back, but he still kept his arms around her waist.

'What happened?' Robert asked them. 'Why were you running away?'

Gwen exchanged a glance with Piers. A simple answer was best, instead of trying to explain all of it. And so she said, 'My father was trying to stop us from getting married. He sent soldiers to bring me back and kill Piers.'

It wasn't exactly the truth, but it was the easiest explanation. She glanced over at Morwenna, suddenly realising that the young woman didn't know that she'd been imprisoned in her chamber. She must have believed that Gwen had abandoned her when that wasn't the truth at all.

Morwenna had been flogged for no reason, except for pretending to be a noblewoman. And Gwen wanted to reach out and offer friendship again. 'I am so sorry I could not free you when you were his prisoner,' she said in regard to her father. 'He locked me away in my room, and I had no idea that he had you flogged.' Her expression grew pained. 'I blame myself for it.'

'You couldn't have stopped him,' Morwenna answered. She turned back to Robert and said, 'We cannot stay out here in the open. We need to find shelter.'

'It will be dawn soon,' Robert agreed. 'But we're not far from Stansbury.'

Gwen had no idea where that was, but anywhere was better than out in the open.

'I agree,' Piers said. He met her gaze and, though

it was hard to read his expression in the darkness, she heard the warmth in his voice. 'Good shooting. I'm glad you brought your bow.'

She detected admiration in his voice, but even so, she couldn't push back the emotions rising higher. In a short time, she'd shot several men, and she couldn't suppress the chilling truth of taking a life. It wasn't something she'd ever imagined she could do. But there had been no choice in it.

'Thank you,' she murmured. His arms were around her, making him aware of her trembling. At his questioning glance, she answered his unspoken question. 'I just…never thought I would have to shoot a man.' Both yesterday and today—it seemed impossible what she'd done.

'I'm glad you did,' Piers answered, tightening his grip on her waist in a silent embrace of support. She sensed that he was trying to absolve her of the guilt. It wasn't something she'd ever imagined, but she could not change it now. She'd made the decision never to go back to her father, and though she hadn't wanted to kill the men, she blamed Alfred for sending them.

Piers glanced over at Morwenna and added, 'And I'm glad you knew how to fight with a sword. Even if you never liked it.'

The young woman met his gaze, but there was a wry smile on Piers's face, as if he knew Morwenna's reasons. Gwen suspected it had to do with Robert, which was confirmed by Morwenna's blush.

The men retrieved the horses and all their belongings before Piers helped her on her mount. He joined

Robert near the front, and Gwen rode alongside Morwenna, following them.

'Are you really getting married?' Morwenna asked her. 'It seems so soon.'

She didn't miss the note of wariness in the young woman's voice but really didn't know how to answer. Piers's offer of marriage wasn't based on love or feelings. It was a vow to protect her, but she didn't truly know why. He had told her so little about himself. Did he hope to regain Penrith through the union, if he was the earl's son? He'd sworn he would answer her questions and keep no more secrets between them. She intended to hold him to that vow.

Morwenna was waiting for her answer, so Gwen admitted, 'Piers has promised to take care of me. My father is…not who I thought he was. Both for the way he treated you and our people. I didn't realise he was that terrible until I saw the serfs with my own eyes.' She paused while they rode and added, 'I don't know where we'll go yet, but I suppose eventually we'll have to return to Penrith. If my father leaves.'

It *was* too soon to marry Piers; she knew that. But he'd done everything in his power to give her the freedom she wanted. Never had he treated her like a woman incapable of making her own decisions.

Of all the husbands she could choose, he was the one who made her feel empowered. And that was something she might never find with any other man. He did care—she could see it in the way he watched her. And at least by marrying him, she would have a choice.

Piers drew his horse back to ride alongside her. Morwenna took the hint and urged her horse forward to join Robert at the front. His expression held concern and he asked, 'How are you, Gwen?'

'It's been a long night.' She reached out to him, and he took her hand in his. For a moment, they rode together in silence.

'I'm going to leave you with Robert and Morwenna at Stansbury while I find a priest,' he admitted. 'If you're still willing to wed me, that is. There's not much time.'

A sudden rush of uncertainty washed over her, for Gwen was afraid of what lay ahead. She needed to build trust between them, and she still sensed he was holding back secrets.

'I will wed you if you keep your promise,' she said. 'Tell me something you've never told me before.'

Piers squeezed her hand and met her gaze. 'On the morrow, as I promised. After we are wedded, I will tell you everything you want to know.'

'But you won't tell me now.'

His posture stiffened, and he released her hand. 'There are things about my past…that I'm not proud of. Choices I made. And I'd rather marry you before you know all of it.'

'You want to keep the illusion a little longer,' she predicted. The darkness was starting to fade into morning, reminding her of how tired she was. In the shadows of the waning night, she caught a glimpse of his face by moonlight. Piers had shielded his emotions, not saying anything. And she realised that there was hurt beneath it all. He believed if he told her the truth, she would turn her back on him.

But even if there was a raw past that haunted him, she sensed that this man needed her. No one ever had before, and it humbled her. She drew her horse beside him and reached for his hand again.

'Go and find a priest,' she said.

Chapter Eight

It took all day to find a priest, though he'd started searching at Colford Abbey. Piers was exhausted from the journey, but he had no intention of stopping to rest. He'd learned from the monks that King John was travelling north to Scotland, and likely his brother Robert would go to plead his case there soon.

When he'd asked for a priest to come with him back to Stansbury, Father Oswald had voiced his disapproval of the marriage. Most of the other brethren followed suit. There was only one priest from a nearby village who was willing to wed them, and the man was so drunk, he swayed on the ancient mare he rode. His robes were dishevelled, and he had two drinking horns strapped to the mare. Piers wasn't entirely certain the priest knew what was happening, but the man was his only option.

Even then, he wasn't entirely certain this marriage to Gwen would be legal. Without a formal betrothal and with only Robert and Morwenna as witnesses, he didn't know. But it was better than nothing, and he wanted her to feel safe again.

He'd sworn to tell Gwen the truth about his past, but the shame of it weighed upon him. Despite her claim that she was willing to wed him, once she learned of his lies of omission, she would hate him for the ruse he'd played. She'd believed *he* was the heir to Penrith, not Robert. And no explanation could justify what he was about to do.

It was growing dark when they arrived back at Stansbury. Although Piers was hungry, he'd been unable to eat during most of the journey back. Gwen would not look at him in the same way after tonight, and he couldn't relinquish the guilt. The priest dismounted from his mare and stumbled before righting himself.

But the moment they arrived Piers couldn't take his eyes off his bride. Though her silk gown was rumpled, Gwen's hair was braided and there were small wildflowers tucked between the strands. A soft flush upon her cheeks revealed her shyness, and his apprehensions tripled. He had no right to marry someone like her. She deserved the life of a noblewoman, one where she ruled over her people.

Yet, when she reached out her hands to his, he could not deny her. If she was willing to give him a chance, so be it.

The priest took another drink and began speaking Latin words Piers didn't recognise. Though he thought they were part of the marriage rite, he could not be certain. Gwen was smiling at him, but he sensed a slight strain in her eyes. Something was troubling her. But whatever it was, she was still going through with the marriage.

They spoke their vows, though he was fairly certain the priest had left out the entire marriage Mass. And when it was done, Piers leaned in to give Gwen a kiss of peace.

Morwenna and Robert clapped, and within moments they were bringing out a feast that they'd prepared while he was away. Morwenna had baked small flat cakes, and Robert cooked fish over a spit that he'd caught earlier. While it roasted, he passed out wine to Piers and Gwen.

'Is that the bottle I stole from Penrith?' Piers muttered.

Robert only smiled. 'I wish you both good health and many children.' He raised his drinking horn in a toast, and they all drank.

Gwen gave Piers her cup, and then she returned from the horses with a small bundle. She unwrapped it in front of Morwenna and said, 'This was your mother's, wasn't it? The one you left behind.'

Piers hadn't realised that Gwen had brought the gown with her, but it made Morwenna smile while she nodded. Then a moment later, some tears escaped as she took the gown. 'Thank you for bringing it back to me.'

'I knew you'd want it,' Gwen answered.

'I wish you'd given it to me sooner so I wouldn't have worn the monk's habit to your wedding.' Morwenna laughed.

Gwen smiled and said, 'I should have, but I was distracted by Piers.' The look in her eyes held mischief, but when he returned her stare, she suddenly grew shy and looked away. It reminded him that they were now wedded, and he could finally make her his. The thought sent a sudden flare of heat through him. He went to stand beside her and touched the small of her back. 'Shall we go?'

The last of the sunlight rimmed through the leaves, casting beams of gold. For the first time, Piers felt an uncertainty undermining the future that lay ahead. But then Gwen glanced up at him, and her eyes held an emotion he didn't quite understand. 'Yes,' she breathed.

It humbled him that she had married him. He didn't know why or how this had happened. Yet, tonight, he wanted to be worthy of Gwen…even for one moment.

They walked to the edge of the ruins, and he led her down a path that bent around a broken stone wall. Their future was as uncertain and unstable as this crumbling wall. And yet, he intended to push past their troubles and reach for what he wanted.

Piers silenced the voices of doubt, pressing Gwen back gently against the wall as he stole a kiss. He tasted the familiar warmth of her mouth, and when her arms came around his neck, a rush of desire evoked a craving he couldn't deny.

His tongue slid against hers, and she answered the touch, opening to him while her hands threaded through his hair.

She laughed softly against his mouth. 'Not here.'

Piers pulled back from the kiss, keeping his hands upon her hips. 'Come with me.' He led her downhill to the pool of water where he and Robert had bathed after sword fighting all day. A small waterfall cascaded over the rocks, spilling into the pool.

'Do you want to swim?' he asked.

She shook her head. 'Not just now. It looks cold.'

'It's freezing,' he admitted. 'But Robert and I did swim there often after we trained.'

Her expression grew pensive as she studied him. Her blue eyes held suspicion as she said, 'You're not just friends, are you?'

He shook his head but gave her the truth she wanted. 'He's my half-brother.'

For a time, he couldn't discern Gwen's emotions. She was waiting for more, but he'd already decided that, while he would answer her questions, he didn't plan to volunteer any information. The silence stretched between them until at last, she said, 'Tell me the rest, Piers.'

He didn't answer but took her by the hand and led her down by the pool. Then he spread out a blanket and said, 'I'll build a fire for us. Then I'll answer your questions.'

She seemed to accept this, and it gave him time to think of what to say. He wanted to avoid telling her he was a bastard. He didn't want to ruin their wedding day by revealing that they had nowhere to go or any wealth at all.

As he built the fire, he thought of half-truths or reasons to delay telling her all of it. She sat with her knees drawn up beneath her gown, and he couldn't stop from staring at her.

'What is it?' she asked at last.

'You're beautiful,' he admitted, 'and I cannot believe you're my wife.'

Her lips curved in a soft smile, but the wariness remained in her eyes. He moved to sit beside her and, God help him, all he wanted to do was savour her body, pleasuring her again and again.

'Who are you, Piers?' she repeated. 'You promised me an answer.'

He had, but he wanted a few hours without the past to come between them. Already he could see the doubts in her eyes, and he didn't want to shatter the fragile bond between them.

And so, he answered, 'I'm your husband.' With that, he kissed her, unleashing all the desire he'd been holding back. He pulled at the laces of her gown, loosening the bliaud until he could kiss her shoulder. She let out a sigh, and he sensed her frustration. But for now, he wanted to give her the answers a little at a time. He desired her with every breath he took, but he'd never been with a lady before, only a few castle maids. He wanted to pleasure her, but he could sense her nervousness from the rise of goosebumps upon her skin.

'My mother was Wenda of Grevershire,' he murmured against her shoulder. 'I am her only son.'

The words seemed to reassure her, and Gwen rose up to her knees. He continued loosening her gown until it fell to the ground, and she wore only her shift. The linen was so fine, he could see the faint outline of her nipples pressing against the delicate cloth. He pulled off his tunic, and her eyes held apprehension when she saw him.

'Touch me,' he commanded. He needed her hands upon him to give him the courage to say more. She rested her hands upon his chest, her fingers splayed out as she explored him. His heartbeat quickened as she stroked his muscles, and her caress was like fire, haunting him. It seemed like a dream that she was here with him now, that she was his wife. He would never be good enough for her, not in a thousand years. But he wanted to try.

As she explored him, he cupped her breasts, stroking the tips with his thumbs. She inhaled sharply at his touch, biting her lip. Then she closed her eyes, moving her hands around his neck. 'Tell me more, Piers.'

'My father was the Earl of Penrith,' he said. 'I am Robert's older half-brother.' He'd told her part of that truth before, but he hoped this would be enough to satisfy her curiosity. He didn't want her to ask anything more.

With that, he lowered the delicate linen and bared her breasts. They were perfect, with rose nipples and skin softer than he'd ever seen. He laid her back on the blanket, admiring her beauty before he bent to taste her.

She reached for his hair, her fingers gripping him as he swirled his tongue over her nipples. Her back arched, and she let out a tremulous moan while he suckled at her.

But when he was about to cover her body with his own, she stopped him. 'Piers, wait.'

Her body was blazing with needs he'd awakened, but Gwen knew Piers was still holding back the truth from her. Earlier today, Morwenna had helped her prepare for the wedding—and Gwen couldn't stop thinking of their conversation.

'Don't listen to what others say or even what he tells you,' Morwenna had reassured her. 'Listen to your heart and how he makes you feel.'

Gwen had smiled at that. 'Then I know the answer. It won't be easy, and we've made an enemy of my father.

But I do want to marry Piers. He needs me.' Of that, she was certain. Whenever she caught him staring at her, he looked at her as if he could not believe she had chosen him. He was a strong protector, and she wanted to wed a man who treated her as his equal. She turned to face Morwenna, hoping that her friend would also marry. Perhaps it could be a wedding for all of them. 'But what of you and Robert?'

'Robert cares for me, but he cannot marry a miller's daughter, Lady Gwendoline. He is the rightful heir to Penrith.'

And with those words, Morwenna's revelation had changed everything. Piers had admitted that he was Robert's older half-brother…but he hadn't told her the greatest secret of all—that he was not the heir to Penrith. Which meant he was a bastard.

In some ways, the knowledge hadn't surprised her. She had guessed that he was uncomfortable with nobility and, although he knew the estate well, he'd never treated Penrith as if it were his.

She'd almost reconsidered marrying him. The secret was beyond anything she'd imagined, though she knew why he hadn't told her. And though it hurt that he had not trusted her with the truth, she considered his actions over his words.

During the past few weeks, Gwen had caught glimpses of the man he truly was. Piers had been willing to sacrifice himself to let her escape. He would have died if she hadn't surrendered to her father first. It wasn't the action of a man who only wanted land.

And when the soldiers had come to take her back a

second time, Piers had defended her from all of them. There was no doubting his courage or strength.

For those reasons, she had decided to take a chance and follow her heart.

But there were still so many secrets between them. She couldn't ignore what she'd learned, and she needed to hear the truth from his lips. She wanted to believe that Piers would tell her everything, but how could she build a marriage upon dishonesty?

His eyes were hooded with desire, but Gwen had his full attention. She pressed him to sit down while she rested her hands on his chest.

'I married you because I believe you will keep me safe,' she said, reaching up to touch his face. 'And because I see something in you.'

'Don't try to make me into a hero, Gwen,' he said. 'I can't be who you want me to be.' In his eyes, she could see that he believed it. And for a man who was a bastard, it wasn't surprising.

'All I want is your honesty,' she said.

'I've told you who I am.'

'You've told me parts of the truth,' she conceded. 'But you swore to tell me everything. Will you go back on your word now?' All she wanted was an end to the secrets. If he could simply tell her the truth, they could get past the deception and move forward.

From the stubborn set to his jaw, she could see that he had no intention of giving her answers. He was going to cling to the story he'd concocted. And although she was raging with desire for this man, she was not about to surrender a wedding night to a man who lied.

He pulled her into a hard kiss, and she recognised it for what it was—another distraction.

'Piers, stop.' This time, she shoved him back and stood. 'I will not consummate this marriage until you tell me the rest.'

His eyes had gone dark, and a hard cast came over his face. 'You already know the truth, don't you? That I'm a bastard.'

The anger in his voice made her falter, but she forced herself to face him. Beneath his harsh tone, she saw a man whose pride had burned into ashes. He resented his life and would rather lie than admit who he was.

She didn't know how to change that. Or even if she could. 'Yes, I know,' she murmured. 'Robert is the heir, isn't he?'

'He is. And my noble brother has always had everything he's ever wanted. I suppose you thought you were marrying a man like him.'

She didn't miss the note of resentment beneath his words. 'I chose to marry you.'

'And now you know that was a mistake.'

She didn't know how to respond to that. Piers's low station was a greater problem than she'd realised. Not only because of finding a place to live—but because Piers seemed to despise himself.

His eyes turned cold, and he tossed her a blanket. 'You'll want this. It's getting cold.'

She took the blanket and wrapped it around her. 'It doesn't have to be like this between us, Piers. Your past doesn't matter to me—'

'You don't know anything about what my life was like,' he shot back. 'And I don't need your pity.' It was evident now that there would be no wedding night, nothing save a breach between them that she didn't know if she could span.

'It's not pity,' she protested. But he had already stood up and was starting to walk away. 'Where are you going?'

'For a walk. You have a fire and a blanket.'

'But when will you return?'

'When you're asleep.' The words were cool and emotionless before he turned his back and left the camp.

Gwen had never imagined he would abandon her here. At the moment, it felt as if he'd struck a blow to her stomach. In all their time together, not once had he left her alone. But then, a prickle of annoyance caught her. Piers truly believed she considered him beneath her, that she thought less of him because of his birth.

The only reason she thought less of him now was because he was running away. Her anger kindled hotter, and she let the blanket fall. Why was he behaving like this? She'd done nothing wrong, and now that she knew the truth, he acted as if she was to blame for demanding answers.

Did he expect her to huddle by the fire and weep until he returned? Or did he plan to treat her as if she were a high-born noblewoman who was utterly useless? Gwen stared at her retreating husband, wondering if she should follow him.

But no, he'd gone off to sulk. Let him. Until he was ready to talk, there was no sense in trying to coax him into relenting. She tossed another log on the fire, watching as the sparks danced in the darkness.

And though she tried to shield her bruised feelings, she understood that the distance between them was far greater than she'd realised.

* * *

Piers kept his word and didn't return until Gwen was asleep. Though he still ached with desire for his wife, it was a fitting punishment for him. He'd dared to wed a noblewoman and, now that she knew who he was, she regretted the decision.

The only part that didn't make sense was why she'd gone through with the marriage. If Morwenna had told her the truth beforehand, then Gwen had married him while knowing he was a bastard. Why would she do it? Had she mistakenly believed that Morwenna had lied? It made little sense.

He sat down beside the fire, adding more wood while he gathered his cloak around himself. Gwen lay upon the ground, wrapped in the blanket with her back to him, facing the fire. Her golden hair had fallen free of its braids, and he wanted nothing more than to pull back the blanket and feel the warmth of her body in his arms.

But no, she'd already refused to lie with him. He'd seen the look of anger on her face, and it came as no surprise that she didn't want him any more. It was a torment to be bound to her, and yet a thousand invisible walls lay between them.

Better to lock away the useless emotions and accept the truth—that she didn't want to be with someone like him. An honourable man would annul the marriage and send her home again. But he wasn't honourable at all.

He wanted to keep her. The thought of her marrying a man like Gareth of Watcombe, or any other man touching his wife, filled him with fury. He'd known the risk of her disappointment when he'd married her, but he hadn't expected it to happen so soon.

Gwen's breathing was even in sleep, and Piers chose a spot opposite from her. In the morning, he would take her to Grevershire to put more distance between them and her father's men. He knew better than to believe they were safe now.

But as he curled up in his cloak, he couldn't help but wish things were different.

In the morning, Piers awakened to the scent of food. He was startled to realise that Gwen had heated some of the oat cakes Morwenna had cooked yesterday. She gave him some without speaking to him, and he accepted the food. For a long moment, they ate in silence. It was strange, for he was accustomed to her conversation and warmth.

This was the first time she'd shut him out, and he should have expected it. The cold emptiness was so unlike Gwen, he didn't know how to respond. It reminded him of the loneliness he'd endured as an adolescent— the sense of being invisible. But he forced back the useless feelings and faced her.

He helped her pack up their belongings on to the horses and then said, 'We'll ride to Grevershire today. We should arrive there within two days.'

But Gwen regarded him and shook her head. 'No, I have a different plan in mind. If we keep travelling alone, my father's men will only track us down. We're going to Tilmain instead.'

Tilmain? He blinked a moment at that. 'Your father's men are at Tilmain. We can't go there, or I'll be dead within a day.'

She ignored his protests. 'They know nothing of who

you are. But I grew up at Tilmain. The people know me well, and when I order them to accept you as my husband, they will. I will say that you won the competitions, and we married afterwards.'

He thought it was entirely too naive to imagine the people would simply accept that story. 'Why would they believe such a thing?'

She straightened. 'Because I will demand it of them. And if you're going to learn to rule by my side, you might as well begin in a place where I have authority. My father will never expect us to go to Tilmain—we'll be hiding in plain sight.'

Piers mounted his horse and drew it beside hers. 'It's too dangerous. They would learn who I am, and I'd be imprisoned or killed.'

But Gwen turned back to him and the anger in her eyes caught him unawares. 'I am tired of being ordered around. My father has done it all my life. Everyone treats me as if I am too fragile to make a decision or to know what I'm doing. I *am* going to Tilmain, and if you don't want to go with me, the road is over there.'

Her blue eyes flashed with fury, and he was entirely too distracted by her flushed cheeks and the way she glared at him. He'd never known someone so beautiful in all his life, and it only tightened his desire for her.

He stared at her. 'Why are you so certain this plan will work?'

'I'm not,' she admitted. 'But we need allies right now. And if we take command at Tilmain, then we can gain men who will travel back with us to Penrith when we claim it.'

'We'll never win the land by trying to seize it,' he

admitted. 'The only way to conquer Penrith is with the king's consent.'

'We still need men of our own as protection,' she pointed out. 'And I have gold at Tilmain that I can use to pay them. Or the jewels I brought with me.' She led her horse in the right direction and asked, 'Now are you coming or not?'

It was a strong risk, but it might be one worth taking. If nothing else, he could be certain she had a place to stay where she was safe. He moved his horse closer to hers while she stared back at him. Her defiant demeanour intrigued him, along with her flushed cheeks and glaring eyes. For a moment, he admired her openly, letting his gaze pass from her face down to her body. Gwen bit her lip and looked away.

He followed behind her, but as they rode east, he couldn't help but wonder about the greater implications of her actions. She would formally recognise him as her husband among her people. And more than that, she was demanding that he take his place at her side to rule over them. Although he'd planned to seize Penrith, at least he knew the people there. They might accept him as a leader, knowing that he was their lord's bastard son. But no one at Tilmain knew him at all.

By presenting him as her husband, it made it more difficult to annul their marriage. And that made him wonder whether she might one day come to accept him.

They travelled for nearly a sennight without being followed. When Gwen saw the River Ribble at last, a weight seemed to lift from her shoulders for it meant they were nearly there. She guided them over the bridge and then turned to Piers. 'We can travel along the river the rest of the way. No one will follow us. There's a place farther along where the water is deeper. We can hire a boat there.'

'Should we keep the horses or sell them?' he asked.

Gwen hadn't expected him to ask her opinion, but she answered, 'I think we should sell them. It will be easier to sail without them.' And once they reached the outskirts of Tilmain, she could send for more horses.

He agreed, and within a few hours they had managed to find buyers for the horses and were on a boat sailing east. She sat near the front of the vessel, and the wind blew her hair back from her face.

Though she tried to keep a serene expression, it was entirely false. She'd lied to Piers, letting him believe she had served as Lady of Tilmain. The truth was, she'd never had any authority there—her father hadn't allowed her to make any decisions at all. The only reason she'd wanted to come here was because she hoped to gain men to support them.

But now, she was starting to question the wisdom of this. What if no one listened to her? What if they treated her like the invisible daughter she'd always been? How could she possibly show Piers how to lead when she didn't know how to do it herself?

Gwen clenched her hands together, trying to push back the nerves. She would simply have to pretend she knew what she was doing and hope the people would obey.

During the journey here, Piers had hardly spoken to her. His silence bothered her deeply, though she should have expected it. He'd never wanted to tell her about his past. He'd admitted that he was a bastard, but beyond that, she knew little about him.

Yet she wanted to know more. She wanted to understand what he'd suffered over the years so she could begin to make a marriage with him—if that was even possible.

She heard footsteps approaching from behind her and then he came and wrapped his cloak around her. 'The wind is strong,' he said. 'You must be cold.'

The thoughtful gesture was entirely unexpected, but she could feel the heat of his body in the wool. His scent clung to the cloak, and it made her feel as if she were in his embrace. Somehow it hurt even more to be this close to him…and yet a thousand more miles seemed to stretch between them.

It was clear that Piers didn't trust her enough to tell her more about himself, as if she would think less of him for knowing his secrets. She wasn't ashamed of his low birth. He wasn't to blame for his father's choices, but it seemed that he couldn't set the past aside. His pride would never soften, and she was beginning to wonder whether she'd asked the impossible of him by wanting him to reign at her side. She was trying to bridge the distance, but every time she tried, he pushed her away. His entire attention remained fixed upon an uncertain future. And she didn't know if he meant for her to be part of it.

'How much farther will we travel?' he asked, after they had sailed a few hours.

'We should reach Tilmain by morning,' she said. Piers continued to sit beside her, and she was certain that the brisk wind might bother him. 'Do you…want to share the cloak?'

'No. Keep it.'

His words cut through her, for it was as if he didn't want to be close to her. Or perhaps he simply didn't need it. But Gwen lowered her shoulders and focused on the water ahead, trying to decide how they could find a way to live together as husband and wife. This was nothing like the marriage she'd imagined, and she had no idea how to fix what was broken between them.

She studied him for a moment, noting the worn leather he wore over the chainmail armour. The cloak he'd given her was made from wool, but she could feel a few places where small holes had worn through.

'We'll need to find better clothes for you,' she said at last. 'Especially if you are to appear like a nobleman.' She knew of a merchant not far from Tilmain who had made many garments for her father.

'There's no need to spend coins on me,' he said. 'This is all I have, and it will be enough.'

Gwen didn't answer, knowing that it was his pride talking once again. But she wanted him to appear like a wealthy lord. They had roles to play, and their clothing mattered. Though she didn't know if Piers would willingly wear the garments, she had to try.

'And *I* need new clothes,' she added. 'I cannot arrive at Tilmain looking like this.'

He glanced at her as if he saw nothing wrong. But she lifted the hem of her gown, revealing the mud and torn edges. She'd removed all the gemstones from the hem before they'd sailed, and the edge of the gown was in tatters.

Finally, Piers shrugged. 'If we must.' Strange that he would deny himself new clothing but not her. Her need for garments wasn't as strong as his. Although most of her clothes were at Penrith, there were a few gowns she'd left behind. She could purchase one gown from the merchant for now.

The idea of outfitting Piers as a lord was intriguing. She couldn't deny that she liked the way he filled out his chainmail armour. And while it projected power and strength, she also wanted him to experience another side to life—the wealth he'd never had.

She wanted him to wear silk or fine wool. Perhaps a golden chain or even a ring. She was about to suggest it, but he turned his face away, staring back at the shoreline.

His silence cut through her, making her wonder how she could begin to change matters between them. Even if she did share his bed, she sensed that he would hold himself apart. She didn't care about his birthright…but he did. It festered within him, and she worried that it would cause the breach to widen even more.

She'd gone through with this marriage because she believed that Piers cared for her. He'd sacrificed himself, time and again. She'd hoped that one day the barriers would come down between them, but she couldn't have been more wrong. Now, she didn't even know how to talk to him any more.

With a sidelong glance, she saw her husband watching the shoreline, as if he were searching for enemies. Never did he let down his guard, as if he trusted no one. And perhaps that was the problem. He'd never had much of a family or anyone to take care of him.

His secrets were the only protection he had, she was starting to realise. He didn't want anyone to know of his low birth or his poverty. And for him to compete among the other suitors for her hand in marriage must have been the greatest risk he'd ever taken.

She turned to look at Piers openly, studying him. The only trace of vulnerability she'd ever seen in him was when he'd kissed her. He'd looked upon her as if he'd never imagined she would desire someone like him. And when she'd refused to consummate their marriage, it had only put up more walls between them.

Something had to change if she ever wanted a true partner and friend as her husband. Perhaps *she* was the one who had to take that first step, no matter that it frightened her. And though she didn't know what to do, she could start by removing the physical barriers. If she offered him affection in some way, would that help?

Gwen unfastened the cloak and put it back on his shoulders, tying it in place.

'I said I don't need it,' he started to argue.

But she ignored him and instead sat on his lap, pulling the cloak around her once more. His body stiffened the moment she did, and he put his hands on her hips. 'Don't,' he warned.

'The wind is cold,' she said. 'This way, we'll both be warm.' But she was fully aware from her position that he was growing aroused. She could feel the length of him growing, pressing against her backside, and the unfamiliar sensation made her imagine what it would be like if he were touching her. The rocking of the boat intensified the feelings, and her breasts tightened against her gown. She could feel her own desire rising as the rhythmic motion brought a sweet ache between her legs.

The cloak covered both of them, and they were seated at the front of the boat where no one could see them.

'Sit beside me,' he started to say with his hands around her waist. He was about to lift her away, but she wanted his touch.

'Wait.' She took his hands from her hips and drew them to her breasts beneath the cloak. From behind her, she heard a sharp intake of his breath.

'What are you doing, Gwen?' he murmured against her ear. His warm breath made her tremble, but he obeyed her silent command, cupping her breasts against the gown. His voice was gruff, but she noticed that he hadn't pushed her away.

'Do you want me to leave you alone?' she asked. 'Should I go sit somewhere else?'

In response, he adjusted her position on his lap so she could feel his thick length pressed between her legs. Against her gown, he found her erect nipples and circled them with his thumbs. She held back a moan and, with every caress, she seemed to grow wetter.

She'd come to him, hoping to have his arms around her. But somehow it had shifted into far more than she'd imagined. Knowing that the ship's crew was behind him made their liaison even more arousing. Although no one could see what they were doing, she was aware of the men rowing behind them. The forbidden touching grew even hotter because she had to be careful that no one would suspect what was happening.

Piers adjusted the cloak so it fully enveloped both of them. Then with one hand, he reached beneath her skirts while the other continued to stroke her breast. She was biting her lip, trying hard not to release a single word. But when his hand moved between her bare legs and found her wetness, she couldn't stop the muffled cry that broke forth.

'Do you want me to leave you alone?' he asked against her ear. The echo of her own words thrown back at her was unexpected, but she turned to him.

In a low whisper she answered, 'No. I don't want you to stop.'

It was shockingly arousing to feel his fingers against her intimate folds, and she suddenly wondered if she'd pushed matters too far.

'You want this, don't you?' Piers said in a rough whisper. 'You remember how I made you feel that night in the cave.' And then he slid two fingers inside her. Her hands dug into his thighs as she gasped. She was slowly dying of pleasure, overwhelmed by his touch.

'Yes,' she whispered, turning back to look at him. 'I remember.' Then she reached back and cupped him through his trews. 'Do you?'

Chapter Nine

His wife was torturing him beyond everything he'd imagined. Piers didn't know what had prompted this, but the voyage had suddenly become far more interesting. The rocking of the boat made him want to bury himself deep within her flesh, letting the rhythm of the waves take them both towards release.

God above, but this woman was his weakness. He didn't know why she had started this after a sennight of barely speaking to him. Though he'd tried to keep his distance because she'd never wanted a bastard in her bed, he didn't know what to think of her sudden change of heart. What did she want from him?

Gwen reached beneath the cloak to unlace his trews, and when her hand curled over his rigid erection, he held back the urge to shout. She squeezed him gently, and he showed her how to move her hand against him.

He was burning up at her touch, and it wouldn't take long to finish him. But he intended to send her over the edge first.

'Is this what you wanted from me?' he said against

her ear. 'Do you want me to bring you pleasure?' He began moving his fingers inside her, and her inner walls clenched against him. She caressed the blunt head of him, and she was breathing in quick pants.

'Yes,' she whispered. 'And I want you to feel the same way.'

'Why?' he demanded. He found the centre of her desire and began to circle the hooded flesh. Her eyes closed, and she had a pained expression on her face even as she pressed against him. But he needed to know why she'd begun this.

'Because I want this marriage to work,' she said. 'I'm not giving up on us.'

Her words weren't at all what he thought she'd say— and he didn't trust her reasons. 'Dressing me up as a lord won't change anything,' he insisted. He continued to touch her intimately, and she strained against him, clenching against his fingers. She was close now, and he could feel her body trembling.

'I thought you wanted to be Lord of Penrith.' When she began to move her hand up and down, he nearly groaned aloud. 'This is your chance to change who you are. No one knows you at Tilmain. They will believe anything you tell them.'

Piers understood what she was trying to do, but he couldn't simply don the identity of a lord the way he put on a cloak. The clothes would change nothing at all.

'I will teach you what you need to know about ruling over an estate. All you need to do is try.' She stroked him, and he was so close to release, his mind was reeling.

Though he'd wanted to win a lordship over Penrith,

part of him had never imagined it was a possibility. She was giving him the chance to learn what he needed to know.

And yet, he couldn't push back the danger. Her father might learn of their presence and order him killed. Regardless of what she tried to do, it wouldn't last.

He continued to caress Gwen and, when she reached the edge, he leaned over to kiss her. She was shaking in his arms, and he stifled her moan with his mouth as the pleasure tore through her. God above, but he loved touching this woman.

She startled him by squeezing him hard, and his own release erupted without warning. His fingers were buried deep inside her, and it took everything in him to remain silent. For a while, her breathing remained unsteady, though she relaxed against him. He fastened his trews again, and she cleaned off her hand.

'If I do what you ask of me, you're going to sleep in my bed,' he said.

She turned to face him, and her cheeks were still flushed from their love play. But then her expression grew serious. 'I will, but only if you help me make this marriage work. And that means we need to trust one another.'

She had laid down her own gauntlet, and he hesitated at her offer. She believed she already knew the worst of his secrets—but there was far more she didn't know.

And he had no desire to see her response to the man he truly was.

Piers stood while the merchant searched through his wares for new clothing. Though he was careful to keep his expression neutral, he listened to Gwen's conversation. She'd invented a story about how their trunk of belongings had fallen into the river and been ruined.

'Most of your tunics will have to be fitted to my husband, I know,' she was saying. 'But of course, you will have something he can wear today when we arrive at Tilmain.'

Piers remained at her side, feeling ill at ease while she spoke with the merchant. While he understood what she was doing, they only had some of the coins from selling the horses after they'd spent the rest on their voyage. How did she expect to pay for these clothes? He didn't need to dress up like a nobleman, pretending to be someone he wasn't. The armour he wore would suffice.

'Do they know you are coming, my lady?' the merchant asked. 'I had not heard of your arrival. We thought you would remain at Penrith.'

Gwen let out a sigh of annoyance. 'My father asked me to bring my husband to Tilmain first. Of course, he would have come himself, except that there was some unrest he had to manage at Penrith. And we both know how he likes to be in command.'

At that, the merchant appeared amused. 'That he does.' He withdrew a crimson tunic and held it out to Piers. 'Will this suit you?'

Was the man in earnest? Piers glanced at Gwen, not knowing whether to reveal his true feelings. But he could see the doubt in her eyes, and so he turned to the merchant and answered, 'No. It will not suit.' He crossed his arms and stared back at the man, who took a step backwards.

'Oh. I suppose it's…too colourful,' the merchant offered.

'I prefer black,' Piers said. He had no interest in being dressed up in these garments, but he was enduring this for Gwen's sake.

'Of course you do,' the man muttered.

'Will you allow me to choose something for you, my lord husband?' Gwen asked quietly. Piers gave a slight nod but with an underlying warning. To the merchant, she lied, 'My husband is a warrior and fought among the king's men. He will want to wear his armour. Show me tunics and cloaks that can be fitted around his chainmail.'

At that, the merchant's demeanour shifted. 'At once, my lady.' He showed her a table filled with different tunics of all colours, and Piers could only hope she would choose something appropriate.

'This will do,' he heard her say. But before he could see it, she asked, 'My lord, will you close your eyes? I would like to put it on you before you say anything.'

Piers wasn't at all sure about that, but at last, he relented and closed his eyes. He smelled the scent of her skin as she drew near. 'Lift your arms,' she ordered. When he did, he felt her remove his old garment and replace it with another. She slid it over his head, and then said, 'Keep your eyes closed.'

He did, and then he felt her remove his cloak and replace it with another. The weight was different, but he felt her fasten a chain to hold it in place.

'Now open your eyes,' she said.

He glanced down and saw a blue overtunic the colour of a midnight sky with a silver embroidered edge.

The cloak itself was black but made of a finely woven fabric that cost more than he'd ever owned in his life.

'You look handsome, my lord,' she said with a warm smile. 'I like it very much.'

So did he, but he had no idea how they would pay for such finery. Before he could say a word, Gwen turned to the merchant. 'You will come to Tilmain this evening as my guest,' she told the merchant, 'and you will be paid for this, as well as the other garments Lord Grevershire will need.'

The merchant appeared satisfied with her offer. 'What of you, my lady? Would you like to choose a gown for yourself?'

'I would, yes,' she answered. 'Will you send for a girl to help me dress? And horses we may borrow on our journey to Tilmain.'

'I will,' he agreed. 'And you may use two of my own horses.' He disappeared for a moment, and Piers took the opportunity to speak with Gwen.

In a low voice, he said, 'We cannot afford these. We can barely pay for one horse.'

'We can pay for all of it,' she answered. 'My father has more than enough gold at Tilmain. And I have jewels, if we need them.' She showed him the pouch at her waist. 'When you are of a noble family, your name pays for everything.'

The thought was humbling and made him realise that their stations were more different than he'd ever imagined. He understood now that he'd been woefully unprepared to rule over Penrith, even if her father had approved of their marriage. Gwen's plan of using Tilmain to practise was a wise decision, although they could not stay long.

The merchant returned with a young girl and a gown of bright blue silk. 'I think you will like this bliaud, Lady Gwendoline.'

'You remembered my favourite colour.' She smiled and took it from him. To Piers she said, 'My lord, if you'll see to the horses, I will change my gown.'

Piers caught her hand in his and held it for a moment. She squeezed it in return, but he saw the sudden uncertainty beneath her feigned confidence. Neither knew exactly how the people of Tilmain would respond to their arrival.

But he would protect her, no matter what happened.

Gwen braved a smile at Piers as they rode closer to Tilmain. Though she'd tried to maintain her confidence, her nerves were twisting into knots. She'd never commanded the people of Tilmain, and she had no idea whether they would listen to her. She knew what she was *supposed* to do, but her father had never allowed her a voice. Although she tried to maintain an expression of calm, her fears heightened as they approached the gates.

The guards stared at her with confusion but neither moved. Gwen was about to give orders when one asked, 'Is Lord Tilmain—?'

'He remains at Penrith for now,' she answered. 'My husband and I have come to ensure that all is well here.'

'No one sent word of your arrival,' the other guard said. He glanced at the other soldier as if they weren't certain what to do.

But then Piers intervened. 'My wife is weary from our travels. Open the gates.' His voice held a stern authority for which she was grateful.

You cannot be soft, she reminded herself. *You must speak with authority and confidence.*

Yet confidence was something she lacked. Piers's presence made her want to show him what to do, how to lead. But how could she do that when she barely knew how to behave among her own people?

'You don't have the stomach for what must be done to maintain peace,' her father had accused.

All her insecurities came flooding back, though she tried to paste a smile on her face. Many of the castle folk stopped and stared at them. Piers drew his horse beside hers, and she grew aware of how he studied everything—the people and their surroundings, as if he was committing them to memory.

She drew her horse to a stop, and Piers dismounted first before he helped her down. He took the reins of her mare and when a stable boy came forward, Gwen instructed him to care for the horses and ensure that they were returned to the merchant.

For a heart-stopping moment, it seemed as if the people were waiting for her to speak to them, to address everyone with information about why they were here. An inner voice warned her that she had to make the decisions and give orders, but she didn't know how to begin.

She avoided it by taking Piers's arm as they ascended the stone stairs and went inside the main keep. They had already missed the main meal of the day, but she saw her father's steward, John, waiting near the dais. He came forward to greet her, and she held out her hands to him.

'John, this is my husband Piers, the Earl of Grevershire,' she lied. Piers gave a nod to the man and moved closer to her side.

'Welcome back to Tilmain, my lady,' John said. He glanced at Piers as if uncertain what to do. 'I am sorry we were not prepared for your arrival. Will you want food and drink?'

'Yes, please,' she agreed. While he went to make the arrangements, Gwen walked alongside Piers towards the table upon the dais. She gestured for him to take his place at the centre of the table while she took her usual seat beside him. A servant brought them both wine, and she took a sip to steady herself.

'You're nervous,' Piers said in a low voice. 'Why is that?'

'I don't know,' she answered. Most likely because she'd never truly been an equal to her father. It felt wrong somehow, giving orders. She straightened and tried to evoke an air of authority she didn't feel.

When the food arrived, Piers remembered and offered her the first portion before taking bread and pheasant for himself.

She was starving, and it took all her years of training not to stuff the food in her mouth as quickly as possible. When Gwen caught him staring, she flushed and said, 'It's so good.'

But to her surprise, Piers motioned for the servant to return. 'Bring more food for Lady Grevershire.'

At first, she was embarrassed by her hunger, but then she realised what Piers had said. He'd given her his mother's name, asserting her as his wife.

'I shouldn't be eating so much,' she said softly after the servant had given her more bread and meat.

'You're not used to going hungry,' was all he said.

Unlike me, were the unspoken words. She wanted to ask him about it but stopped herself. He didn't want to reveal anything more about himself than was absolutely necessary. Instead, she said, 'I'm glad we have enough. And we should ensure that the people here also have enough to eat.'

He gave a nod of agreement and she reached out to touch his hand. There was no mistaking the sudden flare of desire in his eyes. Then Piers motioned for the steward to come forward.

John approached and asked, 'Was the food to your liking, my lord and my lady?'

Gwen nodded. 'It was excellent.'

'You'll want to rest after your journey, I'm certain,' the steward said. 'I've asked a maid to prepare your chamber.'

Her mood dimmed, for once again it felt like she was being sent to her room. She tried to think of a way to assert herself and glanced over at Piers. Before she could speak, Piers intervened. 'My wife and I would prefer to see Tilmain first.'

'We did not know you would be arriving today, my lord,' the steward began. 'We've not had time to prepare.'

'And if an army attacked, would you be prepared to defend the lands?' Piers accused. He stood from the table, and continued, 'The earl left the estate in your care these past few months. I want to inspect your defences, the dwellings of the people here, and your food stores for the winter.'

His voice carried complete authority, and she was proud of him for taking on the role of leader. And yet, at the same time, she grew aware of her own faults. She needed to take command. But whenever she was about to speak, she could hear her father's chiding voice in her head.

'If you'll just follow me, my lord.' John waited for them, and Piers rested his palm upon her back.

They stood from the table and, before they joined John, she whispered in his ear, 'You seem like you belong here, Piers.'

The compliment was no exaggeration. The new clothing they'd purchased made him look like a warrior nobleman. His muscles filled out the midnight-blue tunic and the dark cloak accentuated his fierce features. She noticed that his gaze continually searched the castle keep, as if learning every face and determining more about the person.

They followed John outside, and Piers kept his hand to her spine. She could feel the silent warning to everyone and his promise of protection to her. 'I want to see the stables,' he said.

The steward appeared confused and answered, 'I thought you wanted to see our defences and our guards first?'

'You will take us there next,' Piers answered.

Gwen wondered why the stables were so important, but the steward obeyed and led them inside. It was dark, and a strong odour emanated from the interior. She covered her nose immediately and saw the reason why.

'The stable boys will take care of that,' the steward promised. 'We have many horses.'

Piers said nothing but returned to the inner bailey, his expression masked. Even so, she could tell that he was displeased. It might be a small chore, but perhaps it revealed other signs of neglect.

Throughout their walk, Gwen asked questions of the steward and acknowledged his praise of the people and especially their guards.

'May we have a demonstration of the soldiers' fighting skills?' Piers asked.

'Aye, my lord.' The steward walked over to the guards and spoke to them for a moment. When he returned, he said, 'They will show you some of their sparring skills with a sword.'

'I would also like to see their archery,' Piers added.

She tensed at that, sensing that there was more he wanted. But she said nothing, for fear that it would undermine his leadership.

The soldiers sparred among themselves, and Piers watched, his gaze taking in everything. Then the men lined up with bows to shoot at straw targets. They were not quite as accurate as she remembered.

Then her husband turned to her. In a low voice, he asked, 'Will you demonstrate your skill for them?'

She hesitated, not understanding what he wanted at first. But at least he was giving her a choice. 'Why?'

'Because you are more skilled than any of them. And they should know it if they don't already.'

'I don't think these men do know,' she admitted. 'I practised in secret in the barley field.' But she was wary of shooting, for fear of insulting them. 'What if I miss my mark?'

'You won't. But if they don't know of your skills,

then it won't matter if you do miss. Wait here.' He left her for a moment and went to speak to the men. Then he returned with the bow and a quiver of arrows. He tested it, pulling back the bowstring as if he meant to shoot. The men lined up nearby, some with amused looks on their faces. They believed Piers was about to aim at the target.

Then he turned to her and smiled. 'Shall we have fun with them?' His eyes gleamed, and she held back a laugh.

'This distance is much farther than what I'm used to,' she whispered.

'But you can do it, can't you?'

'Easily.' She eyed him as he chose an arrow. 'What will you give me if I hit the centre? It seems like a wager is in order.'

'Two answers,' he said. 'To your questions.'

Which was exactly what she was hoping for. 'And you promise to be honest with me?'

He gave a slight nod, and she took the bow from him. For a moment, he rested his hands on her hips while she adjusted her stance.

The steward appeared confused. 'My lady?'

With a single shot, Gwen struck the centre of the target. The men gaped at her arrow before there came murmurs of amazement, followed by polite applause. Then she eyed Piers. 'Another? For a third question?'

He nodded. She chose a second arrow and hit her mark again. This time, the applause was louder, and a few men cheered. 'Your turn.'

Piers took the bow from her and fired three arrows in

succession. All struck the target, and the last one split Gwen's arrow in two.

The men's response was shocked silence. Piers handed the bow to the steward and took Gwen's hand in his as he went to address the men. He studied their faces and then asked quietly, 'Did you know that Lady Gwendoline could shoot like that?' All shook their heads. Gwen felt an awkward embarrassment while they stared at her.

'She wanted to learn, so she trained in secret,' Piers continued. 'You may not have natural skill, but if you work hard, you can master anything. I will expect you to continue practising, the way she did.'

Gwen sensed that Piers wanted to talk more with the men, but her presence would make it difficult for him to get the answers he was seeking. She leaned in and said, 'I'll return to the keep if you want to talk more with them.'

But before she could pull away, he held her hand in his. 'Will you speak to the cooks and ask them to prepare a feast for later tonight? Is there time?'

She nodded. 'I think so. I'll see to it.'

'Everyone should come,' Piers insisted. 'Every servant, every stable boy, every soldier will eat his fill tonight. We will celebrate our marriage.'

She understood then that he was building alliances. The men seemed gladdened by his announcement, but the steward appeared uneasy. It made her wonder whether their food supplies were as strong as he'd claimed.

'Before they join us, I want the boys to muck out the stables and the men to train for another hour,' he said.

To the soldiers, he added, 'I will watch your training while you do.'

The men seemed satisfied by that, but Piers came over to Gwen before she went to order the feast preparations. 'I'm going to learn more from the men while I train with them. There has been neglect here, and I want to know what is happening.'

'It's a good idea,' she agreed quietly. He carried himself like a lord, and she was certain no one suspected the truth. 'You're doing well, Piers.'

'I watched my father for many years.' But there was a tightness around his eyes when he spoke of it. She didn't ask him more, but simply reached out to take his hand. He held it for a moment and then turned back to the men.

Her own nerves gathered in her stomach as she wondered how long they could stay here before Alfred learned what they'd done. She simply didn't know.

After hours of feasting with the people of Tilmain, Piers entered his wife's chamber only to find a hot bath waiting and a fire at the hearth. She was sitting in a chair, warming herself nearby. Her braids were undone, her hair falling across her shoulders. Her beauty stole his very breath.

He closed the door behind him and walked closer.

'The water's still hot,' she said quietly. 'Get in, and I'll bathe you.'

Her offer sent a jolt of desire through him, and he warned himself not to think of her hands upon him. No one had ever offered to do such a thing.

He stared at the water, wondering what it would be

like to sink into the tub and feel heat surrounding him. Or to have Gwen's touch upon his bare skin. She would ask her questions, but he knew better than to expect her to consummate the marriage. He had already resigned himself to a night sleeping alone on the floor.

Piers unfastened his cloak, and she took it from him. Then he removed the overtunic and the heavy chainmail armour, setting it upon a chest in the corner.

'How was the training with the men earlier?' she asked. They hadn't had a chance to talk since she'd departed to make arrangements for the feast.

'It was good,' he answered. 'We worked on their shooting, and some sword fighting.' He'd trained with several of the men, showing them what he knew, and an older guard had taught him some new footwork as well. But his real reason for working with the men was to encourage them to talk. He'd asked them questions about Tilmain and about the earl. After several rounds of practice and ale to quench their thirst, most were comfortable sharing tales.

The earl had governed Tilmain with a strict hand, it seemed. Some of their standards had loosened in his absence, and Piers hoped to make changes for the better. He wasn't certain whether they would accept his authority—especially when they couldn't stay. He was a stranger to them, and he was wary of overstepping. But he'd learned where the earl was now, and he needed to tell Gwen.

'Some of the soldiers said that your father travelled to meet with the king,' he told her. 'King John is travelling to Scotland, and Alfred sent trunks of gifts from Tilmain. An escort of men left a few days ago to join the earl. They think the king is about a sennight's journey from here.'

Though he didn't know why Alfred was meeting with the king, it did reduce the threat hanging over them.

'So, we have a little more time,' she said. Her shoulders relaxed some of the tension when he nodded in agreement.

Gwen removed her bliaud and wore only her underdress and shift. Then she tied her hair back with a ribbon and came forward with a cloth in her hand. 'Take off your trews and get into the tub.'

Piers didn't miss her nervousness, but he didn't tease her about undressing him. Instead, he stripped off his remaining garments and stepped into the small wooden tub. The hot water seemed to sink into his bones, and he closed his eyes, savouring the warmth. He breathed a sigh of utter contentment—but his attention was entirely fixed upon his wife. She spread out a large drying cloth before the fire to warm it. Then she came forward to the tub, dipped her cloth into the water and lathered it with soap.

Piers sat up and offered, 'Do you want to join me?'

But Gwen averted her eyes. 'The tub is too small.' She reached out and began to wash his back. The touch of her hands upon him ignited his desire, a sweet torment that made him ache with need.

As a distraction, he asked her, 'For someone as skilled as you are with archery, why didn't the men know what you could do?'

Her face sobered, and she admitted, 'My father would have humiliated me in front of everyone for daring to touch a bow.' Her hands passed over his shoulders, and Piers tensed, gripping his fists beneath the water. 'When I was a girl and he was away, I spoke with the archery master and asked him to teach me. I brought him extra food and drink, and he agreed, as long as I promised never to reveal him as the one who had taught me. He also took me outside the castle grounds so fewer people would see.'

'How long was he your teacher?' Piers asked.

'Five years.' She moved to wash his chest and admitted, 'His daughter was my age when she died. I think he agreed to teach me because I reminded him of her.' Then she regarded him and asked, 'Are you ready to answer my questions yet?'

'Go on.'

'Lean back,' she told him. When he obeyed, she scooped warm water over his hair and began to wash it. The touch of her fingers massaging his scalp was soothing in a way he'd never expected.

He didn't know what she was going to ask him, but for now, he was enjoying the bath. The only problem was that he wanted a larger tub with her in it.

'How did your father treat you after you first arrived at Penrith?' she asked as she rinsed the soap from his hair. 'When he learned you were his son.'

At least this question wasn't too difficult. Piers chose his words carefully. 'Like a dog he didn't particularly want.' He thought a moment and said, 'He allowed me to stay at Penrith, but gave me nothing. During the summer I slept in the stables, and in the winter, I slept in a corner of the Great Hall among the animals.'

'I suppose, if you had to live in the stables, that's why you wanted ours to be cleaner.'

'Aye,' he admitted. 'You get used to the smell, but it's been neglected here.' He paused a moment and added, 'My father often forgot about me at Penrith. I never meant anything to him besides another mouth to feed. And sometimes I had to fight for whatever scraps of food I could get.'

'You went hungry, then.'

'Often. And after Robert and I were exiled, we had to hunt to survive. It's why we both learned to shoot well. We had to make our own arrows.'

'Why were you exiled?'

'The king's men came for Robert that night, likely planning to kill him. I was captured with him, along with Morwenna and Brian. We were chained together in a wagon…but Robert managed to free us.' Piers paused for a moment when she washed his shoulder and arm, fighting to regain control of his response. Having her hands upon him was a sweet torment.

'After we went into exile at Stansbury, and Robert lost everything…we became equals for the first time. I taught him to survive, and he taught me how to fight.' He let out a slow breath as her hands moved lower.

She began washing his other leg, and he caught her blush when she raised his knee too high and caught a glimpse of his erection. It was a slight consolation that she used a cloth—had she used her hands, he might have lost what little control he had. His need heightened with every touch, but he would not ask her for more than this.

'I thought you were going to kill Robert during the competitions,' she remarked.

'We've been at each other's throats most of our lives,' he admitted. 'There was a time when I hated him. He was always so noble, wanting to do the right thing. I despised him for it.'

'Because he acted as if he were better than you?'

'Because he *was* better than me,' Piers admitted. 'He helped us escape the soldiers on the night we fled. I would be dead or imprisoned, were it not for him.' His brother had always been fascinated by mechanical things, taking them apart. On the night they'd been taken by soldiers, chained in a wagon, his brother had found a way to remove the hinges from the door. Part of him had admired his brother's intellect, while another part of him remained jealous of Robert's privileged world.

'Do you resent him?' Gwen asked.

'No, we're even now. He would be dead if I hadn't saved him that night at Penrith. He'll owe me a favour for the rest of his life.'

She stood and brought the drying cloth over to the tub. 'Stand up.'

He did, and the water slid down his bare skin. Gwen averted her gaze while she held out the cloth. Though he wanted her to look at him, to see the desire raging through him, he reminded himself of what he was—a man who didn't deserve her.

He stepped into the drying cloth while she wrapped it around him. 'This is the first hot bath I've ever had, Gwen. Robert and I usually washed by swimming in that pool of water I showed you.' The linen was warm from the fire, and he reached out to her waist.

She seemed taken aback by his confession and ventured, 'Did you…like the bath?'

'I did.' He stroked her hair back and tilted her chin up to face him. 'The only question is whether you want me to wash you now?'

Chapter Ten

Gwen swallowed hard at the thought. Though a refusal came to her lips, she hesitated. Piers had touched her before, and she knew where this would lead.

'Answer my other questions first, and then…perhaps.'

His eyes grew dark and possessive. 'Two more questions.'

She took a breath and met his gaze. 'Is there anything left at Grevershire? Do you even have a home there?'

He shook his head. 'It's in ruins. As far as I know, it was abandoned years ago.'

Then she truly had married a man with nothing. Piers had no title, no wealth, no lands. He'd intended to bring her to a place where they had nowhere to live. She was starting to realise that if she could not convince her father to accept Piers, she had two choices—either learn to live in poverty or turn her back on the marriage.

The very thought made her heart ache. She wanted so badly to believe that they could find a way to make peace with Alfred. She wanted to rule over either Penrith or Tilmain at Piers's side. But she had no idea how she could make that dream into a reality.

She pushed back the feelings of failure and turned to her last question, the one that had no true answer. 'You've kept so many secrets from me, Piers. You let me believe you were the heir, that you had lands at Grevershire. I care about you…but how can we build a marriage upon lies?'

His expression grew shielded, and he released her. In his blue eyes, she saw a yearning that echoed her own. But he admitted, 'We can't. I have nothing to give you except a life of misery.' He walked over to the bed and sat down, staring out at the small window.

Hot tears rose up and spilled over her cheeks at the aching knowledge that he was giving up. Though it was foolish, she'd let herself begin falling in love with Piers. First, because he'd offered her the freedom she craved. Then he'd made her feel safe and beloved. She wanted a lifetime of feeling valued as a woman.

But ever since she'd turned her back on her family, putting her trust in him, he'd begun shoring up his defences. He'd kept his past a secret, never revealing the truth. And it felt like such a betrayal.

'Are you giving up on us?' she whispered.

She crossed the room and went to sit beside him. Her underdress was damp from the water, and her body ached with unspoken grief.

He turned to her, and the raw pain in his face startled her. 'You were the only good thing that ever happened to me. I knew you were more than I deserved, but when I saw you, I wanted you. More than Penrith, more than anything else—I wanted you.'

Gwen started to touch his shoulder, but he eased back. 'Let me finish.' His expression was haggard, and he took a breath. 'When I tell you the rest, you won't want to stay married to me.' He rested his hands on his knees, and she waited.

'I was sent to Penrith to kill my brother,' he said. 'My mother abandoned me there when I was eleven and gave me a vial of medicine for Robert. I didn't know at the time that it was poison.'

His words chilled her to the bone, but she forced herself to remain silent. If she spoke now, he might never tell her the rest.

'My mother said it was meant for Robert because he'd been ill, and she gave instructions for the maid to make more.'

His mouth tightened, and he said, 'Wenda wanted it to look like an accident. I don't even know what was in the medicine, but Robert would sometimes get well, only to fall sick again. They kept him inside the castle for two years, and everyone thought he would die.'

Gwen wondered how Robert had ever survived the poisoning. It was nothing short of a miracle.

Guilt laced Piers's words, and she was starting to understand why he'd done everything to save his brother's life. He blamed himself for Robert's illness. And she could no longer hold her silence.

'But he didn't die,' she reassured him.

Piers turned to face her, and he said, 'I wanted him to.' He closed his eyes and confessed, 'I went to see Robert after I learned he was my brother. I wanted him to know who I was. I thought…we could become friends. But when I came to see him, he was so sick, he wanted me to go. He told me he didn't want to be my brother or my friend.'

Gwen could only imagine the loneliness Piers had felt, and she was starting to understand why the animosity had begun.

'I got so angry at him for his fine clothes, his bed, and the food they brought to him. He was living the life of a king while I was sleeping with dogs and horse dung.' A wry expression twisted his mouth. 'I threw away his medicine that day and replaced it with water.'

Understanding dawned upon her. 'You saved his life.'

He nodded. 'And yet, at the time, I thought I was killing him by giving him water and not the medicine. Sometimes he did get sick again, after the maid found a way to give him the poison.' A hardness crossed his face, turning his expression to stone. 'Then one day, I slipped several doses of the poisoned medicine into her own wine. She wasn't strong enough to survive, and she was dead by morning.'

Although he kept his voice steady, Gwen didn't miss the pain and guilt within his tone. She couldn't imagine the nightmare he'd endured, even though it was a fitting justice for the woman who had tried to kill Robert.

'After that, Robert got stronger,' he said. 'But neither he nor my father wanted anything to do with me. I was nothing to them.'

She was starting to understand the complexity of their relationship. 'Your mother was trying to make you the heir,' she guessed. 'If Robert died, she thought the earl would let you inherit.'

'Only for herself,' he said. 'She wanted to be Lady of Penrith, and she hated Robert's mother. If Robert's mother hadn't died years earlier, I don't doubt that Wenda would have poisoned her immediately.'

He let out a slow breath of air. 'I am a bastard in every sense of the word, Gwen. Not only because of my birth, but because I wanted to take away my brother's future. I wanted him to know what it was like to sleep with the dogs, go without food, and have nothing. Even now, I want to take Penrith away from him. And I was going to use you to do it.'

He stared at the wall again, unable to look at her. 'It's better if I let you go.'

She knew he was right. And yet, there were pieces missing in his story. Not secrets—she believed he'd told her everything now. But she wanted to know if he felt anything for her at all.

'You were going to take me to Grevershire,' she said quietly. 'Why?'

'Because I didn't know what else to tell you,' he admitted. 'I wanted to keep you with me, but there's nothing there but ruins.'

But a man who cared only about claiming Penrith wouldn't have bothered to take her somewhere else. He'd known of the unrest among the people and could easily have led a rebellion against her father. He might have succeeded in taking Penrith, had he asked the serfs to join him.

Instead, Piers had nearly given himself up to her father, in order to let her escape. He'd been willing to die for her before she'd stepped in and surrendered herself. His words and his actions didn't match.

From the moment he'd arrived at Tilmain, aye, Piers had played the role of overlord. But she could see that he genuinely wanted to make it a better place for the people. He'd shown interest in the soldiers and their training. Whether he knew it or not, Piers would make a strong leader because he could understand the people in a way a nobleman never could.

What if…she made that possible for him? What if she fought with her father to gain the life she wanted? It meant confronting Alfred and making him see reason. But…what if she could somehow change everything?

Her heart was pounding, but she wanted a very different life, one where her husband gave her freedom and respected her opinion. Piers had always treated her as an equal, and he'd proven himself capable of becoming a leader.

She couldn't imagine any other man allowing her to make decisions and rule beside him. But with Piers, she could voice her opinion, and he would never treat her as if she were good for nothing, save embroidering garments. He'd even asked her to demonstrate her archery for the men, as if he were proud of her.

I don't want to give him up, she realised.

And that meant taking matters into her own hands. If she wanted Piers to remain her husband, she would have to fight. She was frightened of what lay ahead, but if she yielded to her father's commands, it meant taking the coward's path. She had to reach for what she wanted instead.

And what she wanted was *him*.

Her heart pounding, she stood from the bed and walked over to the wooden tub. There was an iron pot near the hearth, and she lifted it with a cloth and poured the remaining hot water into the tub. Slowly, she unlaced her underdress and let it fall to the floor. Then she lifted her shift above her head and turned back to her husband while she stood naked before him.

'Will you help me with my bath?'

It was the last thing he expected her to say. If anything, after what he'd told her, Piers had anticipated sleeping on the floor far away from Gwen. But he stood transfixed as she stepped into the bath. She took her ribbon and tied her hair out of the way before she lowered herself into the water.

Her breasts were small and delicate, her waist slender, but she had generous hips. Piers took a breath and walked closer towards the bath. Gwen leaned back, resting her nape against the edge of the tub. When he reached her side, her blue eyes met his.

Just as she'd done for him, he laid out a drying cloth before the fire. Then he tightened the cloth at his waist so it wouldn't fall to the ground. When he came to her, she said, 'There's another cloth you can use to wash me.'

But he had no intention of that. Instead, he reached for the soap, dipped his hands in the water, and began to lather them. 'I'm going to use my hands, Gwen.'

Her face flushed, but nothing in the world would stop him from this. He planned to give her such pleasure, she would never forget him.

Piers eased her from the back of the tub and used his palms to wash her. Her skin was smooth and slippery from the bath, and he caressed her gently. She let out a soft gasp, and he saw the prickle of gooseflesh rising while her nipples tightened. He rinsed her back, cupping water that he spilled over her skin.

She bit her lip when he reached for the soap again. Slowly, he began washing her shoulder blades, moving lower. Piers was aching to touch her, wanting this woman so badly. He knew he'd never be good enough for her. For the life of him, he didn't know why she'd agreed to this. But he was not going to let the opportunity escape.

He grazed the side of her ribs, down to her waist. Then he lathered her stomach in circles. With both hands, he soaped her delicate skin before he moved his hands higher to her breasts. He didn't touch them yet but washed her everywhere else. He wanted to build her anticipation to a fever pitch, to make her feel as he did. And if this was all he'd ever have from her—to touch and caress her skin—he would savour every moment.

But then, she reached up to draw him into a kiss, and he was lost. Piers devoured her mouth hungrily while he lowered his hands to her breasts. He soaped them, sliding his palms over her curves and gently stroking her nipples. She gasped, leaning into his touch. Her tongue slid against his, and she kissed him as if she couldn't get enough.

'More,' she demanded. Her arms went around his neck, and he obeyed. While he kissed her, he poured water over her breasts with his palms, tantalising her as he continued to circle the nipples. Her fingers dug into his hair, and he lowered his mouth to her throat.

'What else do you want from me, Gwen?' He moved his hands down into the water, gently sliding his palms over her bottom. She rose up to her knees, and he moved his hand between her legs.

He experimented with touching her, changing the pressure of his fingers as he explored every inch.

'Taste me,' she begged, guiding his head to her breast. He obeyed and took her nipple into his mouth. Her breathing grew hitched, and he parted her intimately, circling his thumb.

'Do you want me inside you?' he asked against her breast, pressing his fingers to her opening. As he used his tongue and mouth to arouse her more, he continued to caress the intimate place between her legs.

'I…want you, Piers. Inside me,' she agreed. She arched her back, and then he slid a finger inside. Then a second finger, gently guiding them in and out. Her breathing was ragged, and he could feel her rising towards the edge.

'Oh, my… I just—Piers—' She broke off, her body trembling. He kept his touch gentle, but he could feel her need intensifying. The water lapped at her skin, and she gripped the edge of the wooden tub.

His body was aching with his own need, his erection raging. And then he saw her face fill up with ecstasy as he continued his movements. He bent to her other breast and used his mouth and tongue upon her nipple. Within seconds, she let out another gasp and shattered beneath him. She clenched his fingers deep inside her body, and he lifted her out of the water. To his surprise, she wrapped her legs around his waist. A darker side of him imagined dropping his own drying cloth and sinking deep inside before he plunged and withdrew. He was rigid with need for her, and he fought for control.

He'd been with a few maids when he was an adolescent, but this was different. He'd already promised himself to leave her a virgin. At least then, it would not be hard for her to get an annulment. For tonight, he would spend the rest of the hours touching her, and he didn't want her to ever be afraid of him.

The drying cloth lay upon a stool, and he reached for it, still holding her. Her breasts were pressed against his chest, and he brought her to the bed, spreading the drying cloth upon the coverlet. He laid her down, intending to wrap her in the warm linen.

But instead, she remained at the edge of the bed, her hips near the edge. When he bent down, she unfastened his own drying cloth and used it to pull him closer.

He was on a razor's edge, fighting for control. 'We can't do this, Gwen. I won't be able to stop.'

'I don't want you to stop,' she said. And she reached out for his erection, stroking it within her palm. Her silken hand curled over him, and the pleasure was so intense, he didn't think he could last much longer.

And then she guided him to her entrance. She was so slick, the head of him went inside easily and, God above, it was heaven. Her tightness gripped him, and it took everything to keep from sinking in deep.

'This wasn't what I'd planned,' he said, his voice rough.

Gwen sensed him pulling away, out of concern. But if she wanted to fight for this marriage, consummation was necessary. She didn't care about any pain. He'd made her feel so good already, this was something she could give to him.

'I need you, Piers.' She reached to cup him, and he pressed gently, a little deeper. The pain would come when she lost her virginity, but she was ready for him. Instead, he pulled back.

'Don't stop,' she begged.

But he startled her by pushing in a little deeper. He adjusted her hips and drew her knees up so her heels were on the edge of the bed. She felt so exposed, so vulnerable. And yet, with every shallow penetration, she felt the desire rising. His eyes were locked upon hers. 'Am I hurting you?'

'No,' she whispered. 'It's good.'

She braced herself again, but instead, he found the hooded flesh above her entrance and pressed gently against it as he continued the short thrusts. Her breathing began to shift again, matching the rhythm of his body.

And then the sweetness beckoned again, the shimmering ache deepening as his body entered hers. She strained against him, overwhelmed as another release began. But she couldn't stop the cry that broke forth from her as she arched, shaking as the pleasure broke over her in waves.

She didn't care about anything else, but she reached for his waist and pulled him in. There was a slight pain, but the mind-searing pleasure blocked it out, and she marvelled at their joining.

They were one now, and she could feel his body deep inside. She couldn't stop herself from squeezing him, and he let out a hiss as she took him. She wrapped her legs around his waist, and he started his thrusts again.

'I'm sorry,' he said. 'I don't think I can last much longer.'

Longer for what? she wondered. But then he began to deepen his strokes, and she understood what he needed.

She lifted her hips, meeting his thrusts, and she could tell he was trying so hard to be gentle.

His face was a mask of exertion, so tense, she wanted to break past that. And so, she lowered her legs and grabbed his backside, pulling him deep and hard.

'You want to go faster, don't you?' she guessed.

'God help me, yes.'

Though she couldn't suppress the slight pain, neither did she want him to hold back. 'Show me.'

And with that, he unleashed his control. He gripped her waist and penetrated deep, over and over, until she was crying out with another release. He bent to suckle her breast, and she bit back a scream as she came again. The pleasure was blinding, and she met his thrusts until he groaned and spilled himself deep inside. His body collapsed on top of hers and, despite the soreness, she'd never felt more satisfied in her life.

She didn't care what lay ahead. She would do everything to keep Piers as her husband. And although she knew the worst confrontation was yet to come, she intended to enjoy whatever time they had left.

Piers had never imagined a night like the last one. He'd expected Gwen to turn away from him after what he'd told her about Robert and killing the maid. Instead, she had welcomed him into her arms. He didn't understand why, but he'd paid no heed at all and had simply enjoyed the lovemaking.

Daylight streamed through the cracks of the window, and they would have to rise soon. He slid his hand over her shoulders, down to her breast, and she stirred, snuggling close to him. Immediately his arousal flared, even as a voice inside him warned, *This cannot last.*

The earl would discover their presence at Tilmain and order his men to capture or kill him. The only person who could intervene on their behalf was King John. And the earl was with him now.

Gwen reached up to him, lifting her leg over his hip as she kissed him. He went rigid at her touch, but she seemed well aware of what she was doing. 'Good morn, my husband.'

'It is a good morn,' he agreed, reaching down to touch her. He hadn't planned on another round just yet, but she surprised him by guiding his length inside her silken depths.

'What will we do today?' she asked, inhaling as he sank deep.

'I don't think I care any more,' he admitted. 'You have my full attention.' He leaned down and kissed her nipple, swirling his tongue over it while he began to thrust. She squeezed him deep inside in response.

'I like that,' she admitted.

'So do I.' He couldn't stop his smile as he pressed her back. 'You're not too sore?'

'A little, but I don't care.' She began to lift her hips in rhythm, and he continued to suckle at her while caressing the other breast.

'What made you change your mind,' he asked against her skin, 'about consummating our marriage?'

She was squirming beneath him, but he needed to know. Something had changed after he'd told her everything.

'Your honesty,' she admitted. 'All I ever wanted from you was the truth.'

'The truth that I'm no one, and I can give you nothing,' he ventured, reaching down between her legs to find the nodule of her pleasure.

'Regardless of your birth, you're my husband now,' she said. 'And you can give me something. A child.'

He stilled at that, but she continued, 'Our best chance of remaining married is to conceive an heir as quickly as possible.'

She reacted instantly when he began to circle her hooded flesh. 'Piers.' Her voice came in a hushed gasp. 'Yes, there.'

She gripped his backside, trying to get him to increase his thrusts. But instead he stopped moving, stroking her intimately to make her even hotter. She was shaking, trying to move against him as he stimulated her. He withdrew so that only the head of him remained inside, waiting for her to lose control. When she cried out, he thrust deep and felt her spasm against him. It turned raw and rough as she locked her legs around his waist, meeting his penetrations as her release crashed over her. His mind went numb as he felt her seize up, and then his own pleasure broke forth.

Even when he collapsed on top of her, he couldn't deny his hesitation. Though she might want a child, it wouldn't solve their problems. If anything, it would put a price on his head, for her father would never accept an heir conceived by a bastard husband.

'Gwen,' he breathed against her hair. 'We have time for now…but we can't stay here for too much longer.'

'I know.' She reached up and drew a lock of his hair

behind one ear. 'But for today, I want to enjoy this moment. We'll pretend that Tilmain is ours.'

In her voice, he heard the note of dismay, but he understood her reasons for wanting to avoid what lay ahead. Although he wanted to believe they could find a way to be together, it was nearly impossible.

The only way they could live was for her father to die. And if he dared to strike down Alfred, she would never forgive him for it.

'A sennight,' he conceded. 'Or a fortnight at the most.'

But she reached up to touch his face. 'I have to face him, Piers. I have to tell him what we've done and somehow get him to accept it. If I talk to my father, perhaps he might see reason. Especially if I am with child.'

Her voice held hope, but beneath her optimism, she likely suspected the truth. He rested his head against hers and said at last, 'I don't know if your father will ever accept this marriage. But if the king does, then we have a chance. I need to meet with King John—after your father is gone—and pledge my fealty.' He didn't know if it would aid their cause, but it might help. 'Do you want to come with me when I do?'

She touched his cheek. 'I think it would be better if I stayed here. Then my father won't threaten you.'

Her reasoning made sense, but he still didn't believe that Alfred would ever accept him. What he needed was to gain the respect of these men. If the people of Tilmain became his allies and he asked them to stand against the earl—it was their best hope. And yet, there was no time. The people here were strangers to him, and they had no reason to take such a risk.

A chilling premonition caught him, that these were the last moments he might have with Gwen. Though he didn't want to imagine it, he had a strong feeling that after he left, he would never see her again.

He leaned in to capture her lips, kissing her deeply. She responded to him and, after he pulled back, she admitted, 'I wish we could stay in this bed for ever.'

'It's the first time I've slept in a bed before,' he confessed.

She stared at him in disbelief. 'A bath and now a bed? What other things haven't you done?'

He didn't know how to answer that, but Gwen was already pulling away from him and tossing the coverlet aside. She pulled on her shift and underdress. 'I am going to change that today, Piers. If there is anything you've never done or experienced, then we will do that…until we have to leave.'

She appeared adamant about it, and he had no intention of arguing, if it made her happy. The sands were slipping through the hourglass. And it might be that the days ahead would have to give him enough memories for a lifetime.

Chapter Eleven

The first sennight passed by quickly, and for a time, Gwen felt as if she were standing on the edge of a mountain. Each day with Piers had brought her such happiness, she kept waiting for the ground to fall out beneath them. Though she knew it couldn't last, she couldn't help but cling fast to whatever time they had left. And she wanted him to experience the same joy she felt.

She'd arranged for all manner of foods to be served at table so Piers could try them and feel comfortable dining on the dais. Some of his new tunics had arrived from the merchant, whom she had paid handsomely from her father's coffers. Today, Piers wore a tunic of deep forest green, and she watched as he spoke with more of the men.

Somehow, he seemed to have earned their respect in just a short time. He saw everything, from a fence that needed repairing, to the way a young lad struck a straw target with an arrow for the first time. He was as quick to give a kind word as he was a correction.

And he ensured that every last one of the people had enough to eat, which endeared him to all of them.

The steward, John, came up behind her and cleared his throat. 'My lady,' he greeted her after she turned around.

'Good morn to you.' She waited for him to speak, for clearly there was something troubling him.

He watched the training for a while, as Piers corrected some of the fighters. 'His lordship has had a great deal of fighting experience, hasn't he?'

'He and his brother sparred often when they were boys.' She wondered where this was leading.

'There's…been talk. We were wondering about the earl and his return to Tilmain. He went to speak with the king, but will he return here? Or does he intend to travel to Penrith?'

'I have no way of knowing my father's plans.' She kept her expression neutral, pushing back her own insecurities. 'But there's something else, isn't there? What is it that troubles you, John?'

'Some of Lord… Grevershire's commands are different from the earl's. It might not be wise to make too many changes here.' In other words, he was cautioning her not to rule over Tilmain.

'I don't believe there have been any changes,' she pointed out. 'We've only been here a sennight.'

'Yes, but we have had more feasting than usual, and we need to be careful with our winter supplies.'

His warning was not lost on her, although she did not think they'd consumed an excessive amount of food. 'A wedding feast is to be expected. But it sounds as if you do not have enough to feed the people through the winter. I want to see what you have.'

'It's not necessary,' he backtracked. 'There is enough.'

Piers was walking towards them, and she decided to take the opportunity to bring him into the conversation. 'John is going to take us to see the winter stores,' she told him. 'We need to be certain the people have enough food to keep them through the season.'

But John shrugged. 'It's nothing, my lord. Nothing to worry about.'

Piers rested his hand upon her shoulder. 'My wife gave an order.' His voice was calm, but she sensed the edge of iron beneath it. 'Take us both to see the supplies.'

The steward paled and said, 'Of course, we don't have the harvest yet, and we will be adding dried meat to the stores.'

Gwen exchanged a look with Piers, and he gestured towards the steward to lead them. But her husband gave an imperceptible nod that he agreed with her—something must be wrong.

The steward led them to a ladder that descended below ground. He took a torch with him, and Piers did the same. Gwen climbed down the ladder first, and then Piers joined her.

The air was cooler here, and there were dozens of barrels lined up, along with clay containers.

'Is this all you have?' Piers asked.

'Thus far,' the steward agreed. 'Of course, Lord Tilmain sent many barrels of wine to His Highness, King John.'

'Did he send food as well?' Gwen asked.

The steward nodded. 'He always takes food and gifts

with him whenever he travels. Which is his right,' he added.

'I will see to it that your stores are replenished,' Gwen said. 'Give me a full accounting of what you need to feed everyone here. And it should be enough that all can have their fill.'

'We should increase it by half again,' Piers suggested. 'There is no need for anyone to go hungry.' His gaze hardened. 'We will buy more sheep or cattle, if need be. I am also travelling within another sennight to meet with King John. I will need escorts to join me. Lady Gwendoline will remain here.'

Although they had already planned this, she felt a pang that he was leaving without her. But it was better this way. If she had to meet with her father, at least Piers would be safe.

The steward appeared somewhat relieved that they intended to replace the supplies. 'I will make the arrangements for your journey whenever you are ready, my lord.' To Gwendoline, he added, 'May I speak with you about some other household matters? In the meantime, Lord Grevershire, you may wish to choose the men you want to accompany you.'

Gwen nodded to Piers. 'I can handle the rest from here.'

He helped her back up the ladder, but after they had both ascended, his hands lingered on her waist. 'Are you all right?'

'Just…trying not to think about when you leave,' she confessed. But more than that, it was the confrontation that lay ahead.

He turned to the steward and commanded, 'Leave

us.' After the man had gone, Piers pulled her into his arms. 'You'll be safe here, Gwen. I promise you.'

It wasn't that. It was the knowledge that she had to stand up to her father, once and for all, without Piers at her side. A horrible premonition crept over her of all the terrible things that could happen.

But she forced herself to say, 'I know. I just...want you to come back.'

'Even if I don't return, these past few days have been the best I've ever had.' He held her tightly, and her fears only multiplied.

'What do you mean, "Even if I don't return"?' She didn't want to imagine the possibility of him not returning.

He drew back to look at her. 'I will speak to the king. But we both know he may support your father's case over mine. Alfred has likely already spoken with him.'

She stared at him, and the sinking feeling in the pit of her stomach worsened. 'If the king does not help us, are you coming back for me?'

Piers reached out to touch her face, and in his eyes, she saw the truth. He was going to leave her here.

'I don't have a future to offer you, Gwen. All I have is ruins. You deserve better than that.'

She stepped out of his arms, feeling the coldness take root. Oh, God. Was he giving up already? This went far deeper than she'd imagined.

'Don't you dare,' she warned. 'You swore you wouldn't leave me again.'

'Gwen.' He reached out to catch her waist, but she pulled back.

'No. You made a promise to me.' A hard lump caught

in her throat. 'I am trying so hard to fight for this marriage. I want to be with you. I want this to be our life.' She gestured all around the castle grounds. 'But I need you to fight *with* me.'

The solemnity in his face terrified her. Instead, he took her in his arms and held her. She clung to him, but her body was shaking.

'It will be all right, Gwen.'

But she heard the finality in his voice. He truly believed that they could not be together—that his lack of wealth or a name meant they could not win this battle. She'd been willing to surrender everything for him, to face the father who had belittled her and made her feel as if she could never reign over anyone. She would fight with every breath in her body for Piers because she'd fallen in love with him.

And yet, nothing she'd done during the past sennight had made a difference. No matter how she tried to bridge the distance between them, he still saw himself as a bastard serf who slept among the dogs. No words or fine clothes would change that.

'Go and see to the men,' she said quietly. He kissed her forehead and left. After he'd gone, she turned around and leaned against the wall, letting her tears come. She'd been so naive, imagining that he would fight with her, that he loved her enough to stay.

But in the end, this was all playacting to him. Wearing fine clothes, giving orders, sitting at the high table— he didn't believe this life would ever be his.

She sobbed for the future they wouldn't have. For she knew in her heart that once he left to see the king, he wasn't coming back.

* * *

Piers sensed Gwen's withdrawal during the next few days and nights. She barely spoke to him any more, and he suspected she was afraid. Even after he made love to her, she didn't speak—she only held him. Once, in the middle of the night, he awakened and heard her crying softly.

'What is it, Gwen?' he murmured, pulling her close.

She turned to face him, and he wiped her tears away. 'No matter what I try to do, it's not enough.'

'What do you mean?' He pulled her closer, and the touch of her skin against his made him yearn to join with her again.

'All my life, I did everything I could to please my father. It was never enough. And with you, it's the same. No matter what I say or do, you've already given up on me. And…any child we might have.'

Piers didn't know what to say to console her, for only the king held the power to solve their problems. Even if they attempted to overthrow her father, to seize control of either Tilmain or Penrith, it meant nothing without the support of King John. Otherwise, the king could simply send men on behalf of the earl to slaughter them all.

'I just…don't want to lose you,' she admitted. 'And I feel like there's nothing I can do to change it.'

'It's safer here,' he told her. 'And if you do conceive a child, I can't risk either of you.' He drew his hand over her spine, down to the curve of her backside. Then he reached up to caress her breast.

He heard her intake of breath, but she admitted, 'When my father returns, he will punish me. I'll be imprisoned again, and he will do everything in his power to end our marriage. Even if I am with child.'

He moved her until she was atop him, their bodies pressed close. He wanted to bring her comfort, and he covered her with the furs to warm her skin. The softness of her body against his made him ache with desire, but he suppressed his needs. 'If I come back without the king's approval, your father will give the orders to kill me.'

'He won't listen anyway,' she said, shifting her position until his rigid erection pressed against her opening. It was utter torment, wanting to sink deep within—and yet, he held back.

'I don't want to be left behind,' she insisted.

With that, Gwen guided him inside her. He suppressed a groan as she began to move upon him. Her wetness surrounded him, and he cupped her bottom, overcome as she thrust against him. 'If you cannot return here,' she said, 'then tell me where I can meet you. We'll disappear together.'

She squeezed against him as she made love to him, and he sat up to take her breast in his mouth. He'd begun to learn her body and what she wanted. As she withdrew and sank against him, he used his mouth to tantalise her.

She quickened her pace, moving faster upon him. He was swiftly losing control, a captive beneath her spell.

'You're asking me to bring you into a life of misery,' he argued. 'A life where food is never certain, where we have no home. Don't ask it of me.'

'I'd rather be with you than left behind.' She continued her relentless assault, riding him hard as their hips ground together. 'I would give everything up.'

'You don't know what it's like, Gwen. I would never endanger you like that again. It's not worth it.' He seized her hips and met her thrusts, grinding against her as the blinding pleasure took hold. He leaned in to suckle her breast again as her breathing quickened, and he felt the moment she squeezed hard, her body arching against him as she came. He continued to penetrate her, loving the way she came apart, her body trembling around him, until his own release flooded through her.

His heart was pounding as he lay back, still buried inside her. He knew she wanted him to stand up to the earl and demand that Alfred accept their marriage. But words meant nothing to the earl—only strength and power. And that was something Piers lacked. Even if he sought help from the king, all he could offer was his sword, which might not be enough.

'It's still about money and status, isn't it? You think I cannot live without them.'

'I care enough about you, Gwen, that I don't want you to suffer,' was all he could say. 'I want a better life for you.'

She rose up to look at him. In the darkness, he could only see shadows, but she drew his hand to her stomach. 'I've already missed my courses, Piers.'

Her words sent a multitude of emotions crashing through him—awe, fear, and then determination to protect them both. He rested his hand against her flat stomach, wondering if it was even possible to build a life for them.

'A child?' he questioned.

'Possibly.' She lay back down against him and murmured, 'So you see why I can't accept being left behind. I will need your help if this is true. It's still too soon to know.'

He felt humbled by her confession, but it didn't change his resolve. If Gwen were pregnant, he could not imagine forcing her to travel a great distance, to a place far away from her father where they could live in peace. It simply wasn't possible.

He drew his hands over her body and said, 'I will talk to the king and appeal to him.'

She kissed him softly and then asked, 'And then you'll return to us?'

He could not make that promise. 'If the king grants us his protection, then yes. But if he refuses…'

He felt her body tighten with unease. 'You would turn your back on me and our child if the king refuses to acknowledge our marriage? Because you think I'm afraid to live in poverty?'

But this wasn't about wealth. It was about far more than that. It was about protecting his family.

'This has nothing to do with wealth. It's about keeping you both safe,' he insisted. 'And I will do everything in my power to protect you. No matter what that means.'

'Even if it means giving us up?'

'Anything,' he insisted. 'Without hesitation.'

She withdrew from him and turned away, clutching the coverlet to her nakedness. He knew she was crying again, but in this, he could not yield. Never would he do anything to threaten their lives.

Although he wanted to be with Gwen, he knew how

impossible it might be. Until he met with the king, he could only enjoy whatever time they had left.

Piers was going to die. Gwen knew it deep inside, and the anguish grew stronger each day. She loved her husband, but he had ridden off on a fool's errand. They both knew he would not win the king's support—not without lands or power. He could ask, but it meant nothing. And if Alfred was still travelling with the king's entourage, he would likely demand Piers's death for daring to wed his daughter.

With each day that her courses did not come, Gwen felt more protective over the child she might have conceived. Although she understood her husband's desire to protect them, she couldn't imagine a life where she gave him up without a fight.

Her husband had left days ago, but their final moments remained seared in her memory. He'd taken her in his arms, kissing her before he touched his forehead to hers. 'Be safe, Gwen.'

She managed to hold back the tears when she said farewell, despite all that she wanted to say. He didn't tell her of any feelings he might hold for her, though she sensed that he did care, from the way he held her for a long moment.

It had been a wonderful fortnight with Piers, giving her a taste of the life she wanted. But when her father returned, it would end. The people could not obey her orders over his. She only had a little time left, so she intended to make the most of it while she could.

During the first few days after Piers had gone, she had purchased more cattle and sheep with the jewels she'd brought from Penrith. The fields were abundant with new growth and, come the autumn, she felt confident that there would be enough grain to feed everyone.

But she also told the steward to set aside food separately for the people so that her father's 'gifts' would not cause them undue hardship during the winter.

John appeared grateful for her intervention. 'This will help us a great deal, my lady.' He hesitated for a moment, as if choosing his words. 'I've learned that your father is stopping at Tilmain on his way to Penrith.'

She froze at his words, realising the implications. Alfred could be on the same road as Piers, even now. And from the look of guilt on her steward's face, she guessed more. 'You sent word to him that I was here.'

He gave a single nod, swallowing hard. 'I had no choice, my lady. His messenger arrived here two days ago and he…saw you.'

She took a breath, realising that her time was running out. 'You should have told me about the messenger.'

The steward nodded. 'Aye. But I did not tell him about Lord Grevershire. I don't think he knows.'

That was a small consolation. Yet there was still the risk of her father attacking Piers, if their paths crossed. She had to do something to stop it from happening. 'I am going to find my husband. I want an escort of men. And send a maid to pack my belongings.'

If her father had not found Piers yet, she had an opportunity to appeal to the queen. It was possible that the woman might sympathise with her plight. King John's new wife was young, but she could have influence over him.

Gwen returned to her chamber and began choosing

the gowns she would need. Most of her clothing was still at Penrith, so she ordered the maid to pack one of the newer bliauds.

A thousand doubts crept into her heart, but she silenced them. This was about fighting for the man she loved and their unborn child. She would do everything in her power to save them both.

They would reach the king's encampment within a day. Piers raised his hand to order the soldiers to stop for the night. Six men had joined him, and three were among those he'd trained during the past fortnight. Adam was slightly older than himself, a seasoned warrior who fought well. Rufus was a strong fighter with a temper, while Philip was calm and reasoned. It was a good balance of men, and he trusted them as escorts.

Piers chose a place near a stream so the horses could drink while the men began setting up tents. But as he worked, his thoughts returned to Gwen. He couldn't tell her when he was coming back, for he didn't know the answers.

How could a bastard son ever rise to take the place of an earl? He'd intended to pledge his sword to the king, but unless the king acknowledged their marriage and his fealty, they were lost. Gwen's father would likely try to annul their union. And despite her claim that she wanted to run away with him, Piers didn't want her to endure such hardships. He'd lived through them his entire life, and the last thing he wanted was to bring her down with him.

But there was another way.

If he gave up all rights to Penrith and let his brother

Robert claim it, there was a chance the king might agree. Robert *did* have noble blood and a right to those lands. His brother had offered him a place to stay, and if that meant relinquishing Penrith to protect Gwen and their unborn child, he would set aside his pride and accept. It was their best chance to stay together.

The vision of his wife remained fixed within his mind. The last time he'd seen her, she had stood at the gates, her golden hair streaming behind her from the veil she wore. The time they'd spent together at Tilmain had been like a dream, an illusion of the life he wished he could have. In his mind, he envisioned her growing round with his child. He thought of holding their son, and the thought nearly brought him to his knees.

Adam approached while Piers was busy setting up his own tent. The older warrior waited and when Piers turned to him, he asked, 'My lord, may I speak with you?'

He gave a nod. 'What is it?'

Adam hesitated. 'Does…the earl know that you were at Tilmain with Lady Gwendoline?'

'Why do you ask?' He fixed his gaze upon the road ahead, not wanting to give the man any more information.

'No one at Tilmain had heard of your wedding. News like that…well, the earl would have sent word.' Adam didn't look at him, but he admitted, 'The men and I fear for your safety, my lord. We know the sort of man the earl is.'

Piers sensed that the man's warning was genuine. He decided to reveal part of the truth to gain an ally. 'I did marry Lady Gwendoline before a priest,' he told him.

'She wed me willingly, and we came to Tilmain without her father's knowledge.'

At that, Adam inclined his head. 'We suspected as much. My lord would never allow anyone to give orders without his leave. Especially not his daughter.' He cleared his throat. 'Your decision to avoid the main roads was wise.'

Piers had done so out of necessity. There was always a chance of meeting up with the earl on those roads, even if Alfred was travelling back to Penrith instead. And the closer they came to the king's camp, the higher the possibility of their paths crossing. He needed to address the danger and his expectations for the men, should they encounter the earl.

Piers tightened the rope holding his tent and returned to the fire near the centre of their camp. The soldiers seemed to guess his desire to speak with them, and they came forward. He faced them and said, 'My journey to meet with the king may be dangerous. If any of you wish to return to Tilmain, I do not fault you for it. I know many of you have families.'

Philip moved closer and reassured him, 'My lord, it was our choice to come. We will guard you from danger.'

The others echoed the sentiment, and an ache clenched his gut. Piers needed them to understand that their loyalty would be tested. 'And what if that danger comes from his lordship?'

Rufus smiled and reached for his sword hilt. 'Even better.' It was no secret that he disliked his overlord, and a few of the others laughed.

Piers didn't share that sentiment. Instead, he decided

to be honest with the men. 'I married the earl's daughter against his wishes. If his men find us, you need to abandon me. Pretend to take me prisoner, if you must.' He squared off and faced each one of them. 'This isn't your battle—it's mine. And I would not ask you to give up your lives for me. I'm a stranger you barely know.'

Philip straightened in his saddle. 'I'd rather fight for you than the earl, my lord.'

The others echoed his words and the twinge of gratitude deepened inside Piers. Though he wanted to refuse, Piers understood their pride. Instead, he regarded them and said, 'I am grateful for your willingness to defend me. But there are other ways to fight than raising your sword. Your loyalty means a great deal, but I'd rather have you live.'

'I'd rather have you as our overlord,' Rufus said. 'At least then we wouldn't have to worry about our harvest being given away to other noblemen or the king.' He touched his sword hilt again. 'You have my vow to guard your back, my lord.'

Never in his life had Piers thought men would say that to him. Inwardly, he made a silent promise not to allow anything to happen to them. And after he met with the king, he could only hope that John would support his cause.

Or else it would be the last time he saw Gwen.

A few of the men went out hunting and brought back food for the evening meal. They passed around a horn of ale and shared the rabbits. The camaraderie turned jovial as they talked and Adam asked, 'How did you come to wed Lady Gwendoline?'

'I competed in contests for her hand,' Piers answered. 'Her father had already chosen someone else, but I wooed her in secret. It worked.'

Rufus raised the horn of ale in a toast and passed it to him. 'Well done.'

'She seems pleased with her choice of a husband,' Adam said. 'And far happier than we've ever seen her.'

He realised that Adam had known Gwen for a long time. He must have been there since she was much younger. It was an opportunity to learn more about his wife's past.

Piers passed the horn of ale to Adam and asked, 'What was Gwen like as a young maiden?' He wondered if her father had ever allowed her to give commands or have any freedom at all.

'She spent most of her time with her mother,' one answered. 'The two of them were very close.'

That didn't surprise him, but he asked, 'How did her mother die?'

The question brought an immediate pause to their conversation, and several men wouldn't meet his gaze.

'She fell,' Philip answered at last.

Piers didn't miss the uncertain tone to the man's voice. There was far more to this story, and he waited for them to continue. When no one did, he asked, 'How did she…fall?' Again, the silence stretched out among them.

Rufus dared to venture, 'Some say—'

'Enough.' Adam cut the man off. 'Let our lady rest in peace. It matters not how she died. Only that she's gone, and Lady Gwendoline grieved for the loss of her mother.' Then he turned back to Piers. 'It's our hope that the earl returns to Penrith and stays there. You and Lady Gwendoline are a welcome change.'

Piers studied each of them, inclining his head in silent thanks. 'This isn't over yet. Eventually I will have to face the earl, and he wants me dead. He would rather make his daughter a widow than accept me as her husband.'

'You have our swords as protection,' Philip answered. 'We won't fail you.'

Piers was grateful for it. 'In the morning, I plan to seek an audience with the king. I would welcome your eyes and ears in the encampment if you hear of anything that could help my cause.'

'Aye, my lord,' Philip answered.

The evening waned into night, and Rufus promised to keep first watch while they slept. But as Piers went inside his tent, his instincts went on edge. He couldn't quite understand why, but sleep would not come. It was likely foolish, but he couldn't relinquish the feeling of uncertainty.

Perhaps it was the forthcoming meeting that he hoped to have with the king. He tossed and turned within the tent, trying to figure out a better plan, but sleep would not come. No matter how hard he tried, he could think of no means of gaining what he wanted. Not unless it meant leaving everything behind and starting over with Gwen in a place where no one could ever find them.

He heard the soft sound of footsteps approaching. Silently, he reached for his dagger and crouched low. The tent flap lifted, and he pressed the blade to the man's throat.

Adam lifted his hands. In a low voice, he commanded, 'Come with me. The earl's men are near.'

Piers lowered the blade and followed. The fire still burned, and he saw Philip sleeping nearby. 'Where is Rufus?' he asked quietly.

'I don't know, but Alfred's men have come, and we have to get you out of here.'

Something about the man's demeanour seemed unnatural. Why hadn't he woken Phillip, and why wasn't he searching for Rufus? Piers went to saddle his horse, but Adam stopped him once again. 'It's better if we go on foot. I can lead you out of here, towards the king's encampment.'

Although the man was likely right, something rang false in his words. And Piers hadn't survived this long by setting aside his suspicions.

'I'd prefer to ride.' He lifted the saddle and began preparing the horse.

Adam pressed a hand to his shoulder. 'My lord, no.'

But Piers refused to listen. He finished securing the horse's saddle and prepared to mount. Just as he was about to swing his leg over, he felt a blade at his throat.

'I said no,' Adam repeated. He held the sword steady, keeping the edge in place.

'Where is Rufus?' Piers asked softly. He kept his voice deliberately calm, hiding the fury he felt about Adam's treachery.

'Rufus betrayed his lordship's trust. My orders are to bring you to the earl.'

Piers stared back at Adam. The older warrior's face held a steady resolution of a man who was determined to obey the commands he'd been given. And since Adam hadn't attempted to kill him, it meant he was supposed to bring Piers alive to Alfred.

Piers lifted his hands and turned slowly. He had only one chance to escape, and that time was now.

Gwen rode with her escorts along the road, knowing that the risk of meeting her father was grave. She'd been travelling for days now, hoping to find Piers before Alfred could. But as time passed and there was no sign of her husband, she realised that it might be wiser to seek out her father and negotiate with him.

In the distance, she could see the king's encampment, and her nerves tightened at the sight of it. She had to find and confront her father tonight. They continued riding north, but then their travelling party came across a soldier lying face down near the road. Gwen feared he was dead, but two of her men dismounted to look. They shouted to the others, and it seemed that the victim was still alive.

They helped him to sit up while she rode closer. She overheard one of the men calling the soldier Rufus as they checked him. Gwen dismounted and recognised him as one of the men who had trained with Piers. He'd bled through his tunic, and one of her escorts stripped it off to examine his wound. It appeared that he'd been stabbed.

'Who did this to you?' she asked.

'Adam,' he answered. 'He took your…husband captive. Took him…to your father.'

She closed her eyes, trying to push back the wave of fear. 'Where are they now?'

'They went…to see the king.' Rufus let out a gasp

when one soldier pressed a linen cloth to the wound. 'I heard them fighting. Too many.'

She rose to her feet. 'Two of you stay behind to help Rufus. I want the rest of you to accompany me when I ride to find my husband.'

Her escorts readily agreed, and they helped her mount her horse before they continued on. Her stomach twisted with nausea and terror that Piers was already dead. She didn't know how she would stop her father from killing him. Words and pleas would do no good at all. She needed leverage of a different kind.

They rode farther until they were at the edge of the king's encampment. She slowed her pace, trying to calm her beating heart. There was no sign of Piers or her father, which meant they would have to search among the king's entourage.

And if she made a single mistake, it could mean the difference between her husband's life and death. Gwen pulled her horse to a stop and motioned for her men to come closer. When they encircled her, she reminded them, 'You guard me, not my father. And you must obey my orders, not his.'

They appeared uncomfortable by her command, but she elaborated. 'We are here to rescue Lord Grevershire. I want you to find out where he is being held captive and gather whatever information you can. I realise you may have to join forces with my father's men, but remember where your loyalty lies.'

'With you, my lady,' one answered.

Gwen nodded. 'If you help me save my husband, you will be greatly rewarded. And if you betray us, I will never trust you again.' She levelled a stare at each man, and then she said, 'Follow me, and do as I command.'

It was the first time she had truly felt comfortable giving orders. This was about saving Piers, and she would brook no arguments from any man. And something within her shifted, pushing back the feelings of uncertainty. Instead, she understood that issuing orders was not about power or control—it was about protecting those under her care. It made it easier to assume the reins of leadership, and she believed the men sensed it, too.

She rode towards the entrance of the king's encampment where the guards were waiting. Two of her escorts rode beside her, and the rest stayed behind. One of the king's guards rode forward to greet them.

'I am here to find my father Alfred, the Earl of Penrith and Tilmain,' she said quietly. 'I understand he came to pledge his fealty to His Majesty.'

The guard answered, 'He is here, my lady. I can bring you to him.'

'I have been travelling for days and would like to refresh myself beforehand,' she lied. 'Is there a tent for the queen's ladies?'

'There is,' he answered. 'We can bring you there first.'

She smiled, playing the role of the demure noblewoman. 'I thank you. If you would, could you escort the rest of my men to join the earl's guards, and tell my father that I am here?'

He inclined his head. Gwen turned back to the others and gave a single nod, reminding them of their purpose here. She took only one guard with her to the queen's ladies, and he helped her dismount outside the tent.

She opened the tent and walked inside to join the other women. All conversation ceased when they saw her, and she pushed back her nerves. She introduced herself, 'I am Gwendoline of Grevershire.'

She noticed that the queen was not among her ladies, but when a few of the ladies gave their names, she met a few noblewomen whose estates sounded familiar.

But even so, she felt like an intruder here. She tried to talk with some of the ladies and most told her that their husbands were seeking audiences. It seemed that King John needed men to fight for him in France, and he was demanding more taxes from his noblemen. Gwen detected a note of annoyance from among the ladies.

'Are you here with your family?' one woman asked her.

Gwen nodded. 'My father, the Earl of Penrith, is here. And also my husband, Lord Grevershire. He came to pledge his fealty to King John.'

'I hope he brought chests of gold with him,' one of the ladies remarked drily, handing her a cup of wine. 'That is, if he wants to speak with King John at all.'

Gwen accepted the wine and drank, but her sense of uneasiness was rising. It didn't bode well for her own future if the king was in need of funds.

'I was hoping to speak with the queen,' she said, but one of the ladies shook her head.

'Queen Isabelle may return later, but she's with His Majesty now.'

Gwen wasn't about to be deterred. 'Do you think I could gain an audience with her?' She was still hoping the queen could help support her cause with Piers.

The woman shook her head. 'It's unlikely.'

Gwen pretended to accept this, but she would try. She took her meal with the ladies and grew quiet, listening to their conversations to learn what she could. But everything centred around their own troubles.

None of her soldiers returned or even any of the king's men. She wasn't certain whether she should try to find any of them. As time crept on, her worries deepened. Where was Piers, and what had her father done to him? She prayed he was a captive and not dead.

She tried to calm herself. The men would find out what had happened—she had to keep faith in them. If she left the tent or tried to ask questions, it would only draw more attention.

After a while, she heard voices approaching outside the tent, her father's among them. Her stomach knotted in fear, but she forced herself to calm down. She rested her hands below her waist, reminding herself that she was not only fighting for Piers. This was also a battle to guard their unborn child.

Gwen waited, wondering what to say to Alfred. In vain, she tried to gather the remnants of her courage. She heard the earl asking the guard whether she was inside. Then a moment later, her father entered the tent and saw her. Alfred's face darkened with rage, and he demanded, 'Come with me.'

Gwen hesitated, for it would be more difficult for him to chastise her in front of the queen's ladies. But then she realised that his anger would only worsen if she stayed. One of the women sent her a sympathetic look, and Gwen averted her gaze as she left the tent.

Her father looked as if he had been in a fight some time ago. Dark bruises were on his face, and she noticed a healing cut across one cheek. 'What happened to you?'

He ignored the question and said, 'You've caused more trouble than you know. I sent men to find you and bring you home, but all this was your fault, wasn't it? You ran away with the bastard willingly.'

Fear iced her heart, but she managed to answer, 'He is my husband now. I married Piers before a priest.'

A slow smile slid over the earl's face. 'Is that what you think?'

She couldn't tell whether his smile was because he'd taken Piers or because he intended to keep her from him. For now, she remained silent and stared back at him. He was trying to intimidate her as he always did, making her feel like a disobedient child.

'What have you done?' she asked quietly.

The smile that remained on his face was chilling, making her fear the worst. Though she tried to keep her composure, she gripped her hands together to stop them from shaking.

'He's going to die,' her father said. 'The only question is whether I grant him a merciful death.'

She gave no response to his threat but simply stared at him. How could she ever have believed she could stand up to this man and win her own victory? Ever since her mother's death, Gwen hadn't been allowed to have any freedom of her own. Her life was bound by invisible chains that could never be broken.

She had to tread carefully to protect her husband. In a low voice, she asked, 'What is it you want from me?' There was a slight tremor in her words, but she managed to hold back her terror.

'You're going to marry Gareth of Watcombe,' he said quietly. 'Willingly.'

She wanted to tell him that she could not do it, but any words she said would bring harm to her husband. Instead, she said, 'I want to see Piers with my own eyes.'

'Don't make demands of me.' He backhanded her with a gloved hand, and the blow radiated pain through her cheek. She hadn't expected it and covered her face in shock. 'You will do as I say.'

Her heart was racing, but she kept quiet. *Piers's life depends on your actions,* she reminded herself. *Be careful.*

Alfred's face turned purple with rage, but he steadied himself. 'Your desires mean nothing to me. Only your obedience.' He cleared his throat and said, 'This so-called marriage was never legal. You whored yourself to a bastard, and it's over now. I will send word to Gareth of Watcombe, and you will marry him before the king himself to bear witness. No one will doubt your union, and you will consummate it immediately.'

Her father continued. 'If you tell the king that your first marriage happened against your will, I might allow the bastard to be beheaded. But if you don't obey me, rest assured, I will make his death painful until the very end.'

She believed him. Alfred was well past the point of

her begging for forgiveness or pleading for Piers's life. He would never see reason. Her only hope was for her men to save Piers and take him far away from here.

Her father gripped her wrist painfully and, when his back was to her, she allowed the tears to slide down her cheeks. A suffocating panic took hold, and she simply didn't know if there was any way to save Piers.

Chapter Twelve

For two days, he'd had little food or water. Piers struggled against the chains at his wrists, wondering if he would ever see Gwen again. His head ached from the blows he'd suffered, and blood caked upon his skin. The vision of his wife kept him focused upon survival. For now, it was all he had as a distraction from the immense thirst and the gnawing hunger.

Two men came and unchained him. This time, they bound his wrists with leather and dragged him outside. Sunlight burned his eyes, but when his vision adjusted, he recognised them from Penrith. He'd known these men since he was a boy, but neither would look at him now. Two more joined behind him, and these were from Tilmain, although they were not the men he'd travelled with. There was a sombre mood, as if they didn't like their orders.

Piers didn't ask questions but went with them, knowing this might be his only chance to escape. He'd been struck unconscious during the last fight, and he didn't know where the men had taken him.

Dozens of tents stood in the distance—so many that he could not count them all. He didn't know where he was, but he guessed it was inside the king's encampment. Some of the tents were large and elaborate, but it was not entirely clear which one belonged to His Majesty.

'Are you planning to kill me?' he asked the men. It wouldn't surprise him. He had dared to marry a woman he didn't deserve. But he held no regrets at all for being with her. Gwen had given him a glimpse of heaven, and he would savour those memories in whatever time he had remaining.

Instead, they brought him outside the encampment towards a small grove of trees. He stumbled as he walked, dizziness washing over him. The lack of food and water had stolen his strength, making an escape impossible.

He heard a soft cry and, when he lifted his gaze, he saw his wife approaching. For a moment, he blinked, wondering whether it was an illusion. Gwen's blonde hair was braided back, and her blue eyes held tears while her father gripped her wrist. The sight of his wife brought a rush of emotions—joy, anguish, and all-encompassing fear. Not for himself, but for her safety.

He'd been brought here to die. He knew that, but he didn't know what would become of Gwen. The earl wanted him gone—and it would not be a painless death if Alfred had brought her here to witness it.

He turned to the two men on either side of him. In a low voice so the earl wouldn't overhear him, he murmured, 'Lady Gwendoline shouldn't be here.'

In their faces, he saw the silent agreement. But they

were afraid to defy orders. The men stripped off his tunic and led him towards the trees.

Piers continued to speak in a low voice. 'If I did anything at all to help you or your families at Tilmain…' he turned and looked at the others who had come from Penrith '…or if any of you were my friends at Penrith, I ask you to take my wife away from this place. Don't let her watch.'

The men remained quiet, but he hoped his words had influenced them in some way. As the men bound him between the two trees, he stared back at the king's encampment. He'd been so close…and now, he would never have the chance to fight for her.

'Let him go,' he heard Gwen say. Her face was white, but she wrenched her hand away from her father. 'You have what you wanted—my obedience.'

'I want far more than that,' Alfred responded. 'I want you to see the consequences of your actions so you will never defy me again.'

There was a flash of rage on her face, and Piers locked eyes with her. For a brief moment, she rested her hands upon her womb and stared back at him.

In the distance, Piers heard the noise of shouting. There seemed to be a gathering of some kind, as noblemen and soldiers strode past the tents.

'What's happening?' he asked a soldier. But the man only shook his head and adjusted the bindings as the earl came closer.

'I want him flogged,' the earl said. 'I want his blood to soak the grass and, when he can no longer stand, I want the flesh flayed from his body.'

Piers refused to look at Alfred. He didn't want the

earl to have that satisfaction. Instead, he fixed his gaze upon Gwen, wanting her face to be the last thing he saw when he died. He gripped the leather bindings, steeling himself for what lay ahead.

A bastard wasn't supposed to love an earl's daughter. She deserved so much more that he could never give. He thought of Gwen's smile, her joy at the thought of an unborn child. At least part of him might live on with her, even if he could not be there.

The noise of unrest grew louder, but the earl seemed not to care. 'My lord, should we take Lady Gwendoline back to the queen?' one of the soldiers suggested, nodding back at the encampment.

'No,' the earl snapped. 'I want her to watch. I want her to hear him scream and know that it was her disobedience that caused this.'

With that, the earl pulled back his cloak and revealed a scourge with metal spikes. Piers stiffened at the sight of it, bracing himself.

'Don't,' Gwen warned. She ran forward towards her father and stepped between them. 'Please.' He could hear the terror in her voice, and she added, 'I beg of you.'

The earl picked up the scourge while Gwen covered his back, standing between them once more. The touch of her body against his was a comfort to savour. Back to back they stood, but he knew not what the earl would do.

He heard the sound of a blade being unsheathed. 'Step away from him, Gwen, or I'll kill him right now.'

Piers rested his head against hers and said softly, 'I will never forget the time we spent together. Be strong. You have to protect—' *Our child,* he almost said. But he held back the words, hoping she would understand. 'Leave, Gwen. Run!'

With reluctance, she pulled away from him and stepped aside. 'I love you,' she whispered.

The words humbled him, and he answered, 'You're everything to me.'

She stumbled forward, as if the earl had shoved her away.

Then he felt the agonising blow of the scourge as the metal spikes dug into his skin and tore the flesh. He gasped at the pain. 'Run!' he repeated. If nothing else, the earl would not have the satisfaction of forcing her to watch. 'Don't stop. Just go.'

Blow after blow came down upon his back, the scourge slicing through skin. Piers felt the blood streaming from his back, but he would not give the earl the satisfaction of hearing him scream.

Instead, he thought of his beautiful wife, and the image gave him strength.

'I'm going to send the healer to my daughter tonight,' the earl said. 'She will give Gwen a cup of wine to help her sleep. There will be herbs in that wine that cause a woman to miscarry. When you die, I want you to know that no part of you will *ever* live on.'

Shock resonated through him, and rage took hold. A rushing filled his ears, and Piers didn't even feel the agony of the whipping any more. He pulled hard against the leather bindings, and his wrists turned white with exertion.

'She will be married to Gareth of Watcombe on the morrow,' the earl swore. 'And then he will give her a child of noble blood.'

Piers had no doubt the earl meant what he said. He had to do something to protect Gwen, and he prayed that she'd managed to escape. His life didn't matter— only hers.

The scourging struck again and, this time, he couldn't stop the roar of pain that tore from him. His knees sagged, and he watched the earl hand the scourge to one of the soldiers. 'Finish him. I'm going after my daughter.'

Gwen was crying so hard, she could barely breathe as she ran. It felt like the act of cowardice, but she understood what Piers had wanted. He wanted her to save their unborn child and leave her father behind. This was her last chance to escape, and she had to take it.

But not before she did everything in her power to save Piers.

The encampment was in chaos. She couldn't tell what was happening, but dozens of men were gathered together, noblemen and soldiers alike, moving towards the centre. Towards the king, she realised. Her heart pounded as she wondered whether he was in danger. Something was happening, but what?

Gwen tried to move among the crowd, but someone shoved her back. She stumbled but tried again. As she did, she overheard someone muttering about too many taxes and how they would put a stop to it.

Then it *was* a rebellion happening against the king. She might be able to use the chaos to her advantage. She could find her men and order them to save Piers and bring him to her. But where were they? There were so many tents, she didn't know where to start.

Then a hand clamped down on hers, and she spun

around. Her father's punishing grip hurt her wrist, and she tried to get away.

'Enough of this,' he snapped. 'My men will finish his punishment.'

Gwen didn't know what Alfred planned to do to her, but she walked beside him, furious at herself for losing the opportunity. If Piers died, she had no one but herself to blame. She should have asked any of the soldiers to help her. For enough coins, they would have. And with every moment that passed, they were beating Piers to death.

She hated herself for being weak. This was her fault.

The crowds of people swelled, and then, suddenly, someone pushed the earl and he stumbled to the ground. He released her wrist, and Gwen stepped back while the crowd surrounded him. Someone else seized her hand, and she turned to see Morwenna.

Hope swelled within her, for if Morwenna was here, then so was Robert. If anyone could save him, it was his brother.

'Where is Piers?' Morwenna asked.

'He's a captive.' Gwen struggled to hold back her tears, but she begged, 'Please ask Robert to help him.'

But her friend turned sombre. 'The king is in danger. I think Robert is trying to defend him.' She took Gwen by the hand and led her deeper into the crowd of soldiers and men. She couldn't even see her father now because so many men surrounded them. 'Robert can't save Piers now…but you could. If you know where he is.'

Fear paralyzed her with doubts, but Morwenna was right. She held the power to save Piers if she could only overcome her terror.

Morwenna handed Gwen her knife. 'Take this. And if you can save him, send him to fight for the king.'

She doubted if Piers was strong enough, but Gwen took the blade and murmured her thanks, sheathing it at her side. Then Morwenna left, hurrying towards the king's tent.

Gwen still couldn't see her father, but she couldn't stay here. Instead of remaining in the crowd, she chose one of the tents and slipped inside. Better to hide from her father and make her plans than to risk being found again.

No one was inside the tent, and from the bare interior, she could tell that soldiers had slept here. Bed rolls lay on the ground, along with leftover food and discarded leather armour. Her mind steadied, and she was determined not lose this new opportunity to save Piers. She studied her surroundings…and saw a bow and a quiver of arrows on the opposite side of the tent. Without hesitation, she armed herself.

The bow gave her a sense of power and the knowledge that she could defend herself. This time, she would save her husband. And God help any man who tried to stop her.

She gathered a few other supplies and tossed a handful of coins on to one of the bed rolls as payment. Then she kept her bow in one hand, an arrow in the other as she exited the tent.

The weapon in her hand brought a strange sense of calm. She took a deep breath as she hurried back to the place where her father had flogged Piers. Though she didn't want to kill anyone, if they dared to defy her orders, she wouldn't hesitate to draw back her bow.

Please let him be alive, she prayed as she ran. She dodged her way past tents and the uprising, hoping there was time to escape. Along the way, she untethered a horse and mounted it. She rode towards the trees and saw the soldiers surrounding Piers. He lay face down on the ground, and Gwen couldn't tell if he was alive or dead.

'Get back!' she commanded, drawing her bow. The men jerked to attention at the sound of her voice. She held her weapon steady.

'He's alive, my lady.'

'How many lashes did he receive after I left?' She kept her voice rigid, trying to push back against the fury.

'None,' another man answered. 'We disobeyed the earl's commands.'

At first, she couldn't tell what they were doing... and then she realised they were tending his wounds. A hard lump formed in her throat when she understood that they'd remained loyal to her. 'Help me get him on to the horse.'

The men had torn up Piers's tunic to stanch the bleeding. Gently, they lifted up his unconscious form, and they brought him over to a different horse.

'I want him to ride with me,' she argued, but the soldier shook his head.

'Forgive me, my lady, but he could fall. I don't know if you're strong enough to hold him.' He eyed her weapon. 'And we may need your bow.'

From the grim expression on their faces, she believed them. 'We have to leave now, while we still can.'

But before she turned her back, she saw a change in their faces, a sudden tension. Without hesitation, she nocked an arrow to her bow and spun her horse around. Her father was striding closer, his sword drawn.

An icy coldness flooded through her. Because of him, her husband was bleeding out from his wounds. Alfred's cruelty enraged her, and she wondered when it would ever end.

He'd made her life nothing but a misery, taking her freedom. She'd mistakenly believed that he loved her, that he wanted only the best for her. Instead, he wanted to control every aspect of her existence.

'Don't move,' she warned.

As she'd expected, he ignored her. Instead, he commanded the men, 'Seize her.'

The soldiers did nothing, and she was grateful for their support. But although she knew she could end it all now, she didn't want to murder her own father. All she wanted was to leave in safety to take care of her husband.

'Let us go,' she said to Alfred, lowering her weapon.

But instead of relenting, her father charged towards her husband, his sword raised. The soldier tried to move out of the way, but Piers started to fall.

And so, she had no other choice but to let her arrow fly.

Piers drifted in and out of consciousness. During the next few days, he barely remembered the swaying of a boat, and he guessed that they were travelling back to Tilmain. His back was on fire with pain, but someone had placed herbs and bandages on the wounds. He was dimly aware of Gwen giving him water and food.

When the fever came, he lost all awareness of the

world around him except that they were now in a chamber instead of in a boat. His body trembled, and his back felt swollen and aching. But as he drifted in and out of darkness, Gwen was there for him. He gripped her hand as if it were a means of clinging to life. He didn't know if he could survive this, in truth. Healers came and went, but the fever only seemed to worsen.

One night, he heard Gwen weeping, and he opened his eyes. 'Don't cry.' His voice came out with a ragged hoarseness, but she took his hand in hers. In the faint lamp light, her golden hair gleamed. It was tangled and falling out of her braid, but she looked beautiful to him.

'Our soldiers have shut the gates to Tilmain,' she told him. 'My father is outside them, demanding that we let him enter.'

'He's alive then?'

She nodded. 'I wounded him with an arrow, but I didn't have the heart to kill him. It was a mistake. I should have finished it. Now, more men will die because of me.'

'They don't have to die,' he said. 'Just open the gates to him.'

'I'm so tired, Piers. For weeks, we've been fleeing from him, fighting his men. I've argued with him, I've begged. He won't relent. He'll never stop.' Her sob cracked apart, and he squeezed her hand as she wept. He reached up to her, and she lay down to face him. He brushed away her tears, and the contrast of her cool skin against his feverish skin was a balm.

'Do you know… God rest her…now I wonder if my mother's death was truly an accident?' Gwen took a breath, and Piers didn't contradict her, for he'd wondered the same thing.

'My father told me she fell. But what if she…took her own life? Or worse, what if he pushed her down those stairs?'

The anguish in her voice bothered him deeply. 'Don't think of it,' he said, resting his hand against her cheek. 'You'll only torment yourself.'

'I don't know what to do,' she admitted. 'I'll never escape him.'

'Just be strong.' He ran his fingers through her hair and rested his forehead against hers. 'You're the strongest woman I know. Lead the men and defend Tilmain. Claim it as yours.'

She touched his hair, moving her hand to his face. 'Piers, you're burning up,' she whispered. 'I'll get the healer again.'

'It's all right,' he answered. 'Stay with me.' He laced his fingers with hers, as if he could somehow heal himself from her touch. She obeyed, but he could feel the tension in her body. 'Gwen, you're going to be all right.'

At his words, she continued crying. 'Don't you dare give up. Don't say I'm going to be all right when I'm not.'

He didn't believe that at all. She would do whatever was necessary, and she had all the people of Tilmain behind her. He'd overheard her issuing orders, and she'd taken full command of the estate.

'You can defeat Alfred,' he said. 'Even if I am gone.'

She brought his hand to her womb. 'You cannot leave me. For if you do, I have nothing left. And no one.' Tears rolled down her cheeks as he realised what she was saying. Her courses must have come.

Her grief broke his heart when he understood that there was no child. He hadn't realised how much he'd hoped for one until now. 'I'm sorry, Gwen.'

She took a moment to gather her composure and said, 'I will order the men to hold our walls a little longer. We can last under siege if we have to. But I am going to get a healer.'

He didn't know if it would be enough. Though he tried to fight back against the fever, he didn't know if he could win this battle. He would try for her sake.

'I love you,' she said, her voice thick with tears. 'And I need you to fight for me. I cannot face my father without you.'

'You can do anything you set your mind to, Gwen,' he answered. He closed his eyes as the weakness overtook him. Sleep threatened to pull him under, and he heard her footsteps retreating towards the door, likely to find the healer. But he forced himself to say the words she needed to hear. His voice came out as a whisper, and he said, 'I love you, too.'

The door closed, and he suspected she hadn't heard him.

He had no idea how much time passed before the healer returned. He heard the woman muttering something about poisoned flesh and fever. And when she pressed her hands against his swollen back, the pain drew a harsh shout from him.

'Stop it,' Gwen insisted. 'You're hurting him.'

'His wounds are not healing,' the old woman said. 'The red skin and that swelling are causing his fever. If we do not cleanse the wounds properly, he will die.'

'What must I do?' Gwen asked. 'Should I fetch garlic or other herbs? Tell me what you need, and I will bring it.' Her voice trembled, revealing her fear.

But their voices grew dim, and soon, he didn't hear them at all. Past blurred with present, and he remembered one night in the cave when he'd fought to save Robert after he'd been wounded. They'd been alone and, that night, Piers had feared for his brother's life.

'You can't die,' he'd told Robert. 'The people need you at Penrith.'

His brother had struggled to open his eyes, and his words had been barely audible. 'You will take care of them. You…know them better.'

Piers didn't know what had happened to Robert since they'd left the king's encampment. Had his brother won command of Penrith? And more than that, what could he do to keep Gwen safe?

All thoughts were cut off when the healer lanced his wounds. He couldn't stop the cry of pain that tore from him before he lost consciousness.

A fortnight later

Gwen stared at her husband, feeling as if she'd fought the battle as fiercely as he had. His fever had broken, and his wounds had begun to heal. She'd kept vigil by his bedside every night, praying for his recovery while she'd changed the poultices and bandages.

Piers had survived, but she could never let down her guard. Her father would return after his own wound healed—and their fight would continue.

For now, they had left Tilmain for a very different

reason. His brother Robert had asked them to travel to Stansbury to witness his wedding vows to Morwenna. And Piers had agreed without hesitation.

Gwen understood why he'd wanted to make the journey, but she was fully aware of the danger. And although they had finally arrived at the ruined fortress for the wedding, she found it difficult to stop searching for signs of her father's men. Piers's mood echoed her own, for the tension weighed down upon them about their unknown future.

Robert came to greet them, and a lump caught in her throat when she saw the brothers embrace. Not only because Piers had survived his wounds, but for the genuine bond between the men.

'You came.' Robert smiled. 'And I see that your wounds have healed.'

'Mostly.' Piers helped her down from her horse, and she embraced Robert as well. He appeared content in a way she'd never seen before. Likely the king had granted him what he'd wanted most of all—his father's lands.

'Will you go back to Penrith after you are wedded?' she asked him.

Robert hesitated and looked uncertain as he eyed both of them. 'The king's ambassadors didn't tell you, did they? I thought they would.'

'Tell us what?' Piers asked. His expression had turned guarded.

'After I saved the king's life, he offered me land.'

'And you now have Penrith again,' Piers said. 'We both know that's what you wanted.'

Robert shook his head slowly. 'I *thought* it was what I wanted. But what I really want is a life with Morwenna.

And if I took Penrith, I'm taking away your future with Gwen. That's not what I want.'

Gwen stared at them both in disbelief. 'I don't understand.'

'I asked the king to give Penrith to you and Piers. I accepted land in Ireland instead. It's an estate in the north.'

She could not have been more stunned. Words utterly failed her as he continued, 'The king agreed that it was better to keep Penrith with you and Piers because then he would not have to strip the earl of his title. Your father should return to Tilmain, while you and Piers live at Penrith.' He offered a half-smile. 'I have the king's seal upon the parchment granting Penrith to you both. I had planned to give it to you after my wedding.'

Never had she imagined that Robert would do such a thing. Piers stared at his brother in utter disbelief. 'You did what?'

'It's yours,' Robert said. 'But you have to help the people there. You know what they need. That's all I ask in return.'

Piers gripped his brother's forearms, and asked quietly, 'Are you certain this is what you want?'

'It's the right thing to do,' Robert answered. 'So, aye. It's what I want.'

Gwen didn't believe for a moment that her father would accept this and return to Tilmain in peace. Alfred was only biding his time, healing from his own wounds while looking for a way to kill Piers. The thought frightened her, but now they would have to travel to Penrith in spite of the danger. If they were going to claim the lands, then they needed to reach the estate before her father did—but she feared their conflict would never end. And the exhaustion of running away, of fighting a battle that could never be won, went so deep, she could barely breathe.

Piers promised Robert that he would restore the lands and bring prosperity back to the people. 'I owe you a debt I can never repay.'

'If you restore their freedom, that will be payment enough,' Robert answered.

She decided to give the brothers a moment alone while she went to greet Morwenna. An older woman was standing with her, and Gwen guessed it was her mother.

'You're here.' Morwenna beamed and held out her arms. Gwen embraced her friend, and in that moment, she pushed away all the fears that haunted her. It was going to be all right, and she would not allow the past to ruin this day.

'I'm so happy for you,' she told her friend. Morwenna was wearing the crimson gown Gwen had given her, and she had a crown of pink wildflowers in her hair.

'Now, the day is perfect,' Morwenna said. 'And this is my mother, Lady Banmouth. I met her for the first time a few weeks ago.'

Even now, Gwen could see how the knowledge of Morwenna's true family had transformed her. No longer did the young woman look at the world as if she were unworthy. Instead, she raised up her face to the man she loved as an equal.

Would Piers ever set aside his past and do the same, ruling at her side? Gwen could only hope so.

Father Oswald, Robert's uncle, walked towards his

nephew to begin the marriage ceremony while several other monks from Colford stood nearby. Piers congratulated his brother and wished him happiness. But their conversation ceased when Morwenna appeared at the entrance to the stone archway. Lady Banmouth stood on one side, and Gwen joined on the opposite side.

Morwenna walked towards Robert slowly, her dark hair flowing freely in soft curls below her shoulders. Her smile held blinding happiness, and Gwen could not help but envy them.

Robert took Morwenna's hands in his and as his uncle began the words to the marriage rite, Gwen went to join her own husband. Piers held her hand, and she thought of their own unconventional wedding. She smiled at the memory of the drunken priest and the night they had spoken their vows.

Piers stared at the wedding, but his hand tightened on hers. In that moment, she sensed the emotion that echoed her own. This should have been a moment of joy and celebration—but the shadow of their own future hung over them still. Robert had given them Penrith, but it meant nothing if they could not defend it from the earl. And that battle was yet to be fought.

After the marriage vows, Robert kissed his bride. Piers leaned over and brushed his mouth against her temple before the priest began the Mass. Throughout the Latin words, she glanced around the ruined fortress, realising that this was where her husband had spent the past two years of his life with Robert, Morwenna, and her brother Brian. Piers had fought to survive, and he'd come out stronger. She could only admire him for the man he'd become.

After the Mass ended, she and Piers cheered while Morwenna's mother dabbed happy tears from her eyes.

'I will come to visit you in Ireland,' Lady Banmouth promised as she embraced her daughter. 'In the spring.' Her smile grew knowing, and when Morwenna rested her hands upon her stomach, a pang of unexpected grief caught in Gwen's throat.

Oh, God. Was Morwenna pregnant? She hadn't expected to be caught unawares like this, and tears spilled over. Gwen tried to smile as if they were tears of happiness. But they were tears of envy and grief. Though it was possible she'd never been pregnant at all, the loss of that dream didn't make the pain any less.

She went to embrace Morwenna and Robert next. 'I wish you both all the happiness in the world.' To Morwenna she added, 'And I am glad that Piers and Robert are half-brothers. For now, we can truly be sisters.'

'If you ever need our help with Penrith, you have it,' Morwenna promised.

Piers put his arm around Gwen's waist and murmured his thanks. Father Oswald, Brother Anselm, and the other monks joined them in a simple feast of bread, cheese, mutton, and fish. Afterwards, they also shared a platter of fresh blackberries.

'It was a lovely wedding,' she said to Piers in a low voice while Brother Anselm began a song in his deep baritone.

'But you're still looking over your shoulder, aren't you?' he mused. 'Are you afraid I can't protect you?'

'No, it's not that. I just don't know what our future will hold,' she admitted. If there could even be a future.

She didn't like to hold fast to doubts, but what other choice was there?

'We will celebrate tonight and journey to Penrith on the morrow,' he promised, reaching for her hands. Another monk had begun playing a tune, and Piers led her near Robert and Morwenna who were dancing.

She hadn't danced since the night of the competitions, and in her husband's arms, she fell captive beneath his spell. Piers kept one arm around her waist while he spun her, and she found herself enjoying the evening. His eyes grew dark with interest, and she suddenly wished for privacy. Or at the very least, a chamber together.

The sun set in the night sky, and she helped Piers light several fires to warm the courtyard. She noticed that Morwenna and Robert were saying their farewells, and she went to fetch a gift she'd wrapped. Gwendoline thanked her for it.

After they'd left, Piers asked, 'What did you give them?'

'Just some things I took from Penrith before I left. Once, I believed they might have been yours, and I brought them for you. But now I know they belonged to Robert. I thought he should have them.'

'You gave him part of his past,' Piers said, drawing her close. 'It's a gift without price.'

'Perhaps.'

He placed his cloak over her shoulders, and they walked past the ruins towards the fire. Morwenna's mother had gone to her own tent to sleep, and the monks departed for the abbey. They were alone at last.

Gwen could feel the warmth of his skin, and she ordered him, 'Take off your tunic so I can tend your back.'

He obeyed, stripping it off. In the firelight, his muscles gleamed, and she felt the urge to press a kiss to his heart. Instead, she went to their belongings and withdrew a small wooden container of salve. When she returned to him, she went to sit behind him. The angry, raw flesh of his back still angered her. Alfred had caused these wounds, for no reason at all.

She was gentle as she spread the salve into his skin. He flinched, but she tried to be careful as she touched him.

'I thought you were going to die,' she admitted. 'It terrified me.'

'I thought I would, too.' He glanced over his shoulder to look at her. 'But I don't regret a single moment we spent together. And I'm going to fight for us. No matter how long it takes.'

Gwen moved in to kiss him, and when his mouth captured hers, she yielded to him. Though a part of her doubted they would ever be able to live in peace with her father, she was grateful for each day with Piers.

'I've asked men to travel from Tilmain to Penrith,' he said. 'We're going to need reinforcements and soldiers we trust.'

'Is there time for them to arrive?' she asked. It would take several days for them to reach Penrith, and she didn't know if any would come.

He nodded. 'I gave orders for them to follow us. They've guarded our backs since the moment we left.'

She stared at him, overwhelmed by the realisation that he had taken command and was already fighting for their future. No longer was he the downtrodden bastard son who slept among the dogs. Instead, he'd become a leader of men. Her heart swelled with love for this man.

Piers stood and led her towards their own tent. 'But for now, we're not going to think about what lies ahead. We're going to enjoy this night together.'

Piers rode with Gwen to the gates of Penrith. The soldiers he'd brought from Tilmain had joined them, and he was grateful for the twenty men who had come. Among them were Rufus and Philip, along with others who had been glad to travel.

Gwen wore a blue gown, and she approached the gate at his side. She appeared nervous, but she raised her chin to gather her courage.

Although they had the king's decree that granted them ownership of Penrith, Piers wondered whether the men here would accept them. When they reached the entrance, the men appeared uncertain, but when they saw Gwen, they opened the gates.

Piers followed behind her, and he waited for the Tilmain soldiers to join them. The men remained alert, and he called out to the captain of the guards. The man's doubts were evident, but Piers showed him the parchment with the king's orders. 'These are our men from Tilmain. They will need food after their journey, and I want them housed among our men.' Although the captain inclined his head, Piers added, 'Tell the soldiers that they will have as much food and drink as they need. Tonight, I will want their help distributing food to the serfs.'

At that, the man started to shake his head. 'The earl—'

'—is no longer in command here,' Piers finished. 'I am.'

'But you're not—' the captain started to say but stopped himself.

Piers knew he was about to accuse him of not being a nobleman. But no longer would he let his past define his future. 'I am who the king wants me to be. And there will be changes at Penrith.'

A faint smile creased the man's face. 'I will let them know.'

Piers dismounted and gave his horse to one of the stable boys. Then he went to help Gwen down. 'Will you see to the food?'

She nodded. 'I'll speak with the steward myself.'

Piers saw several of the onlookers staring, but he knew their time was running out. The sooner they gained allies at Penrith, the better.

For a moment, he glanced at the outbuilding where he'd once gone below ground to reach the tunnels. He'd lived his life in the shadows here, never believing he was good enough. And now, he would never have to use them again. It was strange to realise how different his life would be now.

Slowly, he ascended the stone stairs to the keep. When he reached the top, he stopped to look around. He was glad that Gwen had bought him the finer clothing, for she'd been right about appearances. But more than that, he was starting to realise the immense responsibility on his shoulders now. He had to ensure that everyone had enough to eat, that they had shelter and healers to care for the sick. All of it fell to him. And for the first time, he felt ready to take on the role his mother had wanted for him so many years ago.

He chose Philip and Rufus to join him as they approached the keep. Once inside, he noticed how the Great Hall had fallen into disrepair. The rushes were filthy, and dogs fought in the corner over scraps. The harsh scent of neglect permeated the space, and he saw several soldiers drinking and laughing. He recognised them as some of King John's men.

With a glance back at his own soldiers, he approached the king's men. The soldiers continued to pour ale, and Piers stood before them. 'Get up.'

One scoffed, 'And who's this? Piss off or join us in a drink.'

Piers sent a look towards Rufus and Philip. In one motion, they seized the soldiers and dragged them off the benches, knocking the ale to the ground. Piers unsheathed his dagger and held it to the first man's throat. 'I am the new Lord of Penrith. And you're going to be busy cleaning this keep if you intend to join the others in their feasting tonight.'

'You must not know who we are, *my lord*,' the soldier mocked. 'We take orders from the king.'

'Then it's time you returned to him, isn't it?' Piers seized the man by his tunic and dragged him up, keeping his blade to the soldier's throat. 'Or you can get started cleaning. The choice is yours.' He would tolerate no disrespect from these men.

The second soldier threw a punch at Rufus, who dodged the blow before striking the man hard. Blood trickled from the soldier's mouth, and Rufus said, 'Try that again, and you'll be gone by nightfall.'

There was a moment of confusion among them, and Piers ordered, 'Take their weapons. They won't be needing them.'

The king's soldiers hesitated, and Philip used that moment to seize the man's sword. 'You heard your orders.'

The second soldier handed over his own weapons, and Piers said, 'You will clear out the mess from this room and all the bones and rotting food. I demand your obedience in all things. If you accept my orders, you will have all that you need. But if you defy me, you will go back to King John. He needs soldiers in France, and I will gladly send you there.'

At that, the first man muttered, 'Yes, my lord.'

'You have much to do,' Piers said. 'You'd best get started.'

Gwen entered the keep at that moment, and she was speaking with the steward. For a moment, he watched over his wife. The man began to protest at something she said, but before Piers could intervene Gwen cut off the steward.

'I did not ask for your counsel,' she said. 'It is not your place to question my orders.'

At that, Piers smiled. His wife had become a lioness, the true Lady of Penrith. He moved to her side and glared at the man. Afterwards, the steward hurried away.

Without asking, he took Gwen's hand and began to lead her towards the stairs. She started to protest, 'Piers, there is so much to be done. It's worse than I thought.'

'But they obeyed your orders,' he said, leading her towards her chamber. 'It will be all right.' He opened the door, and the maid inside jerked to her feet. 'Leave us.'

'Do you…need anything, my lord? My lady?' the maid asked. Piers pointed to the door, and the young woman hurried out.

'I wouldn't have minded food and something to drink,' Gwen answered. 'After so much travelling.'

'Later,' he said, leaning in to kiss her. She yielded to him, and he picked her up in his arms. 'There's something else I want right now.' She laughed, but he sensed that there was a great deal bothering her. He pulled her on to his lap and said, 'What troubles you, Gwen?'

'Just…memories, I suppose.' She rested her cheek against his chest and admitted, 'I learned from the steward that my father is travelling to Penrith now. He will be here any day now, and I don't know if we have time to unify our forces. Especially with the king's men to divide us.'

'I've already threatened to send them back to John.' And if any man's loyalty was questionable, Piers wouldn't hesitate to send him away.

'I know. But what if they join my father's forces?' She drew back to face him. 'We have a battle ahead of us, and we will need everyone to fight for us. Otherwise, we will die.'

'No matter what happens, you'll be safe, Gwen.'

Her blue eyes held doubts. Although he wanted to reassure her, he understood her fears. In so many ways, it felt as if they were only pretending to be the Lord and Lady of Penrith, and it didn't seem real. There would be those who opposed them, causing trouble from within the castle. He didn't know whom he could trust, beyond the men who had willingly come from Tilmain.

'Whatever happens, we stay together,' she insisted. 'And we must tighten our defences and prepare for what lies ahead.'

'Leave that to me,' he promised. 'If you will see to it that the serfs have food and supplies, we may be able to bring them to our side. We'll work together, Gwen.' She traced her fingers down his face, and he caught them to his lips. 'Don't be afraid.'

But they both knew that he was not safe here. And when the earl arrived, it would mean war between them.

'They're going to break through the gates today, my lady. They've built a battering ram.'

Gwen met Philip's gaze and nodded. Although they had successfully barred her father from the gates during the past two days, she'd been unwilling to sacrifice her own men. They'd needed time to make their plans, to unify the soldiers from both Penrith and Tilmain, along with the king's soldiers who had chosen to stay. She wanted to keep casualties to a minimum and, thus far, Alfred's siege had been unsuccessful.

'I will speak with my husband.' She left the soldier and went back inside the keep. Piers stood on the far side, donning his chainmail. He sheathed a sword at his side while another soldier held his shield.

Gwen hurried over to him and motioned the men away. In a low voice, she told him what she'd learned about her father's men. 'Philip thinks they will break through today. Some of the men may switch sides if they think we will lose.'

'If they switch sides, they will not stay at Penrith,' he swore. He picked up his helm and regarded her. 'We're going to end this fight today, Gwen. One way or the other.'

She understood what he hadn't said. The only way to end the battle was for her father to die. All night, she hadn't slept because she knew there was no choice but to take Alfred's life. Only then could they claim his lands and give freedom to the people.

'*I* am going to end it,' she promised, 'with the arrow I should have placed in his heart earlier.' She blamed herself for all of this. She'd had the chance to kill her father, and she'd shown him mercy instead. It had been a mistake.

'You don't need that burden,' he said. 'I will face him and fight.'

'You're still healing,' she protested. 'I don't want you to take that risk. No one else needs to die. I'll do what I must.' She had reconciled herself to the truth she should have faced long ago. There would never be any peace as long as Alfred drew breath.

He reached out and cupped her cheek. For a long moment, he stared into her eyes, and she was afraid he might not listen to her. He had the look of a man who intended to fight…and if anything ever happened to Piers, she could not bear it.

'I love you, Gwen,' he said softly, stealing a kiss. 'Let's finish this.'

With those words, her terror only heightened. He'd never said them before, and she feared that he was joining this battle while ensuring that all last words were spoken.

She motioned for a soldier to bring her bow and quiver. 'I'll go to the battlements to take the shot. Make sure everyone else stays far away from him. Tell my father's men to lay down their weapons, and they will not come to harm.'

Her husband met her gaze, but she could not tell what he was thinking. Then Piers gave a nod, and they walked together towards the entrance to the keep. He held her hand in his, but he took his shield from another man.

'Be safe,' she bade him.

'And you.' He kissed her again, and she made her way towards the battlement stairs. On the way there, she signalled for her maid to bring her cloak. She had chosen a mantle of deep crimson so all could see her clearly. When she fastened the cloak across her shoulders, another invisible weight settled upon her.

She didn't want to become a murderer—but what else could she do? So many more would suffer and die if she did not. With every stone step she took, the guilt in her heart deepened. She had a few precious memories of Alfred from when she was a child. Once, he'd let her sit upon his knee, and she'd played with the gold chain he wore. At the time, she had believed her father invincible, a good man who took care of them.

Now, she knew it had always been about power and control. And there was no turning back now.

When she reached the top of the battlements, she saw her father's men gathering at the front of the keep with the battering ram. More men had come, and she wondered how he had accumulated so many forces. But when she looked closer, it appeared that his army was mostly made up of men from Tilmain. It gave her a sense of hope. Perhaps they would lay down their weapons and join her and Piers.

Other soldiers had constructed ladders, and she knew they would try to scale the walls. She nocked an arrow to her bow and called out a warning to her men. Several archers joined her, prepared to fight any man who attempted to penetrate their defences.

Piers walked towards the gates and, as he did, she noticed that the men they'd brought with them from Tilmain stood at his back. She was so proud of her husband. He had accomplished what she had only dared to hope—to win the loyalty of strangers who would now fight by his side.

Now, she had to speak to her father's men and ask them to join them so that no more lives would be lost.

She walked the battlements towards the top of the gates, knowing that everyone could see her clearly. When she reached the top, she called out in a loud voice. 'I am Lady Gwendoline of Penrith. I ask you to lay down your weapons. Do not scale our walls, and do not attempt to break down our gates. You are my men as well. You know me, and you know it is not my wish to harm any one of you.'

She held her bow in one hand, but the men below did not heed her words. The battering ram continued to crash against the wooden gates, and she stared down at her father. Though she could not see him clearly, he had surrounded himself with soldiers and archers. Taking a shot at him would be nearly impossible without striking another man first.

Piers stood shoulder to shoulder with the men below,

and several archers aimed their weapons at the gates. Within moments, they would break through and the battle would begin. Gwen drew back her bow, praying her arrow would find its mark. But before she could release the bowstring, her father gave the signal, and he and his men charged forward.

The gates splintered, and she heard the roar of the men as they broke through. One of the soldiers raised his sword against Piers, and she shot him down without hesitation. The other soldiers poured inside, but instead of attacking Piers and the other men, they kept their shields up and formed a circle around them.

Her father entered on horseback, and Gwen took careful aim. Her heart was pounding, for this was her chance to end it.

Then a shout cut through the courtyard. 'Behind you!' Piers called out.

She turned and saw Adam, the former captain of the guard at Tilmain, who had just climbed over the wall. He broke into a run, heading straight towards her.

Chapter Thirteen

Piers watched as Adam threw himself towards Gwen. She had no time to react, and the battlements were so narrow, he feared the man would push her over. If she fell that distance, she would die.

He rushed towards her, and Gwen did scream as Adam knocked her over. Piers was about to race up the stairs when he saw an arrow protruding from Adam's back. He froze in shock when he saw one of the king's men standing on the opposite side, his bow drawn with a second arrow nocked. It was the soldier he'd ordered to clean the Great Hall on their first day here—and by knocking her over, Adam had just saved Gwen's life. Never had he imagined that the man who had once betrayed him would redeem himself in such a way. There was remorse in Adam's eyes as the life faded from them.

'Stay down!' Piers warned Gwen, and she obeyed. Then Rufus struck down the man who had shot the arrow, ending his life.

The earl charged forward with his men, and chaos erupted in the keep. In that moment, Piers forgot about the pain of his own wounds. This was about facing the past that had held him back and conquering it. Steel clashed against steel, and Piers fought for the woman he loved. In her father's eyes, he saw the hatred and the earl's belief that he would never be good enough for Gwen. Behind him, the soldiers of Tilmain had gathered, but Piers felt their presence in a different way. They were fighting with him, not against him.

Alfred attacked, and Piers noticed him shielding his left shoulder from where Gwen must have wounded him. He used that to his advantage and struck hard, slamming his wooden shield against the man's shoulder.

He cleared his mind of everything, knowing this had to be the end. It didn't matter that he was still regaining his strength from the pain of his own healing wounds. This was about fighting against the man who would never accept him.

In this man's face, he saw the mirror of his own father. He'd never been good enough for the earl, and Degal had barely noticed him. All his life, he'd been found lacking, and Piers was weary of it. He would fight for Gwen, their people, and the family he wanted to build with her. No longer would he believe that he was unworthy.

As his sword sliced towards the earl, he thought of Gwen's devastation that she had not been with child. It had echoed his own grief, and he wanted to give her the legacy of sons and daughters. He wanted to see his wife smile as she held a newborn and feel the sense of awe of being a father.

The earl redoubled his efforts, and Piers circled him, searching for other weaknesses. Though he'd been reluctant to threaten Alfred's life earlier for Gwen's sake, the time for mercy had passed. He quickened his tempo, intending to end this battle now.

Then two other soldiers joined the earl, fighting at Alfred's side. Piers struggled to fight both of them, dodging swords and using his shield while he was prevented from attacking the earl. Numbly, he realised that Alfred would never fight fair. Not with this much at stake.

He continued to defend himself, hacking at his opponents as best he could. But as he struggled to fight three of them, Philip joined at his side. Then Rufus came to the opposite side.

Silently, one by one, the men of Tilmain joined him until the circle widened. Piers was aware of their presence, but he couldn't stop the fight now. Then the men of Penrith joined in with their own weapons, soldiers and serfs alike. A strange sense of unity filled him as one by one, the people chose his side. The earl's face turned purple with fury as they slowly surrounded him.

'It's over,' he told Alfred. 'You will not harm any of these people again.'

But then, he caught a glimpse of Gwen on the battlements with an arrow drawn to her bow. He didn't want her to carry the burden of her father's death, not when there was another way. These soldiers had known the same imprisonment as she had. Over the years, these people had suffered hunger and a lack of freedom. They had countless reasons to be angry with the earl.

Piers lowered his sword and commanded the men, 'Do with the earl as you will. There will be no penalty for your actions.'

With that, the soldiers of Tilmain and Penrith charged forward. They surrounded Alfred and took his life. Piers never saw whose sword penetrated the earl's heart, but he allowed them to express their fury without bounds. A few of Alfred's men tried to escape, but they lost their own lives in the battle.

Piers walked slow steps up the battlements to where Gwen was waiting. He embraced her hard, and she wrapped her arms around his neck. In spite of their victory, she wept, and he understood why. She was crying for what might have been, had her father been willing to surrender.

She murmured against his ear, 'I don't want to see him. I don't care where they bury him.'

'You won't have to see him.' He led her away, and she kept her face averted.

'What will we tell the king?'

He led her into one of the towers and said, 'We'll tell him the truth. That the earl was killed during an uprising. We will tell him that the men responsible are dead.' He lifted her chin to face him. 'No man here will say otherwise.'

He kissed her, wanting her to feel safe again. 'If you want, we can send for a priest and say a Mass for their souls.'

She clung to him and said, 'I just want to forget. About my father, about all of them.'

In her voice, he heard the need for peace. 'Go to our chamber,' he commanded. 'Wait for me there. I need to ensure that our men are safe and that the dead are buried.'

She nodded and let out a slow breath. 'Come to me when it's over.'

'I will,' he promised.

Gwen had arranged for food and wine in their chamber, and she'd ordered the steward to ensure that all the soldiers of Tilmain and Penrith could eat and drink their fill tonight. It was not a celebration feast, but more of a new beginning.

It was nightfall before Piers returned. She had lit several candles around the room, and a fire glowed on the hearth. Shyness overcame her, but she awaited him in their bed. The moment her husband saw her, his gaze grew heated. He stripped off his armour and clothing, leaving it where it fell.

She sat up and let the coverlet fall to her waist, revealing her nakedness. Then she pulled her hair to one side, showing Piers the ribbon she'd used to tie it back. 'You asked me to wear this ribbon for you one day.'

'And nothing else,' he said in a low growl. 'I remember.'

From the intensity of his stare, prickles rose up all over her body. He drank in the sight of her, his gaze lingering upon her bare skin.

'Come here,' he commanded. She moved to the edge of the bed, and he knelt down before her. His hands moved to her waist and then they slid down to her thighs. He rested his hands on her knees and then drew her face to his, where he kissed her deeply. His tongue slid into her mouth, echoing what he would do to her later. Her body broke out into gooseflesh, and she craved his touch.

'Is it finished?' she whispered.

He nodded. 'Some of the men felt that we should… display a few bodies as a warning of punishment. But we know the truth about what happened.'

'I wish it didn't have to be that way,' she admitted. 'I never wanted anyone to die. I only wanted to be free.'

'You are free now.'

She kissed him again, cupping his face before moving her hands down to his shoulders. Although he wasn't fully healed, she needed him right now.

'Piers, will you lie with me?' she whispered.

'Tonight, and every night,' he swore. His hands moved to her flat stomach, and he rested them there a moment. 'Until you grow large with our child inside you.'

She needed this man and said softly, 'I love you.'

'I love you, too.' He bent down to kiss her stomach, and then he lifted her legs on to his shoulders. A sense of anticipation heightened within her, and she saw the wickedness in his eyes as he parted her intimately.

Gwen let out a shuddering breath when he bent down, and his breath warmed her delicate flesh. He moved in and his tongue swirled against her wetness. She gripped the coverlet, moaning as he used his fingers and mouth to torment her. He kissed her, and she touched her breasts, feeling her nipples rise beneath her fingers. Piers's mouth and tongue suckled against her intimately, and she gave a keening cry as he found the place of her pleasure.

He pushed two fingers inside her while he worked her with his tongue. From deep inside, he stroked her, and waves of immense desire took hold and grew. She was nearly sobbing as he pushed her over the edge into a blissful surrender.

As she broke apart, he stood up and pulled her hips close while she lay on the edge of the bed. She felt his velvet length probing at her and helped guide him deep inside. When he was fully embedded, she raised up her knees, and he began steady penetrations. She squeezed him, arching her back as he leaned down.

Gwen brought his hands to her breasts as he quickened his pace. He caressed her erect nipples while he thrust inside her. She was so ready for him, every stroke only made her hotter.

She wrapped her legs around his waist as his hips ground against hers. The lovemaking rose up into a fever pitch until he lost control.

'Gwen… I'm sorry. I can't stop.'

'I don't want you to,' she said. Instead, she drove against him, skin to skin, until she saw his face transform into fierce need. She gloried in his own ecstasy as he gasped and shuddered, spilling his seed deep inside.

Her body trembled with aftershocks, but she let her legs slide back down as he collapsed on top of her.

She didn't think about the horrors of the afternoon or anything else except being in Piers's arms. They would never be apart again, and she believed he would make a better earl than any man.

'I don't want you to get up.' She smiled at him and leaned over to kiss his mouth. 'Not ever.'

He kissed her sweetly, his tongue threading between her lips. 'I'm staying right here.' With his length still inside her, she marvelled at how well they fit together and how much she loved this man.

It might be a challenge to rule over both Tilmain and Penrith, but none of it mattered any more. As long as she and Piers were together, she didn't care what the future held.

Epilogue

There was no terror greater than waiting for your wife to give birth. Piers couldn't stop from pacing the halls, much to his brother Robert's amusement.

'Does it always take this long?' he asked.

Robert sipped his wine and laughed. 'Sometimes longer. But don't worry. Morwenna and the midwife are there for Gwen. She'll come through well enough.'

'I know she wanted this baby more than anything,' Piers said. 'But if I lose her…'

'Don't think of it,' Robert warned. 'You'll go mad if you do.'

During the past year, his brother had settled into his new estate in Ireland. Although Piers had offered him the chance to govern Penrith, Robert had refused, saying that he had made a home at Dunbough. He'd suggested that if Morwenna's brother Brian ever returned from the Crusades, then he could govern Tilmain. In the meantime, Robert was content to remain where he was.

A scream tore through the silence, and Piers ran towards the stairs, only to have Robert drag him back. 'Not yet,' his brother warned.

'But she's in pain.'

'And you can do nothing to stop it,' Robert insisted. 'Gwen is strong, and she will get through this.'

Though he understood that his brother was trying to reassure him, he couldn't stay here any longer. He wrenched off Robert's grip. 'I am going to her now. And you cannot stop me.'

As he hurried up the stairs, he heard his brother laughing but didn't know why. Piers went to Gwen's chamber and opened the door.

The midwife was holding her hand, and Gwen's face was covered in sweat. She was panting heavily, balancing herself on the birthing chair. When she caught sight of Piers, she glared at him. 'This is *your* fault. I hate you for this.' Then she screamed again as she bore down and pushed.

Morwenna came to the door. 'This isn't a good time, Piers. I'll come and fetch you when the baby is here.'

'Just a little longer, my lady,' the midwife coaxed. 'You're doing so well.'

'I don't want a baby any more,' Gwen sobbed. 'It hurts too much.'

Morwenna guided Piers out the doorway and joined him for a moment. 'There's a reason we don't want men in the birthing room. It's very painful, and she will say a great deal that she doesn't mean.'

But then, seconds later, he heard the cry of an infant. He pushed his way past Morwenna and went to Gwen's side.

'It's a girl,' the midwife said. She tied off the umbilical cord and cut it before swaddling the baby and showing the infant to Gwen.

But his wife was still panting, her face bright red with exertion. She tried to smile, but then bore down again.

'Take your daughter,' the midwife urged Piers, handing him the bundle. He took the baby in his arms, startled by how tiny her fingers were. Her face was the size of his palm, and he'd never held anyone so small. But she was the most beautiful thing he'd ever seen in his life.

'I'm going to protect you,' he told the baby. 'You'll always be safe.'

His wife cried out again, and Piers demanded, 'What is happening? Shouldn't the pain be over?'

Morwenna took the baby from him while he went to his wife's side. He'd heard many stories of women dying in childbirth, and if anything happened to Gwen, he would be utterly lost.

'That's it, my lady, push again.'

Push? Was this the afterbirth? But after a few minutes more, he realised that the midwife was guiding a second baby out.

'Twins?' he managed to blurt out.

'And this one's a boy and your heir, my lord.' The midwife helped to cut the cord again, and she used another length of linen to swaddle the child. Gwen was crying, her eyes lit up with joy as he showed her their son.

'I need to hold our children,' she wept.

'Just a moment more,' the midwife said. 'Push out the afterbirth and then you can hold the babies.'

Gwen laboured a little longer, and when it was over,

the midwife helped her back to the bed while he held his son. Then he and Morwenna brought her the babies, and Gwen smiled through her tears as she marvelled at them. 'They're perfect.'

'Well done,' Morwenna said. Then she helped the midwife and, soon after that, they left them alone.

Piers sat beside Gwen as she kissed each child. He'd never known how humbling it would be to bring new life into the world.

'I'm so happy,' she wept.

'A few moments ago, you blamed me and told me you hated me,' he pointed out with a smile.

She pulled him down for a kiss, and then said, 'I still love you.'

'I'm glad to hear it. I love you, too.' He rested his hand upon his daughter's head, then he touched his son. 'And I will guard our children with my life.'

'I want a dozen more,' she informed him. 'I want to fill Penrith with our children, and I want them to know that they are loved.'

She nestled her head against him while he drew his arm around her. This family meant everything to him, and he would love them with every breath he had.

'Is there anything you need?' he offered. 'Anything I can get for you?'

'Everything I need is right here,' she answered.

And he agreed with her wholeheartedly.

* * * * *

If you enjoyed this story, be sure to read the first book in The Legendary Warriors miniseries

The Iron Warrior Returns

And why not also check out Michelle Willingham's Untamed Highlanders miniseries?

The Highlander and the Governess
The Highlander and the Wallflower

HARLEQUIN
PLUS

Try the best multimedia subscription service for romance readers like you!

Read, Watch and Play.

Experience the easiest way to get the romance content you crave.

Start your **FREE TRIAL** at
www.harlequinplus.com/freetrial.